The History of David Grieve

Book III
Storm And Stress

by

Mrs. Humphry Ward

The History of David Grieve
Book III Storm And Stress
by Mrs. Humphry Ward

ISBN: 978-93-62760-98-2

Published by

DOUBLE 9 BOOKS

2/13-B, Ansari Road
Daryaganj, New Delhi – 110002
info@double9books.com
www.double9books.com
Tel. 011-40042856

ABOUT THE AUTHOR

Mary Augusta Ward CBE was a British author who lived from June 11, 1851, to March 24, 1920. She wrote under her married name, Mrs. Humphry Ward. Setting up a Settlement in London to help poor people get better schooling was one way she did this. In 1908, she became the first President of the Women's National Anti-Suffrage League. Mary Augusta Arnold was born in Hobart, Tasmania, Australia. She came from a well-known family of writers and educators. Mary was the daughter of Julia Sorell and Tom Arnold, who taught literature. William Thomas Arnold was a writer and journalist, Ethel Arnold worked for women's right to vote, and Julia Huxley started Prior's Field School for Girls in 1902 and married Leonard Huxley. Their sons were Julian and Aldous Huxley. It was important for British intellectual life to have people like the Arnolds and the Huxleys. Author Matthew Arnold was her uncle, and Thomas Arnold, the famous headmaster of Rugby School, was her grandpa. Tom Arnold, Mary's father, was made head of schools in Van Diemen's Land, which is now Tasmania. He started his job on January 15, 1850.

CONTENTS

CHAPTER I

The brother and sister left Manchester about midday, and spent the night in London at a little City hotel much frequented by Nonconformist ministers, which Ancrum had recommended.

Then next day! How little those to whom all the widest opportunities of life come for the asking, can imagine such a zest, such a freshness of pleasure! David had hesitated long before the expense of the day service *via* Calais; they could have gone by night third class for half the money; or they could have taken returns by one of the cheaper and longer routes. But the eagerness to make the most of every hour of time and daylight prevailed; they were to go by Calais and come back by Dieppe, seeing thereby as much as possible on the two journeys in addition to the fortnight in Paris. The mere novelty of going anything but third class was full of savour; Louie's self-conscious dignity as she settled herself into her corner on leaving Charing Cross caught David's eye; he saw himself reflected and laughed.

It was a glorious day, the firstling of the summer. In the blue overhead the great clouds rose intensely thunderously white, and journeyed seaward under a light westerly wind. The railway banks, the copses were all primroses; every patch of water had in it the white and azure of the sky; the lambs were lying in the still scanty shadow of the elms; every garden showed its tulips and wallflowers, and the air, the sunlight, the vividness of each hue and line bore with them an intoxicating joy, especially for eyes still adjusted to the tones and lights of Manchester in winter.

The breeze carried them merrily over a dancing sea. And once on the French side they spent their first hour in crossing from one side of their carriage to the other, pointing and calling incessantly. For the first time since certain rare moments in their childhood they were happy together and at one. Mother Earth unrolled for them a corner of her magic show, and they took it like children at the play, now shouting, now spell-bound.

David had George Sand's 'Mauprat' on his knee, but he read nothing the whole day. Never had he used his eyes so intently, so passionately. Nothing escaped them, neither the detail of that strange and beautiful fen from which Amiens rises—a country of peat and peat-cutters where the green plain is diapered with innumerable tiny lakes edged with black heaps of turf and daintily set with scattered trees—nor the delicate charm of the forest lands about Chautilly. So much thinner and gracefuller these woods were than English woods! French art and skill were here already in the wild country. Each tree stood out as though it had been personally thought for; every plantation was in regular lines; each woody walk drove straight from point to point, following out a plan orderly and intricate as a spider's web.

By this time Louie's fervour of curiosity and attention had very much abated; she grew tired and cross, and presently fell asleep. But, with every mile less between them and Paris, David's pulse beat faster, and his mind became more absorbed in the flying scene. He hung beside the window, thrilling with enchantment and delight, drinking in the soft air, the beauty of the evening clouds, the wonderful greens and silvers and fiery browns of the poplars. His mind was full of images—the deep lily-sprinkled lake wherein Stenio, Lelia's poet lover, plunged and died; the grandiose landscape of Victor Hugo; Rene sitting on the cliff-side, and looking farewell to the white home of his childhood;—of lines from 'Childe Harold' and from Shelley. His mind was in a ferment of youth and poetry, and the France he saw was not the workaday France of peasant and high road and factory, but the creation of poetic intelligence, of ignorance and fancy.

Paris came in a flash. He had realised to the full the squalid and ever-widening zone of London, had frittered away his expectations almost, in the passing it; but here the great city had hardly announced itself before they were in the midst of it, shot out into the noise, and glare, and crowd of the Nord station.

They had no luggage to wait for, and David, trembling with excitement so that he could hardly give the necessary orders, shouldered the bags, got a cab and gave the address. Outside it was still twilight, but the lamps were lit and the Boulevard into which they presently turned seemed to brother and sister a blaze of light. The young green of the trees glittered under the gas like the trees of a pantomime; the kiosks threw their lights out upon the moving crowd; shops and cafes were all shining and alive; and on either hand rose the long line of stately houses, unbroken by any London or Manchester squalors and inequalities, towering as it seemed into the skies, and making for the great spectacle of life beneath them a setting more gay, splendid, and complete than any Englishman in his own borders can ever see.

Louie had turned white with pleasure and excitement. All her dreams of gaiety and magnificence, of which the elements had been gathered from the illustrated papers and the Manchester theatres, were more than realised by these Paris gas-lights, these vast houses, these laughing and strolling crowds.

'Look at those people having their coffee out of doors,' she cried to David, 'and that white and gold place behind. Goodness! what they must spend in gas! And just look at those two girls—look, quick—there, with the young man in the black moustache—they *are* loud, but aren't their dresses just sweet?'

She craned her neck out of window, exclaiming—now at this, now at that—till suddenly they passed out of the Boulevard into the comparative darkness of side ways. Here the height of the houses produced a somewhat different impression; Louie looked out none the less keenly, but her chatter ceased.

At last the cab drew up with a clatter at the side of a particularly dark and narrow street, ascending somewhat sharply to the north-west from the point where they stopped.

'Now for the *concierge*,' said David, looking round him, after he had paid the man.

And conning Barbier's directions in his mind, he turned into the gateway, and made boldly for a curtained door behind which shone a light.

The woman, who came out in answer to his knock, looked him all over from head to foot, while he explained himself in his best French.

'*Tiens*,' she said, indifferently, to a man behind her, 'it's the people for No. 26—*des Anglais—M. Paul te l'a dit*. Hand me the key.'

The *bonhomme* addressed—a little, stooping, wizened creature, with china-blue eyes, showing widely in his withered face under the light of the paraffin-lamp his wife was holding—reached a key from a board on the wall and gave it to her.

The woman again surveyed them both, the young man and the girl, and seemed to debate with herself whether she should take the trouble to be civil. Finally she said in an ungracious voice—

'It's the fourth floor to the right. I must take you up, I suppose.'

David thanked her, and she preceded them with the light through a door opposite and up some stone stairs.

When they had mounted two flights, she turned abruptly on the landing—

'You take the *appartement* from M. Dubois?'

'Yes,' said David, enchanted to find that, thanks to old Barbier's constant lessons, he could both understand and reply with tolerable ease; 'for a fortnight.'

'Take care; the landlord will be descending on you; M. Dubois never pays; he may be turned out any day, and his things sold. Where is Mademoiselle going to sleep?'

'But in M. Dubois' *appartement*,' said David, hoping this time, in his dismay, that he did *not* understand; 'he promised to arrange everything.'

'He has arranged nothing. Do you wish that I should provide some things? You can hire some furniture from me. And do you want service?'

The woman had a grasping eye. David's frugal instincts took alarm.

'*Merci*, Madame! My sister and I do not require much. We shall wait upon ourselves. If Madame will tell us the name of some restaurant near—'

Instead, Madame made an angry sound and thrust the key abruptly into Louie's hand, David being laden with the bags.

'There are two more flights,' she said roughly; 'then turn to the left, and go up the staircase straight in front of you—first door to the right. You've got eyes; you'll find the way.'

'*Mais, Madame*—' cried David, bewildered by these directions, and trying to detain her.

But she was already half-way down the flight below them, throwing back remarks which, to judge from their tone, were not complimentary.

There was no help for it. Louie was dropping with fatigue, and beginning to be much out of temper. David with difficulty assumed a hopeful air, and up they went again. Leading off the next landing but one they found a narrow passage, and at the end of it a ladder-like staircase. At the top of this they came upon a corridor at right angles, in which the first door bore the welcome figures '26.'

'All right,' said David; 'here we are. Now we'll just go in, and look about us. Then if you'll sit and rest a bit, I'll run down and see where we can get something to eat.'

'Be quick, then—do,' said Louie. 'I'm just fit to drop.'

With a beating heart he put the key into the lock of the door. It fitted, but he could not turn it. Both he and Louie tried in vain.

'What a nuisance!' said he at last. 'I must go and fetch up that woman again. You sit down and wait.'

As he spoke there was a sound below of quick steps, and of a voice, a woman's voice, humming a song.

'Some one coming,' he said to Louie; 'perhaps they understand the lock.'

They ran down to the landing below to reconnoitre. There was, of course, gas on the staircase, and as they hung over the iron railing they saw mounting towards them a young girl. She wore a light fawn-coloured dress and a hat covered with Parma violets. Hearing voices above her, she threw her head back, and stopped a moment. Louie's eye was caught by her hand and its tiny wrist as it lay on the balustrade, and by the coils and twists of her fair hair. David saw no details, only what seemed to him a miracle of grace and colour, born in an instant, out of the dark—or out of his own excited fancy?

She came slowly up the steps, looking at them, at the tall dark youth and the girl beside him. Then on the top step she paused, instead of going past them. David took off his hat, but all the practical questions he had meant to ask deserted him. His French seemed to have flown.

'You are strangers, aren't you?' she said, in a clear, high, somewhat imperious voice. 'What number do you want?'

Her expression had a certain *hauteur*, as of one defending her native ground against intruders. Under the stimulus of it David found his tongue.

'We have taken M. Paul Dubois' rooms,' he said. 'We have found his door, but the key the *concierge* gave us does not fit it.'

She laughed, a free, frank laugh, which had a certain wild note in it.

'These doors have to be coaxed,' she said; 'they don't like foreigners. Give it me. This is my way, too.'

Stepping past them, she preceded them up the narrow stairs, and was just about to try the key in the lock, when a sudden recollection seemed to flash upon her.

'I know!' she said, turning upon them. '*Tenez—que je suis bête!* You are Dubois' English friends. He told me something, and I had forgotten all about it. You are going to take his rooms?'

'For a week or two,' said David, irritated a little by the laughing malice, the sarcastic wonder of her eyes, 'while he is doing some work in Brussels. It seemed a convenient arrangement, but if we are not comfortable we shall go elsewhere. If you can open the door for us we shall be greatly obliged to you, Mademoiselle. But if not I must go down for the *concierge*. We have been travelling all day, and my sister is tired.'

'Where did you learn such good French?' she said carelessly, at the same time leaning her weight against the door, and manipulating the key in such a way that the lock turned, and the door flew open.

Behind it appeared a large dark space. The light from the gas-jet in the passage struck into it, but beyond a chair and a tall screen-like object in the middle of the floor, it seemed to David to be empty.

'That's his *atelier*, of course,' said the unknown; 'and mine is next to it, at the other end. I suppose he has a cupboard to sleep in somewhere. Most of us have. But I don't know anything about Dubois. I don't like him. He is not one of my friends.'

She spoke in a dry, masculine voice, which contrasted in the sharpest way with her youth, her dress, her dainty smallness. Then, all of a sudden, as her eyes travelled over the English pair standing bewildered on the threshold of Dubois' most uninviting apartment, she began to laugh again. Evidently the situation seemed to her extremely odd.

'Did you ask the people downstairs to get anything ready for you?' she inquired.

'No,' said David, hesitating; 'we thought we could manage for ourselves.'

'Well—perhaps—after the first,' she said, still laughing. 'But—I may as well warn you—the Merichat will be very uncivil to you if you don't manage to pay her for something. Hadn't you better explore? That thing in the middle is Dubois' easel, of course.'

David groped his way in, took some matches from his pocket, found a gas-bracket with some difficulty, and lit up. Then he and Louie looked round them. They saw a gaunt high room, lit on one side by a huge studio-window, over which various tattered blinds were drawn; a floor of bare boards, with a few rags of carpet here and there; in the middle, a table covered with painter's apparatus of different kinds; palettes, paints, rags, tin-pots, and, thrown down amongst them, some stale crusts of bread; a large easel, with a number of old and dirty canvases piled upon it; two chairs, one of them without the usual complement of legs; a few etchings and oil-sketches and fragments of coloured stuffs pinned against the wall in wild confusion; and, spread out casually behind the easel, an iron folding-bedstead, without either mattress or bed-clothes. In the middle of the floor stood a smeared kettle on a spirit-stove, and a few odds and ends of glass and china were on the mantelpiece, together with a paraffin-lamp. Every article in the room was thick in dust.

When she had, more or less, ascertained these attractive details, Louie stood still in the middle of M. Dubois' apartment.

'What did he tell all those lies for?' she said to David fiercely. For in the very last communication received from him, Dubois had described himself as having made all necessary preparations *'et pour la toilette et pour le manger.'* He had also asked for the rent in advance, which David with some demur had paid.

'Here's something,' cried David; and, turning a handle in the wall, he pulled a flimsy door open and disclosed what seemed a cupboard. The cupboard, however, contained a bed, some bedding, blankets, and washing arrangements; and David joyously announced his discoveries. Louie took no notice of him. She was tired, angry, disgusted. The illusion of Paris was, for the moment, all gone. She sat herself down on one of the two chairs, and, taking off her hat, she threw it from her on to the belittered table with a passionate gesture.

The French girl had so far stood just outside, leaning against the doorway, and looking on with unabashed amusement while they made their inspection. Now, however, as Louie uncovered, the spectator at the door made a little, quick sound, and then ran forward.

'Mais, mon Dieu! how handsome you are!' she said with a whimsical eagerness, stopping short in front of Louie, and driving her little hands deep into the pockets of her jacket. 'What a head! —what eyes! Why didn't I see before? You must sit to me—you *must!* You will, won't you? I will pay you anything you like! You sha'n't be dull—somebody shall come and amuse you. *Voyons—monsieur!'* she called imperiously.

David came up. She stood with one hand on the table leaning her light weight backward, looking at them with all her eyes—the very embodiment of masterful caprice.

'Both of them!' she said under her breath, *'superbe!'* Monsieur, look here. You and mademoiselle are tired. There is nothing in these rooms. Dubois is a scamp without a sou. He does no work, and he gambles on the Bourse. Everything he had he has sold by degrees. If he has gone to Brussels now to work honestly, it is for the first time in his life. He lives on the hope of getting money out of an uncle in England—that I know, for he boasts of it to everybody. It is just like him to play a practical joke on strangers. No doubt you have paid him already—*n'est-ce pas?* I thought as much. Well, never mind! My rooms are next door. I am Elise Delaunay. I work in Taranne's *atelier.* I am an artist, pure and simple, and I live to please myself and nobody else. But I have a chair or two, and the woman downstairs looks after me because I make it worth her while. Come with me. I will give you some supper, and I will lend you a rug and a pillow for that bed. Then to-morrow you can decide what to do.'

David protested, stammering and smiling. But he had flushed a rosy red, and there was no real resistance in him. He explained the invitation to Louie, who had been looking helplessly from one to the other, and she at once accepted it. She understood perfectly that the French girl admired her; her face relaxed its frown; she nodded to the stranger with a sort of proud yielding, and then let herself be taken by the arm and led once more along the corridor.

Elise Delaunay unlocked her own door.

'*Bien!*' she said, putting her head in first, 'Merichat has earned her money. Now go in—go in!—and see if I don't give you some supper.'

CHAPTER II

She pushed them in, and shut the door behind them. They looked round them in amazement. Here was an *atelier* precisely corresponding in size and outlook to Dubois'. But to their tired eyes the change was one from squalor to fairyland. The room was not in fact luxurious at all. But there was a Persian rug or two on the polished floor; there was a wood fire burning on the hearth, and close to it there was a low sofa or divan covered with pieces of old stuffs, and flanked by a table whereon stood a little meal, a roll, some cut ham, part of a flat fruit tart from the *patissier* next door, a coffee pot, and a spirit kettle ready for lighting. There were two easels in the room; one was laden with sketches and photographs; the other carried a half-finished picture of a mosque interior in Oran—a rich splash of colour, making a centre for all the rest. Everywhere indeed, on the walls, on the floor, or standing on the chairs, were studies of Algeria, done with an ostentatiously bold and rapid hand. On the mantelpiece was a small reproduction in terra cotta of one of Dalou's early statues, a peasant woman in a long cloak straining her homely baby to her breast—true and passionate. Books lay about, and in a corner was a piano, open, with a confusion of tattered music upon it. And everywhere, as it seemed to Louie, were *shoes!*—the daintiest and most fantastic shoes imaginable—Turkish shoes, Pompadour shoes, old shoes and new shoes, shoes with heels and shoes without, shoes lined with fur, and shoes blown together, as one might think, out of cardboard and ribbons. The English girl's eyes fastened upon them at once.

'Ah, you tink my shoes pretty,' said the hostess, speaking a few words of English, *'c'est mon dada, voyez-vous—ma collection!—Tenez*—I cannot say dat in English, Monsieur; explain to your sister. My shoes are my passion, next to my foot. I am not pretty, but my foot is ravishing. Dalou modelled it for his Siren. That turned my head. Sit down, Mademoiselle—we will find some plates.'

She pushed Louie into a corner of the divan, and then she went over to a cupboard standing against the wall, and beckoned to David.

'Take the plates—and this potted meat. Now for the *petit vin* my doctor cousin brought me last week from the family estate. I have stowed it away somewhere. Ah! here it is. We are from the Gironde—at least my mother was. My father was nobody—*bourgeois* from tip to toe, though he called himself an artist. It was a *mesalliance* for her when she married him. Oh, he led her a life!—she died when I was small, and last year *he* died, eleven months ago. I did my best to cry. *Impossible!* He had made Maman and me cry too much. And now I am perfectly alone in the world, and perfectly well-behaved. Monsieur Prudhomme may talk—I snap my finger at him. You will have your ideas, of course. No matter! If you eat my salt, you will hardly be able to speak ill of me.'

'Mademoiselle!' cried David, inwardly cursing his shyness—a shyness new to him—and his complete apparent lack of anything to say, or the means of saying it.

'Oh, don't protest!—after that journey you can't afford to waste your breath. Move a little, Monsieur—let me open the other door of the cupboard—there are some chocolates worth eating on that back shelf. Do you admire my *armoire?* It is old Breton—it belonged to my grandmother, who was from Morbihan. She brought her linen in it. It is cherry wood, you see, mounted in silver. You may search Paris for another like it. Look at that flower work on the panels. It is not *banal* at all—it has character—there is real design in it. Now take the chocolates, and these sardine—put them down over there. As for me, I make the coffee.'

She ran over to the spirit lamp, and set it going; she measured out the coffee; then sitting down on the floor, she took the bellows and blew up the logs.

'Tell me your name, Monsieur?' she said suddenly, looking round.

David gave it in full, his own name and Louie's. Then he walked up to her, making an effort to be at his ease, and said something about their French descent. His mode of speaking was slow and bookish—correct, but wanting in life. After this year's devotion to French books, after all his compositions with Barbier, he had supposed himself so familiar with French! With the woman from the *loge*, indeed, he could have talked at large, had she been conversational instead of rude. But here, with this little glancing creature, he felt himself plunged in a perfect quagmire of ignorance and stupidity. When he spoke of being half French, she became suddenly grave, and studied him with an intent piercing look. 'No,' she said slowly, 'no, at bottom you are not French a bit, you are all English, I feel it. I should fight you—*a outrance!* Grive*—what a strange name! It's a bird's name. You are not like it—you do not belong to it. But *David!*—ah, that is better. *Voyons!*'

She sprang up, ran over to the furthest easel, and, routing about amongst its disorder of prints and photographs, she hit upon one, which she held up triumphantly.

'There, Monsieur!—there is your prototype. That is David—the young David—scourge of the Philistine. You are bigger and broader. I would rather fight him than you—but it is like you, all the same. Take it.'

And she held out to him a photograph of the Donatello David at Florence—the divine young hero in his shepherd's hat, fresh from the slaying of the oppressor.

He looked at it, red and wondering, then shook his head.

'What is it? Who made it, Mademoiselle?'

'Donatello—oh, I never saw it. I was never in Italy, but a friend gave it me. It is like you, I tell you. But, what use is that? You are English—yes, you *are*, in spite of your mother. It is very well to be called David—you may be Goliath all the time!'

Her tone had grown hard and dry—insulting almost. Her look sent him a challenge.

He stared at her dumbfounded. All the self-confidence with which he had hitherto governed his own world had deserted him. He was like a tongue-tied child in her hands.

She enjoyed her mastery, and his discomfiture. Her look changed and melted in an instant.

'I am rude,' she said, 'and you can't answer me back—not yet—for a day or two. *Pardon*! Monsieur David—Mademoiselle—will you come to supper?'

She put chairs and waved them to their places with the joyous animation of a child, waiting on them, fetching this and that, with the quickest, most graceful motions. She had brought from the *armoire* some fine white napkins, and now she produced a glass or two and made her guests provide themselves with the red wine which neither had ever tasted before, and over which Louie made an involuntary face. Then she began to chatter and to eat—both as fast as possible—now laughing at her own English or at David's French, and now laying down her knife and fork that she might look at Louie with an intent professional look which contrasted oddly with the wild freedom of her talk and movements.

Suddenly she took up a wineglass and held it out to David with a piteous childish gesture.

'Fill it, Monsieur, and then drink—drink to my good luck. I wish for something—with my *life*—my soul; but there are people who hate me, who would delight to see me crushed. And it will be three weeks—three long long weeks, almost—before I know.'

She was very pale, the tears had sprung to her eyes, and the hand holding the glass trembled. David flushed and frowned in the vain desire to understand her.

'What am I to do?' he said, taking the glass mechanically, but making no use of it.

'Drink!—drink to my success. I have two pictures, Monsieur, in the Salon; you know what that means? the same as your *Academie? Parfaitement!* ah! you understand. One is well hung, on the line; the other has been shamefully treated—but *shamefully!* And all the world knows why. I have some enemies on the jury, and they delight in a mean triumph over me—a triumph which is a scandal. But I have friends, too—good friends—and in three weeks the rewards will be voted. You understand? the medals, and the *mentions honorables.* As for a medal—no! I am only two years in the *atelier;* I am not unreasonable. But a *mention!*—ah! Monsieur David, if they don't give it me I shall be very miserable.'

Her voice had gone through a whole gamut of emotion in this speech— pride, elation, hope, anger, offended dignity—sinking finally to the plaintive note of a child asking for consolation.

And luckily David had followed her. His French novels had brought him across the Salon and the jury system; and Barbier had told him tales. His courage rose. He poured the wine into the glass with a quick, uncertain hand, and raised it to his lips.

'*A la gloire de Mademoiselle!*' he cried, tossing it down with a gesture almost as free and vivid as her own.

Her eye followed him with excitement, taking in every detail of the action—the masculine breadth of chest, the beauty of the dark head and short upper lip.

'Very good—very good!' she said, clapping her small hands. 'You did that admirably—you improve—*n'est-ce pas, Mademoiselle?*'

But Louie only stared blankly and somewhat haughtily in return. She was beginning to be tired of her silent *role*, and of the sort of subordination it implied. The French girl seemed to divine it, and her.

'She does not like me,' she said, with a kind of wonder under her breath, so that David did not catch the words. 'The other is quite different.'

Then, springing up, she searched in the pockets of her jacket for something—lips pursed, brows knitted, as though the quest were important.

'Where are my cigarettes?' she demanded sharply. 'Ah! here they are. Mademoiselle—Monsieur.'

Louie laughed rudely, pushing them back without a word. Then she got up, and began boldly to look about her. The shoes attracted her, and some Algerian scarves and burnouses that were lying on a distant chair. She went to turn them over.

Mademoiselle Delaunay looked after her for a moment—with the same critical attention as before—then with a shrug she threw herself into a corner of the divan, drawing about her a bit of old embroidered stuff which lay there. It was so flung, however, as to leave one dainty foot in an embroidered silk stocking visible beyond it. The tone of the stocking was repeated in the bunch of violets at her neck, and the purples of the flowers told with charming effect against her white skin and the pale fawn colour of her dress and hair. David watched her with intoxication. She could hardly be taller than most children of fourteen, but her proportions were so small and delicate that her height, whatever it was, seemed to him the perfect height for a woman. She handled her cigarette with mannish airs; unless it were some old harridan in a collier's cottage, he had never seen a woman smoke before, and certainly he had never guessed it could become her so well. Not pretty! He was in no mood to dissect the pale irregular face with its subtleties of line and expression; but, as she sat there smoking and chatting, she was to him the realisation—the climax of his dream of Paris. All the lightness and grace of that dream, the strangeness, the thrill of it seemed to have passed into her.

'Will you stay in those rooms?' she inquired, slowly blowing away the curls of smoke in front of her.

David replied that he could not yet decide. He looked as he felt—in a difficulty.

'Oh! *you* will do well enough there. But your sister—*Tenez*! There is a family on the floor below—an artist and his wife. I have known them take *pensionnaires*. They are not the most distinguished persons in the world—*mais enfin!*—it is not for long. Your sister might do worse than board with them.'

David thanked her eagerly. He would make all inquiries. He had in his pocket a note of introduction from Dubois to Madame Cervin, and another, he believed, to the gentleman on the ground floor—to M. Montjoie, the sculptor.

'Ah! M. Montjoie!'

Her brows went up, her grey eyes flashed. As for her tone it was half amused, half contemptuous. She began to speak, moved restlessly, then apparently thought better of it.

'After all,' she said, in a rapid undertone, '*qu'est-ce que cela me fait? Allons*. Why did you come here at all, instead of to an hotel, for so short a time?'

He explained as well as he was able.

'You wanted to see something of French life, and French artists or writers?' she repeated slowly, 'and you come with introductions from Xavier Dubois! *C'est drole, ca*. Have you studied art?'

He laughed.

'No—except in books.'

'What books?'

'Novels—George Sand's.'

It was her turn to laugh now.

'You are really too amusing! No, Monsieur, no; you interest me. I have the best will in the world towards you; but I cannot ask Consuelos and Teverinos to meet you. *Pas possible*. I regret—'

She fell into silence a moment, studying him with a merry look. Then she broke out again.

'Are you a connoisseur in pictures, Monsieur?'

He had reddened already under her *persiflage*. At this he grew redder still.

'I have never seen any, Mademoiselle,' he said, almost piteously; 'except once a little exhibition in Manchester.'

'Nor sculpture?'

'No,' he said honestly; 'nor sculpture.'

It seemed to him he was being held under a microscope, so keen and pitiless were her laughing eyes. But she left him no time to resent it.

'So you are a blank page, Monsieur—virgin soil—and you confess it. You interest me extremely. I should even like to teach you a little. I am the most ignorant person in the world. I know nothing about artists in books. *Mais je suis artiste, moi! fille d'artiste*. I could tell you tales—'

She threw her graceful head back against the cushion behind her, and smiled again broadly, as though her sense of humour were irresistibly tickled by the situation.

Then a whim seized her, and she sat up, grave and eager.

'I have drawn since I was eight years old,' she said; 'would you like to hear about it? It is not romantic—not the least in the world—but it is true.'

And with what seemed to his foreign ear a marvellous swiftness and fertility of phrase, she poured out her story. After her mother died she had been sent at eight years old to board at a farm near Rouen by her father, who seemed to have regarded his daughter now as plaything and model, now as an intolerable drag on the freedom of a vicious career. And at the farm the child's gift declared itself. She began with copying the illustrations, the saints and holy families in a breviary belonging to one of the farm servants; she went on to draw the lambs, the carts, the horses, the farm buildings, on any piece of white wood she could find littered about the yard, or any bit of paper saved from a parcel, till at last the old cure took pity upon her and gave her some chalks and a drawing-book. At fourteen her father, for a caprice, reclaimed her, and she found herself alone with him in Paris. To judge from the hints she threw out, her life during thee next few years had been of the roughest and wildest, protected only by her indomitable resolve to learn, to make herself an artist, come what would. 'I meant to be *famous*, and I mean it still!' she said, with a passionate emphasis which made David open his eyes. Her father refused to believe in her gift, and was far too self-indulgent and brutal to teach her. But some of his artist friends were kind to her, and taught her intermittently; by the help of some of them she got permission, although under age, to copy in the Louvre, and with hardly any technical knowledge worked there feverishly from morning to night; and at last Taranne—the great Taranne, from whose *atelier* so many considerable artists had gone out to the conquest of the public—Taranne had seen some of her drawings, heard her story, and generously taken her as a pupil.

Then emulation took hold of her—the fierce desire to be first in all the competitions of the *atelier*. David had the greatest difficulty in following her rapid speech, with its slang, its technical idioms, its extravagance and variety; but he made out that she had been for a long time deficient in sound training, and that her rivals at the *atelier* had again and again beaten her easily in spite of her gift, because of her weakness in the grammar of her art.

'And whenever they beat me I could have killed my conquerors; and whenever I beat them, I despised my judges and wanted to give the prize away. It is not my fault. *Je suis faite comme ça—voilà!* I am as vain as a peacock; yet when people admire anything I do, I think them fools—*fools!* I am jealous and proud and absurd—so they all say; yet a word, a look from a real artist—from one of the great men who *know*—can break me, make me cry. *Demelez ca, Monsieur, si vous pouvez!'*

She stopped, out of breath. Their eyes were on each other. The fascination, the absorption expressed in the Englishman's look startled her. She hurriedly turned away, took up her cigarette again, and nestled into the cushion. He vainly tried to clothe some of the quick comments running through his mind in adequate French, could find nothing but the most commonplace phrases, stammered out a few, and then blushed afresh. In her pity for him she took up her story again.

After her father's sudden death, the shelter, such as it was, of his name and companionship was withdrawn. What was she to do? It turned out that she possessed a small *rente* which had belonged to her mother, and which her father had never been able to squander. Two relations from her mother's country near Bordeaux turned up to claim her, a country doctor and his sister—middle-aged, devout—to her wild eyes at least, altogether forbidding.

'They made too much of their self-sacrifice in taking me to live with them,' she said with her little ringing laugh. 'I said to them—"My good uncle and aunt, it is too much—no one could have the right to lay such a burden upon you. Go home and forget me. I am incorrigible. I am an artist. I mean to live by myself, and work for myself. I am sure to go to the bad— good morning." They went home and told the rest of my mother's people that I was insane. But they could not keep my money from me. It is just enough for me. Besides, I shall be selling soon,—certainly I shall be selling! I have had two or three inquiries already about one of the exhibits in the Salon. Now then—*talk*, Monsieur David!' and she emphasised the words by a little frown; 'it is your turn.'

And gradually by skill and patience she made him talk, made him give her back some of her confidences. It seemed to amuse her greatly that he should be a bookseller. She knew no booksellers in Paris; she could assure him they were all pure *bourgeois*, and there was not one of them that could be likened to Donatello's David. Manchester she had scarcely heard of; she shook her fair head over it. But when he told her of his French reading, when he waxed eloquent about Rousseau and George Sand, then her mirth became uncontrollable.

'You came to France to talk of Rousseau and George Sand?' she asked him with dancing eyes—'*Mon Dieu! mon Dieu!* what do you take us for?'

This time his vanity was hurt. He asked her to tell him what she meant— why she laughed at him.

'I will do better than that,' she said; 'I will get some friend of mine to take you to-morrow to "Les Trois Rats."'

'What is "Les Trois Rats"?' he asked, half wounded and half mystified.

'"Les Trois Rats," Monsieur, is an artist's cafe. It is famous, it is characteristic; if you are in search of local colour you must certainly go there. When you come back you will have some fresh ideas, I promise you.'

He asked if ladies also went there.

'Some do; I don't. Conventions mean nothing to me, as you perceive, or I should have a companion here to play propriety. But like you, perhaps, I am Romantic. I believe in the grand style. I have ideas as to how men should treat me. I can read Octave Feuillet. I have a terrible weakness for those *cavaliers* of his. And garbage makes me ill. So I avoid the "Trois Rats."'

She fell silent, resting her little chin on her hand. Then with a sudden sly smile she bent forward and looked him in the eyes.

'Are you pious, Monsieur, like all the English? There is some religion left in your country, isn't there?'

'Yes, certainly,' he admitted, 'there was a good deal.'

Then, hesitating, he described his own early reading of Voltaire, watching its effect upon her, afraid lest here too he should say something fatuous, behind the time, as he seemed to have been doing all through.

'Voltaire!'—she shrugged her little shoulders—'Voltaire to me is just an old *perruque*—a prating philanthropical person who talked about *le bon Dieu*, and wrote just what every *bourgeois* can understand. If he had had his will and swept away the clergy and the Church, how many fine subjects we artists should have lost!'

He sat helplessly staring at her. She enjoyed his perplexity a minute; then she returned to the charge.

'Well, my credo is very short. Its first article is art—and its second is art—and its third is art!'

Her words excited her. The delicate colour flushed into her cheek. She flung her head back and looked straight before her with half-shut eyes.

'Yes—I believe in art—and expression—and colour—and *le vrai*. Velazquez is my God, and—and he has too many prophets to mention! I was devout once for three months—since then I have never had as much faith of the Church sort as would lie on a ten-sous piece. But'—with a sudden whimsical change of voice—'I am as credulous as a Breton fisherman, and as superstitious as a gipsy! Wait and see. Will you look at my pictures?'

She sprang up and showed her sketches. She had been a winter in Algiers, and had there and in Spain taken a passion for the East, for its colour, its mystery, its suggestions of cruelty and passion. She chattered away, explaining, laughing, haranguing, and David followed her submissively from thing to thing, dumb with the interest and curiosity of this new world and language of the artist.

Louie meanwhile, who, after the refreshment of supper, had been forgetting both her fatigue and the other two in the entertainment provided her by the shoes and the Oriental dresses, had now found a little inlaid coffer on a distant table, full of Algerian trinkets, and was examining them. Suddenly a loud crash was heard from her neighbourhood.

Elise Delaunay stood still. Her quick speech, died on her lips. She made one bound forward to Louie; then, with a cry, she turned deathly pale, tottered, and would have fallen, but that David ran to her.

'The glass is broken,' she said, or rather gasped; 'she has broken it—that old Venetian glass of Maman's. Oh! my pictures!—my pictures! How can I undo it? *Je suis perdue*! Oh go!—go! —*go*—both of you! Leave me alone! Why did I ever see you?'

She was beside herself with rage and terror. She laid hold of Louie, who stood in sullen awkwardness and dismay, and pushed her to the door so suddenly and so violently that the stronger, taller girl yielded without an attempt at resistance. Then holding the door open, she beckoned imperiously to David, while the tears streamed down her cheeks.

'Adieu, Monsieur—say nothing—there is nothing to be said—go!'

He went out bewildered, and the two in their amazement walked mechanically to their own door.

'She is mad!' said Louie, her eyes blazing, when they paused and looked at each other. 'She must be mad. What did she say?'

'What happened?' was all he could reply.

'I threw down that old glass—it wasn't my fault—I didn't see it. It was standing on the floor against a chair. I moved the chair back just a trifle, and it fell. A shabby old thing—I could have paid for another easily. Well, I'm not going there again to be treated like that.'

The girl was furious. All that chafed sense of exclusion and slighted importance which had grown upon her during David's *tete-a-tete* with their strange hostess came to violent expression in her resentment. She opened the door of their room, saying that whatever he might do she was going to bed and to sleep somewhere, if it was on the floor.

David made a melancholy light in the squalid room, and Louie went about her preparations in angry silence. When she had withdrawn into the little cupboard-room, saying carelessly that she supposed he could manage with one of the bags and his great coat, he sat down on the edge of the bare iron bedstead, and recognised with a start that he was quivering all over—with fatigue, or excitement? His chief feeling perhaps was one of utter discomfiture, flatness, and humiliation.

He had sat there in the dark without moving for some minutes, when his ear caught a low uncertain tapping at the door. His heart leapt. He sprang up and turned the key in an instant.

There on the landing stood Elise Delaunay, her arms filled with what looked like a black bearskin rug, her small tremulous face and tear-wet eyes raised to his.

'*Pardon*, Monsieur,' she said hurriedly. 'I told you I was superstitious— well, now you see. Will you take this rug?—one can sleep anywhere with it though it is so old. And has your sister what she wants? Can I do anything for her? No! *Alors*—I must talk to you about her in the morning. I have some more things in my head to say. *Pardon!—et bonsoir.* '

She pushed the rug into his hands. He was so moved that he let it drop on the floor unheeding, and as she looked at him, half audacious, half afraid, she saw a painful struggle, as of some strange new birth, pass across his dark young face. They stood so a moment, looking at each other. Then he made a quick step forward with some inarticulate words. In an instant she was halfway along the corridor, and, turning back so that her fair hair and smiling eyes caught the light she held, she said to him with the queenliest gesture of dismissal:

'*Au revoir*, Monsieur David, sleep well.'

CHAPTER III

David woke early from a restless sleep. He sprang up and dressed. Never had the May sun shone so brightly; never had life looked more alluring.

In the first place he took care to profit by the hints of the night before. He ran down to make friends with Madame Merichat—a process which was accomplished without much difficulty, as soon as a franc or two had passed, and arrangements had been made for the passing of a few more. She was to take charge of the *appartement*, and provide them with their morning coffee and bread. And upon this her grim countenance cleared. She condescended to spend a quarter of an hour gossiping with the Englishman, and she promised to stand as a buffer between him and Dubois' irate landlord.

'A job of work at Brussels, you say, Monsieur? *Bien*; I will tell the *proprietaire*. He won't believe it—Monsieur Dubois tells too many lies; but perhaps it will keep him quiet. He will think of the return—of the money in the pocket. He will bid me inform him the very moment Monsieur Dubois shows his nose, that he may descend upon him, and so you will be let alone.'

He mounted the stairs again, and stood a moment looking along the passage with a quickening pulse. There was a sound of low singing, as of one crooning over some occupation. It must be she! Then she had recovered her trouble of the night before—her strange trouble. Yet he dimly remembered that in the farm-houses of the Peak also the breaking of a looking-glass had been held to be unlucky. And, of course, in interpreting the omen she had thought of her pictures and the jury.

How could he see her again? Suddenly it occurred to him that she had spoken of taking a holiday since the Salon opened. A holiday which for her meant 'copying in the Louvre.' And where else, pray, does the tourist naturally go on the first morning of a visit to Paris?

The young fellow went back into his room with a radiant face, and spent some minutes, as Louie had not yet appeared, in elaborating his toilette. The small cracked glass above the mantelpiece was not flattering, and David was almost for the first time anxious about and attentive to what he saw there. Yet, on the whole, he was pleased with his short serge coat and his new tie. He thought they gave him something of a student air, and would not disgrace even *her* should she deign to be seen in his company. As he laid his brush down he looked at his own brown hand, and remembered hers with a kind of wonder—so small and white, the wrist so delicately rounded.

When Louie emerged she was not in a good temper. She declared that she had hardly slept a wink; that the bed was not fit to sleep on; that the cupboard was alive with mice, and smelt intolerably. David first endeavoured to appease her with the coffee and rolls which had just arrived, and then he broached the plan of sending her to board with the Cervins, which Mademoiselle Delaunay had suggested. What did she think? It would cost more, perhaps, but he could afford it. On their way out he would deliver the two notes of introduction, and no doubt they could settle it directly if she liked.

Louie yawned, put up objections, and refused to see anything in a promising light. Paris was horrid, and the man who had let them the rooms ought to be 'had up.' As for people who couldn't talk any English she hated the sight of them.

The remark from an Englishwoman in France had its humour. But David did not see that point of it. He flushed hotly, and with difficulty held an angry tongue. However, he was possessed with an inward dread—the dread of the idealist who sees his pleasure as a beautiful whole—lest they should so quarrel as to spoil the visit and the new experience. Under this curb he controlled himself, and presently, with more *savoir vivre* than he was conscious of, proposed that they should go out and see the shops.

Louie, at the mere mention of shops, passed into another mood. After she had spent some time on dressing they sallied forth, David delivering his notes on the way down. Both noticed that the house was squalid and ill-kept, but apparently full of inhabitants. David surmised that they were for the most part struggling persons of small means and extremely various occupations. There were three *ateliers* in the building, the two on their own top floor, and M. Montjoie's, which was apparently built out at the back on the ground floor. The first floor was occupied by a dressmaker, the *proprietaires* best tenant, according to Madame Merichat. Above her was a clerk in the Ministry of the Interior, with his wife and two or three children; above them again the Cervins, and a couple of commercial travellers, and so on.

The street outside, in its general aspect, suggested the same small, hard-pressed professional life. It was narrow and dull; it mounted abruptly towards the hill of Montmartre, with its fort and cemetery, and, but for the height of the houses, which is in itself a dignified architectural feature, would have been no more inspiriting than a street in London.

A few steps, however, brought them on to the Boulevard Montmartre, and then, taking the Rue Lafitte, they emerged upon the Boulevard des Italiens.

Louie looked round her, to this side and that, paused for a moment, bewildered as it were by the general movement and gaiety of the scene. Then a *lingerie* shop caught her eye, and she made for it. Soon the last cloud had cleared from the girl's brow. She gave herself with ecstasy to the shops, to the people. What jewellery, what dresses, what delicate cobwebs of lace and ribbon, what miracles of colour in the florists' windows, what suggestions of wealth and lavishness everywhere! Here in this world of costly contrivance, of an eager and inventive luxury, Louise Suveret's daughter felt herself at last at home. She had never set foot in it before; yet already it was familiar, and she was part of it.

Yes, she was as well dressed as anybody, she concluded, except perhaps the ladies in the closed carriages whose dress could only be guessed at. As for good looks, there did not seem to be much of *them* in Paris. She called the Frenchwomen downright plain. They knew how to put on their clothes; there was style about them, she did not deny that; but she was prepared to maintain that there was hardly a decent face among them.

Such air, and such a sky! The trees were rushing into leaf; summer dresses were to be seen everywhere; the shops had swung out their awnings, and the day promised a summer heat still tempered by a fresh spring breeze. For a time David was content to lounge along, stopping when his companion did, lost as she was in the enchantment and novelty of the scene, drinking in Paris as it were at great gulps, saying to himself they would be at the Opera directly, then the Theatre-Francais, the Louvre, the Tuileries, the Place de la Concorde! Every book that had ever passed through his hands containing illustrations and descriptions of Paris he had read with avidity. He, too, like Louie, though in a different way, was at home in these streets, and hardly needed a look at the map he carried to find his way. Presently, when he could escape from Louie, he would go and explore to his heart's content, see all that the tourist sees, and then penetrate further, and judge for himself as to those sweeping and iconoclastic changes which, for its own tyrant's purposes, the Empire had been making in the older city. As he thought of the Emperor and the government his gorge rose within him. Barbier's talk had insensibly determined all his ideas of the imperial regime. How much longer would France suffer the villainous gang who ruled her? He began an inward declamation in the manner of Hugo, exciting himself as he walked—while all the time it was the spring of 1870 which was swelling and expanding in the veins and branches of the plane trees above him—May was hurrying on, and Worth lay three short months ahead!

Then suddenly into the midst of his political musings and his traveller's ardour the mind thrust forward a disturbing image—the figure of a little fair-haired artist. He looked round impatiently. Louie's loiterings began to chafe him.

'Come along, do,' he called to her, waking up to the time; 'we shall never get there.'

'Where?' she demanded.

'Why, to the Louvre.'

'What's there to see there?'

'It's a great palace. The Kings of France used to live there once. Now they've put pictures and statues into it. You must see it, Louie—everybody does. Come along.'

'I'll not hurry,' she said perversely.' I don't care *that* about silly old pictures.'

And she went back to her shop-gazing. David felt for a moment precisely as he had been used to feel in the old days on the Scout, when he had tried to civilise her on the question of books. And now as then he had to wrestle with her, using the kind of arguments he felt might have a chance with her. At last she sulkily gave way, and let him lead on at a quick pace. In the Rue Saint-Honore, indeed, she was once more almost unmanageable; but at last they were safely on the stairs of the Louvre, and David's brow smoothed, his eye shone again. He mounted the interminable steps with such gaiety and eagerness that Louie's attention was drawn to him.

'Whatever do you go that pace for?' she said crossly. 'It's enough to kill anybody going up this kind of thing!'

'It isn't as bad as the Downfall,' said David, laughing, 'and I've seen you get up that fast enough. Come, catch hold of my umbrella and I'll drag you up.'

Louie reached the top, out of breath, turned into the first room to the right, and looked scornfully round her.

'Well I never!' she ejaculated. 'What's the good of this?'

Meanwhile David shot on ahead, beckoning to her to follow. She, however, would take her own pace, and walked sulkily along, looking at the people who were not numerous enough to please her, and only regaining a certain degree of serenity when she perceived that here as elsewhere people turned to stare after her.

David meanwhile threw wondering glances at the great Veronese, at Raphael's archangel, at the towering Vandyke, at the 'Virgin of the Rocks.' But he passed them by quickly. Was she here? Could he find her in this wilderness of rooms? His spirits wavered between delicious expectancy and the fear of disappointment. The gallery seemed to him full of copyists young and old: beardless *rapins* laughing and chatting with fresh maidens; old men sitting crouched on high seats with vast canvases before them; or women, middle-aged and plain, with knitted shawls round their shoulders, at work upon the radiant Greuzes and Lancrets; but that pale golden head— nowhere!

AT LAST!

He hurried forward, and there, in front of a Velazquez, he found her, in the company of two young men, who were leaning over the back of her chair criticising the picture on her easel.

'Ah, Monsieur David!'

She took up the brush she held with her teeth for a moment, and carelessly held him out two fingers of her right hand.

'Monsieur—make a diversion—tell the truth—these gentlemen here have been making a fool of me.'

And throwing herself back with a little laughing, coquettish gesture, she made room for him to look.

'Ah, but I forgot; let me present you. M. Alphonse, this is an Englishman; he is new to Paris, and he is an acquaintance of mine. You are not to play any joke upon him. M. Lenain, this gentleman wishes to be made acquainted with art; you will undertake his education—you will take him to-night to "Les Trois Rats." I promised for you.'

She threw a merry look at the elder of her two attendants, who ceremoniously took off his hat to David and made a polite speech, in which the word *enchante* recurred. He was a dark man, with a short black beard, and full restless eye; some ten years older apparently than the other, who was a dare-devil boy of twenty.

'*Allons!* tell me what you think of my picture, M. David.'

The three waited for the answer, not without malice. David looked at it perplexed. It was a copy of the black and white Infanta, with the pink rosettes, which, like everything else that France possesses from the hand of Velazquez, is to the French artist of to-day among the sacred things, the flags and battle-cries of his art. Its strangeness, its unlikeness to anything of the picture kind that his untrained provincial eyes had ever lit upon, tied his tongue. Yet he struggled with himself.

'Mademoiselle, I cannot explain—I cannot find the words. It seems to me ugly. The child is not pretty nor the dress. But—'

He stared at the picture, fascinated—unable to express himself, and blushing under the shame of his incapacity.

The other three watched him curiously.

'Taranne should get hold of him,' the elder artist murmured to his companion, with an imperceptible nod towards the Englishman. 'The models lately have been too common. There was a rebellion yesterday in the *atelier de femmes*; one and all declared the model was not worth drawing, and one and all left.'

'Minxes!' said the other coolly, a twinkle in his wild eye. 'Taranne will have to put his foot down. There are one or two demons among them; one should make them know their place.'

Lenain threw back his head and laughed—a great, frank laugh, which broke up the ordinary discontent of the face agreeably. The speaker, M. Alphonse Duchatel, had been already turned out of two *ateliers* for a series of the most atrocious *charges* on record. He was now with Taranne, on trial, the authorities keeping a vigilant eye on him.

Meanwhile Elise, still leaning back with her eyes on her picture, was talking fast to David, who hung over her, absorbed. She was explaining to him some of the Infanta's qualities, pointing to this and that with her brush, talking a bright, untranslatable artist's language which dazzled him, filled him with an exciting medley of new impressions and ideas, while all the time his quick sense responded with a delightful warmth and eagerness to the personality beside him—child, prophetess, egotist, all in one—noticing each characteristic detail, the drooping, melancholy trick of the eyes, the nervous delicacy of the small hand holding the brush.

'David—*David*! I'm tired of this, I tell you! I'm not going to stay, so I thought I'd come and tell you. Good-bye!'

He turned abruptly, and saw Louie standing defiantly a few paces behind him.

'What do you want, Louie?' he said impatiently, going up to her. It was no longer the same man, the same voice.

'I want to go. I hate this!'

'I'm not ready, and you can't go by yourself. Do you see' —(in an undertone)—'this is Mademoiselle Delaunay?'

'That don't matter,' she said sulkily, making no movement. 'If you ain't going, I am.'

By this time, however, Elise, as well as the two artists, had perceived Louie's advent. She got up from her seat with a slight sarcastic smile, and held out her hand.

'*Bonjour*, Mademoiselle! You forgave me for dat I did last night? I ask your pardon—oh, *de tout mon cœur!*'

Even Louie perceived that the tone was enigmatical. She gave an inward gulp of envy, however, excited by the cut of the French girl's black and white cotton. Then she dropped Elise's hand, and moved away.

'Louie!' cried David, pursuing her in despair; 'now just wait half an hour, there's a good girl, while I look at a few things, and then afterwards I'll take you to the street where all the best shops are, and you can look at them as much as you like.'

Louie stood irresolute.

'What is it?' said Elise to him in French. 'Your sister wants to go? Why, you have only just come!'

'She finds it dull looking at pictures,' said David, with an angry brow, controlling himself with difficulty. 'She must have the shops.'

Elise shrugged her shoulders and, turning her head, said a few quick words that David did not follow to the two men behind her. They all laughed. The artists, however, were both much absorbed in Louie's appearance, and could not apparently take their eyes off her.

'Ah!' said Elise, suddenly.

She had recognised some one at a distance, to whom she nodded. Then she turned and looked at the English girl, laughed, and caught her by the wrist.

'Monsieur David, here are Monsieur and Madame Oervin. Have you thought of sending your sister to them? If so, I will present you. Why not? They would amuse her. Madame Cervin would take her to all the shops, to the races, to the Bois. *Que sais-je?*

All the while she was looking from one to the other. David's face cleared. He thought he saw a way out of this *impasse*.

'Louie, come here a moment. I want to speak to you.'

And he carried her off a few yards, while the Cervins came up and greeted the group round the Infanta. A powerfully built, thickset man, in a grey suit, who had been walking with them, fell back as they joined Elise Delaunay, and began to examine a Pieter de Hooghe with minuteness.

Meanwhile David wrestled with his sister. She had much better let Mademoiselle Delaunay arrange with these people. Then Madame Cervin could take her about wherever she wanted to go. He would make a bargain to that effect. As for him, he must and would see Paris—pictures, churches, public buildings. If the Louvre bored her, everything would bore her, and it was impossible either that he should spend his time at her apron-string, flattening his nose against the shop-windows, or that she should go about alone. He was not going to have her taken for 'a bad lot,' and treated accordingly, he told her frankly, with an imperious tightening of all his young frame. He had discovered some time since that it was necessary to be plain with Louie.

She hated to be disposed of on any occasion, except by her own will and initiative, and she still made difficulties for the sake of making them, till he grew desperate. Then, when she had pushed his patience to the very last point, she gave way.

'You tell her she's to do as I want her,' she said, threateningly. 'I won't stay if she doesn't. And I'll not have her paid too much.'

David led her back to the rest.

'My sister consents. Arrange it if you can, Mademoiselle,' he said imploringly to Elise.

A series of quick and somewhat noisy colloquies followed, watched with disapproval by the *gardien* near, who seemed to be once or twice on the point of interfering.

Mademoiselle Delaunay opened the matter to Madame Cervin, a short, stout woman, with no neck, and a keen, small eye. Money was her daily and hourly preoccupation, and she could have kissed the hem of Elise Delaunay's dress in gratitude for these few francs thus placed in her way. It was some time now since she had lost her last boarder, and had not been able to obtain another. She took David aside, and, while her look sparkled with covetousness, explained to him volubly all that she would do for Louie, and for how much. And she could talk some English too—certainly she could. Her education had been *excellent*, she was thankful to say.

'*Mon Dieu, qu'elle est belle!*' she wound up. 'Ah, Monsieur, you do very right to entrust your sister to me. A young fellow like you—no!—that is not *convenable*. But I—I will be a dragon. Make your mind quite easy. With me all will go well.'

Louie stood in an impatient silence while she was being thus talked over, exchanging looks from time to time with the two artists, who had retired a little behind Mademoiselle Delaunay's easel, and from that distance were perfectly competent to let the bold-eyed English girl know what they thought of her charms.

At last the bargain was concluded, and the Cervins walked away with Louie in charge. They were to take her to a restaurant, then show her the Rue Royale and the Rue de la Paix, and, finally—David making no demur whatever about the expense—there was to be an afternoon excursion through the Bois to Longchamps, where some of the May races were being run.

As they receded, the man in grey, before the Pieter de Hooghe, looked up, smiled, dropped his eyeglass, and resumed his place beside Madame Cervin. She made a gesture of introduction, and he bowed across her to the young stranger.

For the first time Elise perceived him. A look of annoyance and disgust crossed her face.

'Do you see,' she said, turning to Lenain; 'there is that animal, Montjoie? He did well to keep his distance. What do the Cervins want with him?'

The others shrugged their shoulders.

'They say his Maenad would be magnificent if he could keep sober enough to finish her,' said Lenain; 'it is his last chance; he will go under altogether if he fails; he is almost done for already.'

'And what a gift!' said Alphonse, in a lofty tone of critical regret. 'He should have been a second Barye. *Ah, la vie Parisienne—la maudite vie Parisienne!*'

Again Lenain exploded.

'Come and lunch, you idiot,' he said, taking the lad's arm; 'for whom are you posing?'

But before they departed, they inquired of David in the politest way what they could do for him. He was a stranger to Mollie. Delaunay's acquaintance; they were at his service. Should they take him somewhere at night? David, in an effusion of gratitude, suggested 'Les Trois Rats.' He desired greatly to see the artist world, he said. Alphonse grinned. An appointment was made for eight o'clock, and the two friends walked off.

CHAPTER IV

David and Elise Delaunay thus found themselves left alone. She stood a moment irresolutely before her canvas, then sat down again, and took up her brushes.

'I cannot thank you enough, Mademoiselle,' the young fellow began shyly, while the hand which held his stick trembled a little. 'We could never have arranged that affair for ourselves.'

She coloured and bent over her canvas.

'I don't know why I troubled myself,' she said, in a curious irritable way.' Because you are kind!' he cried, his charming smile breaking. 'Because you took pity on a pair of strangers, like the guardian angel that you are!'

The effect of the foreign language on him leading him to a more set and literary form of expression than he would have naturally used, was clearly marked in the little outburst.

Elise bit her lip, frowned and fidgeted, and presently looked him straight in the face.

'Monsieur David, warn your sister that that man with the Cervins this morning—the man in grey, the sculptor, M. Montjoie—is a disreputable scoundrel that no decent woman should know.'

David was taken aback.

'And Madame Cervin—'

Elise raised her shoulders.

'I don't offer a solution,' she said; 'but I have warned you.'

'Monsieur Cervin has a somewhat strange appearance,' said David, hesitating.

And, in fact, while the negotiations had been going on there had stood beside the talkers a shabby, slouching figure of a man, with longish grizzled hair and a sleepy eye—a strange, remote creature, who seemed to take very little notice of what was passing before him. From various indications, however, in the conversation, David had gathered that this looker-on must be the former *prix de Rome*.

Elise explained that Monsieur Carvin was the wreck of a genius. In his youth he had been the chosen pupil of Ingres and Hippolyte Flandrin, had won the *prix de Rome,* and after his three years in the Villa Medicis had come home to take up what was expected to be a brilliant career. Then for some mysterious reason he had suddenly gone under, disappeared from sight, and the waves of Paris had closed over him. When he reappeared he was broken in health, and married to a retired modiste, upon whose money he was living. He painted bad pictures intermittently, but spent most of his time in hanging about his old haunts—the Louvre, the Salon, the various exhibitions, and the dealers, where he was commonly regarded by the younger artists who were on speaking terms with him as a tragic old bore, with a head of his own worth painting, however if he could be got to sit—for an augur or a chief priest.

'It was *absinthe* that did it,' said Elise calmly, taking a fresh charge into her brush, and working away at the black trimmings of the Infanta's dress. 'Every day, about four, he disappears into the Boulevard. Generally, Madame Cervin drives him like a sheep; but when four o'clock comes she daren't interfere with him. If she did, he would be unmanageable altogether. So he takes his two hours or so, and when he comes back there is not much amiss with him. Sometimes he is excited, and talks quite brilliantly about the past—sometimes he is nervous and depressed, starts at a sound, and storms about the noises in the street. Then she hurries him off to bed, and the next morning he is quite meek again, and tries to paint. But his hand shakes, and he can't see. So he gives it up, and calls to her to put on her things. Then they wander about Paris, till four o'clock comes round again, and he gives her the slip—always with some elaborate pretence of other. Oh! she takes it quietly. Other vices might give her more trouble.'

The tone conveyed the affectation of a complete knowledge of the world, which saw no reason whatever to be ashamed of itself. The girl was just twenty, but she had lived for years, first with a disreputable father, and then in a perpetual *camaraderie,* within the field of art, with men of all sorts and kinds. There are certain feminine blooms which a *milieu* like this effaces with deadly rapidity.

For the first time David was jarred. The idealist in him recoiled. His conscience, too, was roused about Louie. He had handed her over, it seemed, to the custody of a drunkard and his wife, who had immediately thrown her into the company of a man no decent woman ought to know. And Mademoiselle Delaunay had led him into it. The guardian angel speech of a few moments before rang in his ears uncomfortably.

Moreover, whatever rebellions his young imagination might harbour, whatever license in his eyes the great passions might claim, he had maintained for months and years past a practical asceticism, which had left its mark. The young man who had starved so gaily on sixpence a day that he might read and learn, had nothing but impatience and disgust for the glutton and the drunkard. It was a kind of physical repulsion. And the woman's light indulgent tone seemed for a moment to divide them.

Elise looked round. Why this silence in her companion?

In an instant she divined him. Perhaps her own conscience was not easy. Why had she meddled in the young Englishman's affairs at all? For a whim? Out of a mere good-natured wish to rid him of his troublesome sister; or because his handsome looks, his *naivete*, and his eager admiration of herself amused and excited her, and she did not care to be baulked of them so soon? At any rate, she found refuge in an outburst of temper.

'Ah!' she said, after a moment's pause and scrutiny. 'I see! You think I might have done better for your sister than send her to lodge with a drunkard—that I need not have taken so much trouble to give you good advice for that! You repent your little remarks about guardian angels! You are disappointed in me!—you distrust me!'

She turned back to her easel and began to paint with headlong speed, the small hand flashing to and fro, the quick breath rising and falling tempestuously.

He was dismayed—afraid, and he began to make excuses both for himself and her. It would be all right; he should be close by, and if there were trouble he could take his sister away.

She let her brushes fall into her lap with an exclamation.

'Listen!' she said to him, her eyes blazing—why, he could not for the life of him understand. 'There will be no trouble. What I told you means nothing open—or disgusting. Your sister will notice nothing unless you tell her. But I was candid with you—I always am. I told you last night that I had no scruples. You thought it was a woman's exaggeration; it was the literal truth! If a man drinks, or is vicious, so long as he doesn't hurl the furniture at my head, or behave himself offensively to me, what does it matter to me! If he drinks so that he can't paint, and he wants to paint, well!—then he seems to me another instance of the charming way in which a kind Providence has arranged this world. I am sorry for him, *tout bonnement!* If I could give the poor devil a hand out of the mud, I would; if not, well, then, no sermons! I take him as I find him; if he annoys me, I call in the police. But as to hiding my face and canting, not at all! That is your English way—it is the way of our *bourgeoisie*. It is not mine. I don't belong to the respectables—I would sooner kill myself a dozen times over. I can't breathe in their company. I know how to protect myself; none of the men I meet dare to insult me; that is my idiosyncrasy—everyone has his own. But I have my ideas, and nobody else matters a fig to me.—So now, Monsieur, if you regret our forced introduction of last night, let me wish you a good morning. It will be perfectly easy for your sister to find some excuse to leave the Cervins. I can give you the addresses of several cheap hotels where you and she will be extremely comfortable, and where neither I nor Monsieur Cervin will annoy you!'

David stared at her. He had grown very pale. She, too, was white to the lips. The violence and passion of her speech had exhausted her; her hands trembled in her lap. A wave of emotion swept through him. Her words were insolently bitter. Why, then, this impression of something wounded and young and struggling—at war with itself and the world, proclaiming loneliness and *Sehnsucht*, while it flung anger and reproach?

He dropped on one knee, hardly knowing what he did. Most of the students about had left their work for a while; no one was in sight but a *gardien*, whose back was turned to them, and a young man in the remote distance. He picked up a brush she had let fall, pressed it into her reluctant hand, and laid his forehead against the hand for an instant.

'You misunderstand me,' he said, with a broken, breathless utterance. 'You are quite wrong—quite mistaken. There are not such thoughts in me as you think. The world matters nothing to me, either. I am alone, too; I have always been alone. You meant everything that was heavenly and kind—you must have meant it. I am a stupid idiot! But I could be your friend—if you would permit it.'

He spoke with an extraordinary timidity and slowness. He forgot all his scruples, all pride—everything. As he knelt there, so close to her delicate slimness, to the curls on her white neck, to the quivering lips and great, defiant eyes, she seemed to him once more a being of another clay from himself—beyond any criticism his audacity could form. He dared hardly touch her, and in his heart there swelled the first irrevocable wave of young passion. She raised her hand impetuously and began to paint again. But suddenly a tear dropped on to her knee. She brushed it away, and her wild smile broke.

'Bah!' she said, 'what a scene, what a pair of children! What was it all about? I vow I haven't an idea. You are an excellent *farceur*. Monsieur David! One can see well that you have read George Sand.'

He sat down on a little three-legged stool she had brought with her, and held her box open on his knee. In a minute or two they were talking as though nothing had happened. She was giving him a fresh lecture on Velazquez, and he had resumed his role of pupil and listener. But their eyes avoided each other, and once when, in taking a tube from the box he held, her fingers brushed against his hand, she flushed involuntarily and moved her chair a foot further away.

'Who is that?' she asked, suddenly looking round the corner of her canvas. '*Mon Dieu!* M. Regnault! How does he come here? They told me he was at Granada.'

She sat transfixed, a joyous excitement illuminating every feature. And there, a few yards from them, examining the Rembrandt 'Supper at Emmaus' with a minute and absorbed attention, was the young man he had noticed in the distance a few minutes before. As Elise spoke, the new-comer apparently heard his name, and turned. He put up his eyeglass, smiled, and took off his hat.

'Mademoiselle Delaunay! I find you where I left you, at the feet of the master! Always at work! You are indefatigable. Taranne tells me great things of you. "Ah," he says, "if the men would work like the women!" I assure you, he makes us smart for it. May I look? Good—very good! a great improvement on last year—stronger, more knowledge in it. That hand wants study—but you will soon put it right. Ah, Velazquez! That a man should be great, one can bear that, but so great! It is an offence to the rest of us mortals. But one cannot realise him out of Madrid. I often sigh for the months I spent copying in the Museo. There is a repose of soul in copying a great master—don't you find it? One rests from one's own efforts awhile— the spirit of the master descends into yours, gently, profoundly.'

He stood beside her, smiling kindly, his hat and gloves in his hands, perfectly dressed, an air of the great world about his look and bearing which differentiated him wholly from all other persons whom David had yet seen in Paris. In physique, too, he was totally unlike the ordinary Parisian type. He was a young athlete, vigorous, robust, broad-shouldered, tanned by sun and wind. Only his blue eye—so subtle, melancholy, passionate—revealed the artist and the thinker.

Elise was evidently transported by his notice of her. She talked to him eagerly of his pictures in the Salon, especially of a certain 'Salome,' which, as David presently gathered, was the sensation of the year. She raved about the qualities of it—the words colour, poignancy, force recurring in the quick phrases.

'No one talks of your *success* now, Monsieur. It is another word. *C'est la gloire elle-même qui vous parle à l'oreille!*'

As she let fall the most characteristic of all French nouns, a slight tremor passed across the young man's face. But the look which succeeded it was one of melancholy; the blue eyes took a steely hardness.

'Perhaps a lying spirit, Mademoiselle. And what matter, so long as everything one does disappoints oneself? What a tyrant is art! —insatiable, adorable! You know it. We serve our king on our knees, and he deals us the most miserly gifts.'

'It is the service itself repays,' she said, eagerly, her chest heaving.

'True!—most true! But what a struggle always!—no rest—no content. And there is no other way. One must seek, grope, toil—then produce rapidly—in a flash—throw what you have done behind you—and so on to the next problem, and the next. There is no end to it—there never can be. But you hardly came here this morning, I imagine, Mademoiselle, to hear me prate! I wish you good day and good-bye. I came over for a look at the Salon, but to-morrow I go back to Spain. I can't breathe now for long away from my sun and my South! Adieu, Mademoiselle. I am told your prospects, when the voting comes on, are excellent. May the gods inspire the jury!'

He bowed, smiled, and passed on, carrying his lion-head and kingly presence down the gallery, which had now filled up again, and where, so David noticed, person after person turned as he came near with the same flash of recognition and pleasure he had seen upon Elise's face. A wild jealousy of the young conqueror invaded the English lad.

'Who is he?' he asked.

Elise, womanlike, divined him in a moment. She gave him a sidelong glance and went back to her painting.

'That,' she said quietly, 'is Henri Regnault. Ah, you know nothing of our painters. I can't make you understand. For me he is a young god— there is a halo round his head. He has grasped his fame—the fame we poor creatures are all thirsting for. It began last year with the Prim—General Prim on horseback—oh, magnificent!—a passion!—an energy! This year it is the "Salome." About— Gautier—all the world—have lost their heads over it. If you go to see it at the Salon, you will have to wait your turn. Crowds go every day for nothing else. Of course there are murmurs. They say the study of Fortuny has done him harm. Nonsense! People discuss him because he is becoming a master—no one discusses the nonentities. *They* have no enemies. Then he is sculptor, musician, athlete—well-born besides—all the world is his friend. But with it all so simple—*bon camarade* even for poor scrawlers like me. *Je l'adore!*'

'So it seems,' said David.

The girl smiled over her painting. But after a bit she looked up with a seriousness, nay, a bitterness, in her siren's face, which astonished him.

'It is not amusing to take you in—you are too ignorant. What do you suppose Henri Regnault matters to me? His world is as far above mine as Velazquez' art is above my art. But how can a foreigner understand our shades and grades? Nothing but *success*, but *la gloire*, could ever lift me into his world. Then indeed I should be everybody's equal, and it would matter to nobody that I had been a Bohemian and a *declassee*.

She gave a little sigh of excitement, and threw her head back to look at her picture, David watched her.

'I thought,' he said ironically, 'that a few minutes ago you were all for Bohemia. I did not suspect these social ambitions.'

'All women have them—all artists deny them,' she said, recklessly. 'There, explain me as you like, Monsieur David. But don't read my riddle too soon, or I shall bore you. Allow me to ask you a question.'

She laid down her brushes and looked at him with the utmost gravity. His heart beat—he bent forward.

'Are you ever hungry, Monsieur David?'

He sprang up, half enraged, half ashamed.

'Where can we get some food?'

'That is my affair,' she said, putting up her brushes. 'Be humble, Monsieur, and take a lesson in Paris.'

And out they went together, he beside himself with the delight of accompanying her, and proudly carrying her box and satchel. How her little feet slipped in and out of her pretty dress—how, as they stood on the top of the great flight of stairs leading down into the court of the Louvre, the wind from outside blew back the curls from her brow, and ruffled the violets in her hat, the black lace about her tiny throat. It was an enchantment to follow and to serve her. She led him through the Tuileries Gardens and the Place de la Concorde to the Champs-Elysées. The fountains leapt in the sun; the river blazed between the great white buildings of its banks; to the left was the gilded dome of the Invalides, and the mass of the Corps Législatif, while in front of them rose the long ascent to the Arc de l'Etoile set in vivid green on either hand. Everywhere was space, glitter, magnificence. The gaiety of Paris entered into the Englishman, and took possession.

Presently, as they wandered up the Champs-Elysées, they passed a great building to the left. Elise stopped and clasped her hands in front of her with a little nervous, spasmodic gesture.

'That,' she said, 'is the Salon. My fate lies there. When we have had some food, I will take you in to see.'

She led him a little further up the Avenue, then took him aside through cunningly devised labyrinths of green till they came upon a little cafe restaurant among the trees, where people sat under an awning, and the wind drove the spray of a little fountain hither and thither among the bushes. It was gay, foreign, romantic, unlike anything David had ever seen in his northern world. He sat down, with Barbier's stories running in his head. Mademoiselle Delaunay was George Sand—independent, gifted, on the road to fame like that great *declassee* of old; and he was her friend and comrade, a humble soldier, a camp follower, in the great army of letters.

Their meal was of the lightest. This descent on the Champs-Elysées had been a freak on Elise's part, who wished to do nothing so *banal* as take her companion to the Palais Royal. But the restaurant she had chosen, though of a much humbler kind than those which the rich tourist commonly associates with this part of Paris, was still a good deal more expensive than she had rashly supposed. She opened her eyes gravely at the charges; abused herself extravagantly for a lack of *savoir vivre*; and both with one accord declared it was too hot to eat. But upon such eggs and such green peas as they did allow themselves—a *portion* of each, scrupulously shared—David at any rate, in his traveller's ardour, was prepared to live to the end of the chapter.

Afterwards, over the coffee and the cigarettes, Elise taking her part in both, they lingered for one of those hours which make the glamour of youth. Confidences flowed fast between them. His French grew suppler and more docile, answered more truly to the individuality behind it. He told her of his bringing up, of his wandering with the sheep on the mountains, of his reading among the heather, of 'Lias and his visions, of Hannah's cruelties and Louie's tempers—that same idyll of peasant life to which Dora had listened months before. But how differently told! Each different listener changes the tale, readjusts the tone. But here also the tale pleased. Elise, for all her leanings towards new schools in art, had the Romantic's imagination and the Romantic's relish for things foreign and unaccustomed. The English boy and his story seemed to her both charming and original. Her artist's eye followed the lines of the ruffled black head and noted the red-brown of the skin. She felt a wish to draw him—a wish which had entirely vanished in the case of Louie.

'Your sister has taken a dislike to me,' she said to him once, coolly. 'And as for me, I am afraid of her. Ah! and she broke my glass!'

She shivered, and a look of anxiety and depression invaded her small face. He guessed that she was thinking of her pictures, and began timidly to speak to her about them. When they returned to the world of art, his fluency left him; he felt crushed beneath the weight of his own ignorance and her accomplishment.

'Come and see them!' she said, springing up. 'I am tired of my Infanta. Let her be awhile. Come to the Salon, and I will show you "Salome." Or are you sick of pictures? What do you want to see? *Ça m'est égal.* I can always go back to my work.'

She spoke with a cavalier lightness which teased and piqued him.

'I wish to go where you go,' he said flushing, 'to see what you see.'

She shook her little head.

'No compliments, Monsieur David. We are serious persons, you and I. Well, then, for a couple of hours, *soyons camarades!*'

Of those hours, which prolonged themselves indefinitely, David's after remembrance was somewhat crowded and indistinct. He could never indeed think of Regnault's picture without a shudder, so poignant was the impression it made upon him under the stimulus of Elise's nervous and passionate comments. It represented the daughter of Herodias resting after the dance, with the dish upon her knee which was to receive the head of the saint. Her mass of black hair—the first strong impression of the picture—stood out against the pale background, and framed the smiling sensual face, broadly and powerfully made, like the rest of the body, and knowing neither thought nor qualm. The colour was a bewilderment of scarlets and purples, of yellow and rose-colour, of turtle-greys and dazzling flesh-tints—bathed the whole of it in the searching light of the East. The strangeness, the science of it, its extraordinary brilliance and energy, combined with its total lack of all emotion, all pity, took indelible hold of the English lad's untrained provincial sense. He dreamt of it for nights afterwards.

For the rest—what whirl and confusion! He followed Elise through suffocating rooms, filled with the liveliest crowd he had ever seen. She was constantly greeted, surrounded, carried off to look at this and that. Her friends and acquaintances, indeed, whether men or women, seemed all to treat her in much the same way. There was complete, and often noisy, freedom of address and discussion between them. She called all the men by their surnames, and she was on half mocking, half caressing terms with the women, who seemed to David to be generally art students, of all ages and aspects. But nobody took any liberties with her. She had her place, and that one of some predominance. Clearly she had already the privileges of an eccentric, and a certain cool ascendency of temperament. Her little figure fluttered hither and thither, gathering a train, then shaking it off again. Sometimes and her friends, finding the heat intolerable, and wanting space for talk, would overflow into the great central hall, with its cool palms and statues; and there David would listen to torrents of French artistic theory, anecdote, and *blague,* till his head whirled, and French cleverness — conveyed to him in what, to the foreigner, is the most exquisite and the most tantalising of all tongues — seemed to him superhuman.

As to what he saw, after 'Salome,' he remembered vividly only three pictures — Elise Delaunay's two — a portrait and a workshop interior — before which he stood, lost in naive wonder at her talent; and the head of a woman, with a thin pale face, reddish-brown hair, and a look of pantherish grace and force, which he was told was the portrait of an actress at the Odeon who was making the world stare — Mademoiselle Bernhardt. For the rest he had the vague, distracting impression of a new world — of nude horrors and barbarities of all sorts — of things licentious or cruel, which yet, apparently, were all of as much value in the artist's eye, and to be discussed with as much calm or eagerness, as their neighbours. One moment he loathed what he saw, and threw himself upon his companion, with the half-coherent protests of an English idealism, of which she scarcely understood a word; the next he lost himself in some landscape which had torn the very heart out of an exquisite mood of nature, or in some scene of peasant life — so true and living that the scents of the fields and the cries of the animals were once more about him, and he lived his childhood over again.

Perhaps the main idea which the experience left with him was one of a goading and intoxicating *freedom.* His country lay in the background of his mind as the symbol of all dull convention and respectability. He was in the land of intelligence, where nothing is prejudged, and all experiments are open.

When they came out, it was to get an ice in the shade, and then to wander to and fro, watching the passers-by — the young men playing a strange game with disks under the trees — the nurses and children — the ladies in the carriages — and talking, with a quick, perpetual advance towards intimacy, towards emotion. More and more there grew upon her the charm of a certain rich poetic intelligence there was in him, stirring beneath his rawness and ignorance, struggling through the fetters of language; and in response, as the evening wore on, she threw off her professional airs, and sank the egotist out of sight. She became simpler, more childish; her variable, fanciful youth answered to the magnetism of his.

At last he said to her, as they stood by the Arc de l'Etoile, looking down towards Paris:

'The sun is just going down—this day has been the happiest of my life!'

The low intensity of the tone startled her. Then she had a movement of caprice, of superstition.

'*Alors—assez*! Monsieur David, stay where you are. Not another step!— *Adieu!*'

Astonished and dismayed, he turned involuntarily. But, in the crowd of people passing through the Arch, she had slipped from him, and he had lost her beyond recovery. Moreover, her tone was peremptory—he dared not pursue and anger her.

Minutes passed while he stood, spell—and trance-bound, in the shadow of the Arch. Then, with the long and labouring breath, the sudden fatigue of one who has leapt in a day from one plane of life to another—in whom a passionate and continuous heat of feeling has for the time burnt up the nervous power—he moved on eastwards, down the Champs-Elysées. The sunset was behind him, and the trees threw long shadows across his path. Shade and sun spaces alike seemed to him full of happy crowds. The beautiful city laughed and murmured round him. Nature and man alike bore witness with his own rash heart that all is divinely well with the world—let the cynics and the mourners say what they will. His hour had come, and without a hesitation or a dread he rushed upon it. Passion and youth—ignorance and desire—have never met in madder or more reckless dreams than those which filled the mind of David Grieve as he wandered blindly home.

CHAPTER V

As David climbed the garret stairs to his room, the thought of Louie flashed across his mind for the first time since the morning. He opened the door and looked round. Yes; all her things were gone. She had taken up her abode with the Cervins.

A certain anxiety and discomfort seized him; before going out to the Boulevard to snatch some food in preparation for his evening at the 'Trois Rats' he descended to the landing below and rang the Cervins' bell.

A charwoman, dirty and tired with much cleaning, opened to him.

No, Madame was not at home. No one was at home, and the dinner was spoiling. Had they not been seen all day? Certainly. They had come in about six o'clock *avec une jeune personne* and M. Montjoie. She thought it probable that they were all at that moment down below, in the studio of M. Montjoie.

David already knew his way thither, and was soon standing outside the high black door with the pane of glass above it to which Madame Merichat had originally directed him. While he waited for an answer to his ring he looked about him. He was in a sort of yard which was almost entirely filled up by the sculptor's studio, a long structure lighted at one end as it seemed from the roof, and at the other by the usual north window. At the end of the yard rose a huge many-storied building which seemed to be a factory of some sort. David's Lancashire eye distinguished machinery through the monotonous windows, and the figures of the operatives; it took note also of the fact that the rooms were lit up and work still going on at seven o'clock. All around were the ugly backs of tall houses, every window flung open to this May heat. The scene was squalid and *triste* save for the greenish blue of the evening sky, and the flight of a few pigeons round the roof of the factory.

A man in a blouse came at last, and led the way in when David asked for Madame Cervin. They passed through the inner studio full of a confusion of clay models and casts to which the dust of months gave the look and relief of bronze.

Then the further door opened, and he saw beyond a larger and emptier room; sculptor's work of different kinds, and in various stages on either side; casts, and charcoal studies on the walls, and some dozen people scattered in groups over the floor, all looking towards an object on which the fading light from the upper part of the large window at the end was concentrated.

What was that figure on its pedestal, that white image which lived and breathed? *Louie?*

The brother stood amazed beside the door, staring while the man in the blouse retreated, and the persons in the room were too much occupied with the spectacle before them to notice the new-comer's arrival.

Louie stood upon a low pedestal, which apparently revolved with the model, for as David entered, Montjoie, the man in the grey suit, with the square, massive head, who had joined the party in the Louvre, ran forward and moved it round slightly. She was in Greek dress, and some yards away from her was the clay study—a maenad with vine wreath, tambourine, thyrsus, and floating hair—for which she was posing.

Even David was dazzled by the image thus thrown out before him. With her own dress Louie Grieve seemed to have laid aside for the moment whatever common or provincial elements there might be in her strange and startling beauty. Clothed in the clinging folds of the Greek chiton; neck, arms, and feet bare; the rounded forms of the limbs showing under the soft stuff; the face almost in profile, leaning to the shoulder, as though the delicate ear were listening for the steps of the wine god; a wreath of vine leaves round the black hair which fell in curly masses about her, sharpening and framing the rosy whiteness of the cheek and neck; one hand lightly turned back behind her, showing the palm, the other holding a torch; one foot poised on tiptoe, and the whole body lightly bent forward, as though for instant motion:—in this dress and this attitude, worn and sustained with extraordinary intelligence and audacity, the wild hybrid creature had risen, as it were, for the first time, to the full capacity of her endowment—had eclipsed and yet revealed herself.

The brother stood speechless, looking from the half-completed study to his sister. How had they made her understand?—where had she got the dress? And such a dress! To the young fellow, who in his peasant and tradesman experience had never even seen a woman in the ordinary low dress of society, it seemed incredible, outrageous. And to put it on for the purpose of posing as a model in a room full of strange men—Madame Cervin was the only woman present—his cheek burnt for his sister; and for the moment indignation and bewilderment held him paralysed.

In front of him a little way, but totally unaware of the stranger's entrance, were two men whispering and laughing together. One held a piece of paper on a book, and was making a hurried sketch of Louie. Every now and then he drew the attention of his companion to some of the points of the model.

David caught a careless phrase or two, and understood just enough of their student's slang to suspect a good deal worse than was actually said.

Meanwhile Montjoie was standing against an iron pillar, studying intently every detail of Louie's pose, both hands arched over his eyes.

'*Peste!* did one ever see so many points combined?' he threw back to a couple of men behind him. 'Too thin—the arms might be better—and the hands a *little* common. But for the *ensemble—mon Dieu!* we should make Carpeaux's *atelier* look alive—*hein?*'

'Take care!' laughed a man who was leaning against a cast a few feet away, and smoking vigorously. 'She likes it, she has never done it before, but she likes it. Suppose Carpeaux gets hold of her. You may repent showing her, if you want to keep her to yourself.'

'Ah, that right knee wants throwing forward a trifle,' said Montjoie in a preoccupied tone, and going up to Louie, he spoke a few words of bad English.

'Allow me, mademoiselle—put your hand on me—*ainsi*—vile I change dis pretty foot.'

Louie looked down bewildered, then at the other men about her, with her great eyes, half exultant, half inquiring. She understood hardly anything of their French. One of them laughed, and, running to the clay Maenad, stooped down and touched the knee and ankle, to show her what was meant. Louie instinctively put her hand on Montjoie's shoulder to steady herself, and he proceeded to move the bare sandalled foot.

One of the men near him made a remark which David caught. He suddenly strode forward.

'Sir! Have the goodness to tell me how you wish my sister to stand, and I will explain to her. She is not your model!'

The sculptor looked up startled. Everybody stared at the intruder, at the dark English boy, standing with a threatening eye, and trembling with anger, beside his sister. Then Madame Cervin, clasping her little fat hands with an exclamation of dismay, rushed up to the group, while Louie leapt down from her pedestal and went to David.

'What are you interfering for?' she said, pushing Madame Cervin aside and looking him full in the eyes, her own blazing, her chest heaving.

'You are disgracing yourself,' he said to her with the same intensity, fast and low, under his breath, so as to be heard only by her. 'How can you expose yourself as a model to these men whom you never saw before? Let them find their own models; they are a pack of brutes!'

But even as he spoke he shrank before the concentrated wrath of her face.

'I will make you pay for it!' she said. 'I will teach you to domineer.'

Then she turned to Madame Cervin.

'Come and take it off, please!' she said imperiously. 'It's no good while he is here.'

As she crossed the room with her free wild step, her white draperies floating, Montjoie, who had been standing pulling at his moustaches, and studying the brother from under his heavy brows, joined her, and, stooping, said two or three smiling words in her ear. She looked up, tossed her head and laughed—a laugh half reckless, half *farouche*; two or three of the other men hurried after them, and presently they made a knot in the further room, Louie calmly waiting for Madame Cervin, and sitting on the pedestal of a bronze group, her beautiful head and white shoulders thrown out against the metal. Montjoie's artist friends—of the kind which haunt a man whose *mœurs* are gradually bringing his talent to ruin—stood round her, smoking and talking and staring at the English girl between whiles. The arrogance with which she bore their notice excited them, but they could not talk to her, for she did not understand them. Only Montjoie had a few words of English. Occasionally Louie bent forward and looked disdainfully through the door. When would David be done prating?

For he, in fact, was grappling with Madame Cervin, who was showing great adroitness. This was what had happened according to her. Monsieur Montjoie—a man of astonishing talent, an artist altogether superior—was in trouble about his statue—could not find a model to suit him—was in despair. It seemed that he had heard of mademoiselle's beauty from England, in some way, before she arrived. Then in the studio he had shown her the Greek dress.

'—There were some words between them—some compliments, Monsieur, I suppose—and your sister said she would pose for him. I opposed myself. I knew well that mademoiselle was a young person *tout-à-fait comme il faut*, that monsieur her brother might object to her making herself a model for M. Montjoie. *Mais, mon Dieu!*' and the ex-modiste shrugged her round shoulders—'mademoiselle has a will of her own.'

Then she hinted that in an hour's acquaintance mademoiselle had already shown herself extremely difficult to manage—monsieur would probably understand that. As for her, she had done everything possible. She had taken mademoiselle upstairs and dressed her with her own hands— she had been her maid and companion throughout. She could do no more. Mademoiselle would go her own way.

'Who were all these men?' David inquired, still hot and frowning.

Madame Cervin rose on tiptoe and poured a series of voluble biographies into his ear. According to her everybody present was a person of distinction; was at any rate an artist, and a man of talent. But let monsieur decide. If he was dissatisfied, let him take his sister away. She had been distressed, insulted, by his behaviour. Mademoiselle's box had been not yet unpacked. Let him say the word and it should be taken upstairs again.

And she drew away from him, bridling, striking an attitude of outraged dignity beside her husband, who had stood behind her in a slouching abstracted silence during the whole scene—so far as her dwarf stature and vulgar little moon-face permitted.

'We are strangers here, Madame,' cried David. 'I asked you to take care of my sister, and I find her like this, before a crowd of men neither she nor I have ever seen before!'

Madame Cervin swept her hand grandiloquently round.

'Monsieur has his remedy! Let him take his sister.'

He stood silent in a helpless and obvious perplexity. What, saddle himself afresh after these intoxicating hours of liberty and happiness? Fetter and embarrass every moment? Shut himself out from freedom—from *her*?

Besides, already his first instinctive rage was disappearing. In the confusion of this new world he could no longer tell whether he was right or ridiculous. Had he been playing the Philistine, mistaking a mere artistic convention for an outrage? And Louie was so likely to submit to his admonitions!

Madame Cervin watched him with a triumphant eye. When he began to stammer out what was in effect an apology, she improved the opportunity, threw off her suave manners, and let him understand with a certain plain brutality that she had taken Louie's measure. She would do her best to keep the girl in order—it was lucky for him that he had fallen upon anybody so entirely respectable as herself and her husband—but she would use her own judgment; and if monsieur made scenes, she would just turn out her boarder, and leave him to manage as he could.

She had the whip-hand, and she knew it. He tried to appease her, then discovered that he must go, and went with a hanging head.

Louie took no notice of him nor he of her, as he passed through the inner studio, but Montjoie came forward to meet the English lad, bending his great head and shoulders with a half-ironic politeness. Monsieur Grieve he feared had mistaken the homage rendered by himself and his friends to his sister's beauty for an act of disrespect—let him be reassured! Such beauty was its own defence. No doubt monsieur did not understand artistic usage. He, Montjoie, made allowance for the fact, otherwise the young man's behaviour towards himself and his friends would have required explanation.

The two stood together at the door—David proudly crimson, seeking in vain for phrases that would not come—Montjoie cool and malicious, his battered weather-beaten face traversed by little smiles. Louie was looking on with scornful amusement, and the group of artists round her could hardly control their mirth.

He shut the door behind him with the feeling of one who has cut a ridiculous figure and beaten a mean retreat. Then, as he neared the bottom of the stairs, he gave himself a great shake, with the gesture of one violently throwing off a weight. Let those who thought that he ought to control Louie, and could control her, come and see for themselves! He had done what he thought was for the best—his quick inner sense carefully refrained from attaching any blame whatever to Mademoiselle Delaunay—and now Louie must go her own gait, and he would go his. He had said his say—and she should not spoil this hoarded, this long-looked-for pleasure. As he passed into the street, on his way to the Boulevard for some food, his walk and bearing had in them a stern and passionate energy.

He had to hurry back for his appointment with Mademoiselle Delaunay's friends of the morning. As he turned into the Rue Chantal he passed a flower-stall aglow with roses from the south and sweet with narcissus and mignonette. An idea struck him, and he stopped, a happy smile softening away the still lingering tension of the face. For a few sous he bought a bunch of yellow-eyed narcissus and stepped gaily home with them. He had hardly time to put them in water and to notice that Madame Merichat had made Dubois' squalid abode look much more habitable than before, when there was a knock at the door and his two guides stood outside.

They carried him off at once. David found more of a tongue than he had been master of in the morning, and the three talked incessantly as they wound in and out of the streets which cover the face of the hill of Montmartre, ascending gradually towards the place they were in search of. David had heard something of the history of the two from Elise Delaunay. Alphonse was a lad of nineteen brimming over with wild fun and mischief, and perpetually in disgrace with all possible authorities; the possessor nevertheless of a certain delicate and subtle fancy which came out in the impressionist landscapes—many of them touched with a wild melancholy as inexplicable probably to himself as to other people—which he painted in all his spare moments. The tall black-bearded Lenain was older, had been for years in Taranne's *atelier*, was an excellent draughtsman, and was now just beginning seriously upon the painting of large pictures for exhibition. In his thin long face there was a pinched and anxious look, as though in the artist's inmost mind there lay hidden the presentiment of failure.

They talked freely enough of Elise Delaunay, David alternately wincing and craving for more. What a clever little devil it was! She was burning herself away with ambition and work; Taranne flattered her a good deal; it was absolutely necessary, otherwise she would be for killing herself two or three times a week. Oh! she might get her *mention* at the Salon. The young Solons sitting in judgment on her thought on the whole she deserved it; two of her exhibits were not bad; but there was another girl in the *atelier*, Mademoiselle Breal, who had more interest in high places. However, Taranne would do what he could; he had always made a favourite of the little Elise; and only he could manage her when she was in one of her impracticable fits.

Then Alphonse put the Englishman through a catechism, and at the end of it they both advised him not to trouble his head about George Sand. That was all dead and done with, and Balzac not much less. He might be great, Balzac, but who could be at the trouble of reading him nowadays? Lenain, who was literary, named to him with enthusiasm Flaubert's 'Madame Bovary' and the brothers Goncourt. As for Alphonse, who was capable, however, of occasional excursions into poetry, and could quote Musset and Hugo, the *feuilletons* in the 'Gaulois' or the 'Figaro' seemed, on the whole, to provide him with as much fiction as he desired. He was emphatically of opinion that the artist wants no books; a little poetry, perhaps, did no harm; but literature in painting was the very devil. Then perceiving that between them they had puzzled their man, Alphonse would have proceeded to 'cram' him in the most approved style, but that Lenain interposed, and a certain cooling of the Englishman's bright eye made success look unpromising. Finally the wild fellow clapped David on the back and assured him that 'Les Trois Rats' would astonish him. 'Ah! here we are.'

As he spoke they turned a corner, and a blaze of light burst upon them, coming from what seemed to be a gap in the street face, a house whereof the two lower stories were wall—and windowless, though not in the manner of the ordinary cafe, seeing that the open parts were raised somewhat above the pavement.

'The patron saint!' said Alphonse, stopping with a grin and pointing. Following the finger with his eye David caught a fantastic sign swinging above him: a thin iron crescent, and sitting up between its two tips a lean black rat, its sharp nose in the air, its tail curled round its iron perch, while two other creatures of the same kind crept about him, the one clinging to the lower tip of the crescent, the other peering down from the top on the king-rat in the middle. Below the sign, and heavily framed by the dark overhanging eave, the room within was clearly visible from the street. From the background of its black oak walls and furniture emerged figures, lights, pictures, above all an imposing *cheminee* advancing far into the floor, a high, fantastic structure also of black oak like the panelling of the room, but overrun with chains of black rats, carved and combined with a wild *diablerie*, and lit by numerous lights in branching ironwork. The dim grotesque shapes of the pictures, the gesticulating, shouting crowd in front of them, the mediaevalism of the room and of that strange sign dangling outside: these things took the English lad's excited fancy and he pressed his way in behind his companions. He forgot what they had been telling him; his pulse beat to the old romantic tune; poets, artists, talkers—here he was to find them.

David's two companions exchanged greetings on all sides, laughing and shouting like the rest. With difficulty they found a table in a remote corner, and, sitting down, ordered coffee.

'Alphonse! *mon cher!*'

A young man sitting at the next table turned round upon them, slapped Alphonse on the shoulder, and stared hard at David. He had fine black eyes in a bronzed face, a silky black beard, and long hair *à la lion*, that is to say, thrown to one side of the head in a loose mane-like mass.

'I have just come from the Salon. Not bad—Regnault? *Hein?*'

'*Non—il arrivera, celui-là,*' said the other calmly.

'As for the other things from the Villa Medici fellows,' said the first speaker, throwing his arm round the back of his chair, and twisting it round so as to front them, 'they make me sick. I should hardly do my fire the injustice of lighting it with some of them.'

'All the same,' replied Alphonse stoutly, 'that Campagna scene of D. 's is well done.'

'Literature, *mon cher*! literature!' cried the unknown, 'and what the deuce do we want with literature in painting?'

He brought his fist down violently on the table.

'*Connu,*' said Alphonse scornfully. 'Don't excite yourself. But the story in D. 's picture doesn't matter a halfpenny. Who cares what the figures are doing? It's the brush work and the values I look to. How did he get all that relief—that brilliance? No sunshine—no local colour—and the thing glows like a Rembrandt!'

The boy's mad blue eyes took a curious light, as though some inner enthusiasm had stirred.

'*Peuh*! we all know you, Alphonse. Say what you like, you want something else in a picture than painting. That'll damn you, and make your fortune some day, I warn you. Now *I* have got a picture on the easel that will make the *bourgeois* skip.'

And the speaker passed a large tremulous hand through his waves of hair, his lip also quivering with the nervousness of a man overworked and overdone.

'You'll not send it to the Salon, I imagine,' said another man beside him, dryly. He was fair, small and clean-shaven, wore spectacles, and had the look of a clerk or man of business.

'Yes, I shall,' cried the other violently—his name was Dumesnil—'I'll fling it at their heads. That's all our school can do—make a scandal.'

'Well, that has even been known to make money,' said the other, fingering his watch-chain with a disagreeable little smile.

'Money!' shouted Dumesnil, and swinging round to his own table again he poured out hot denunciations of the money-grabbing reptiles of to-day who shelter themselves behind the sacred name of art. Meanwhile the man at whom it was all levelled sipped his coffee quietly and took no notice.

'Ah, a song!' cried Alphonse. 'Lenain, *vois-tu*? It's that little devil Perinot. He's been painting churches down near Toulouse, his own country. Saints by the dozen, like this,' and Alphonse drooped his eyes and crossed his limp hands, taking off the frescoed mediaeval saint for an instant, as only the Parisian *gamin* can do such things. 'You should see him with a *cure*. However, the *cures* don't follow him here, more's the pity. Ah! *très bien—très bien*!'

These plaudits were called out by some passages on the guitar with which the singer was prefacing his song. His chair had been mounted on to a table, so that all the world could see and hear. A hush of delighted attention penetrated the room; and outside, in the street, David could see dark forms gathering on the pavement.

The singer was a young man, undersized and slightly deformed, with close-cut hair, and a large face, droll, pliant and ugly as a gutta-percha mask. Before he opened his lips the audience laughed.

David listened with all his ears, feeling through every fibre the piquant strangeness of the scene—alive with the foreigner's curiosity, and with youth's pleasure in mere novelty. And what clever fellows, what dash, what *camaraderie!* That old imaginative drawing towards France and the French was becoming something eagerly personal, combative almost,—and in the background of his mind throughout was the vibrating memory of the day just past—the passionate sense of a new life.

The song was tumultuously successful. The whole crowded *salle,* while it was going on, was one sea of upturned faces, and it was accompanied at intervals by thunders of applause, given out by means of sticks, spoons, fists, or anything else that might come handy. It recounted the adventures of an artist and his model. As it proceeded, a slow crimson rose into the English lad's cheek, overspread his forehead and neck. He sat staring at the singer, or looking round at the absorbed attention and delight of his companions. By the end of it David, his face propped on his hands, was trying nervously to decipher the names and devices cut in the wood of the table on which he leant. His whole being was in a surge of physical loathing—the revulsion of feeling was bewildering and complete. So this was what Frenchmen thought of women, what they could say of them, when the mask was off, and they were at their ease. The witty brutality, the naked coarseness of the thing scourged the boy's shrinking sense. Freedom, passion—yes! but *this!* In his wild recoil he stood again under the Arc de Triomphe watching her figure disappear. Ah! pardon! That he should be listening at all seemed to a conscience, an imagination quickened by first love, to be an outrage to women, to love, to her!

Yet—how amusing it was! how irresistible, as the first shock subsided, was the impression of sparkling verse, of an astonishing mimetic gift in the singer! Towards the end he had just made up his mind to go on the first pretext, when he found himself, to his own disgust, shaking with laughter.

He recovered himself after a while, resolved to stay it out, and betrayed nothing. The comments made by his two companions on the song— consisting mainly of illustrative anecdote—were worthy of the occasion. David sat, however, without flinching, his black eyes hardening, laughing at intervals.

Presently the room rose *en bloc,* and there was a move towards the staircase.

'The manager, M. Edmond, has come,' explained Alphonse; 'they are going upstairs to the concert-room. They will have a recitation perhaps,— *ombres chinoises,*—music. Come and look at the drawings before we go.'

And he took his charge round the walls, which were papered with drawings and sketches, laughing and explaining. The drawings were done, in the main, according to him, by the artists on the staffs of two illustrated papers which had their headquarters at the 'Trois Rats.' David was especially seized by the innumerable sheets of animal sketches—series in which some episode of animal life was carried through from its beginning to a close, sometimes humorous, but more often tragic. In a certain number of them there was a free imagination, an irony, a pity, which linked them together, marked them as the conceptions of one brain. Alphonse pointed to them as the work of a clever fellow, lately dead, who had been launched and supported by the 'Trois Rats' and its frequenters. One series in particular, representing a robin overcome by the seduction of a glass of absinthe and passing through all the stages of delirium tremens, had a grim inventiveness, a fecundity of half humorous, half pathetic fancy, which held David's eye riveted.

As for the ballet-girl, she was everywhere, with her sisters, the model and the *grisette*. And the artistic ability shown in the treatment of her had nowhere been hampered by any Philistine scruple in behalf of decency.

Upstairs there was the same mixed experience. David found himself in a corner with his two acquaintances, and four or five others, a couple of journalists, a musician and a sculptor. The conversation ranged from art to religion, from religion to style, from style to women, and all with a perpetual recurrence either to the pictures and successes of the Salon, or to the *liaisons* of well-known artists.

'Why do none of us fellows in the press pluck up courage and tell H. what we really think about those Homeric *machines* of his which he turns out year after year?' said a journalist, who was smoking beside him, an older man than the rest of them. 'I have a hundred things I want to say—but H. is popular—I like him himself—and I haven't the nerve. But what the devil do we want with the Greeks—they painted their world—let us paint ours! Besides, it is an absurdity. I thought as I was looking at H. 's things this morning of what Preault used to say of Pradier: "*Il partait tous les matins pour la Grèce et arrivait tous les soirs Rue de Breda.*" "Pose your goddesses as you please—they are *grisettes* all the same."'

'All very well for you critics,' growled a man smoking a long pipe beside him; 'but the artist must live, and the *bourgeois* will have subjects. He won't have anything to do with your "notes" —and "impressions" —and "arrangements." When you present him with the view, served hot, from your four-pair back—he buttons up his pockets and abuses you. He wants his stories and his sentiment. And where the deuce is the sentiment to be got? I should be greatly obliged to anyone who would point me to a little of the commodity. The Greeks are already ridiculous,—and as for religion—'

The speaker threw back his head and laughed silently.

'Ah! I agree with you,' said the other emphatically; 'the religious pictures this year are really too bad. Christianity is going too fast—for the artist.'

'And the sceptics are becoming bores,' cried the painter; 'they take themselves too seriously. It is, after all, only another dogmatism. One should believe in nothing—not even in one's doubts.'

'Yes,' replied the journalist, knocking out his pipe, with a sardonic little smile—'strange fact! One may swim in free thought and remain as *banal* as a bishop all the time.'

'I say,' shouted a fair-haired youth opposite, 'who has seen C. 's Holy Family? Who knows where he got his Madonna?'

Nobody knew, and the speaker had the felicity of imparting an entirely fresh scandal to attentive ears. The mixture in the story of certain brutalities of modern manners with names and things still touching or sacred for the mass of mankind had the old Voltairean flavour. But somehow, presented in this form and at this moment, David no longer found it attractive. He sat nursing his knee, his dark brows drawn together, studying the story-teller, whose florid Norman complexion and blue eyes were already seared by a vicious experience.

The tale, however, was interrupted and silenced by the first notes of a piano. The room was now full, and a young actor from the Gymnase company was about to give a musical sketch. The subject of it was 'St. Francis and Santa Clara.'

This performance was perhaps more wittily broad than anything which had gone before. The audience was excessively amused by it. It was indeed the triumph of the evening, and nothing could exceed the grace and point of the little speech in which M. Edmond, the manager of the cafe, thanked the accomplished singer afterwards.

While it was going on, David, always with that poignant, shrinking thought of Elise at his heart, looked round to see if there were any women present. Yes, there were three. Two were young, outrageously dressed, with sickly pretty tired faces. The third was a woman in middle life, with short hair parted at the side, and a strong, masculine air. Her dress was as nearly as possible that of a man, and she was smoking vigorously. The rough *bonhomie* of her expression and her professional air reminded David once more of George Sand. An artist, he supposed, or a writer.

Suddenly, towards the end of the sketch, he became conscious of a tall figure behind the singer, a man standing with his hat in his hand, as though he had just come in, and were just going away. His fine head was thrown back, his look was calm, David thought disdainful. Bending forward he recognised M. Regnault, the hero of the morning.

Regnault had come in unperceived while the dramatic piece was going on; but it was no sooner over than he was discovered, and the whole *salle* rose to do him honour. The generosity, the extravagance of the ovation offered to the young painter by this hundred or two of artists and men of letters were very striking to the foreign eye. David found himself thrilling and applauding with the rest. The room had passed in an instant from cynicism to sentiment. A moment ago it had been trampling to mud the tenderest feeling of the past; it was now eagerly alive with the feeling of the present.

The new-comer protested that he had only dropped in, being in the neighbourhood, and must not stay. He was charming to them all, asked after this man's picture and that man's statue, talked a little about the studio he was organising at Tangiers, and then, shaking hands right and left, made his way through the crowd.

As he passed David, his quick eye caught the stranger and he paused.

'Were you not in the Louvre this morning with Mademoiselle Delaunay?' he asked, lowering his voice a little; 'you are a stranger?'

'Yes, an Englishman,' David stammered, taken by surprise. Regnault's look swept over the youth's face, kindling in an instant with the artist's delight in beautiful line and tint.

'Are you going now?'

'Yes,' said David hurriedly. 'It must be late?'

'Midnight, past. May I walk with you?'

David, overwhelmed, made some hurried excuses to his two companions, and found himself pushing his way to the door, an unnoticed figure in the tumult of Regnault's exit.

When they got into the street outside, Regnault walked fast southwards for a minute or so without speaking. Then he stopped abruptly, with the gesture of one shaking off a weight.

'Pah! this Paris chokes me.'

Then, walking on again, he said, half-coherently, and to himself:

'So vile,—so small,—so foul! And there are such great things in the world. *Beasts!—pigs!*—and yet so generous, so struggling, such a hard fight for it. So gifted,—many of them! What are you here for?'

And he turned round suddenly upon his companion. David, touched and captured he knew not how by the largeness and spell of the man's presence, conquered his shyness and explained himself as intelligibly as he could:

An English bookseller, making his way in trade, yet drawn to France by love for her literature and her past, and by a blood-tie which seemed to have in it mystery and pain, for it could hardly be spoken of—the curious little story took the artist's fancy. Regnault did his best to draw out more of it, helped the young fellow with his French, tried to get at his impressions, and clearly enjoyed the experience to which his seeking artist's sense had led him.

'What a night!' he said at last, drawing a full draught of the May into his great chest. 'Stop and look down those streets in the moonlight. What surfaces,—what gradations,—what a beauty of multiplied lines, though it is only a piece of vulgar Haussmann! Indoors I can't breathe—but out of doors and at night this Paris of ours,—ah! she is still beautiful—*beautiful*! Now one has shaken the dust of that place off, one can feel it. What did you think of it?—tell me.'

He stooped and looked into his companion's face. David was tall and lithe, but Regnault was at least half a head taller and broader in proportion.

David walked along for a minute without answering. He too, and even more keenly than Regnault, was conscious of escape and relief. A force which had, as it were, taken life and feeling by the throat had relaxed its grip. He disengaged himself with mingled loathing and joy. But in his shyness he did not know how to express himself, fearing, too, to wound the Frenchman. At last he said slowly:

'I never saw so many clever people together in my life.'

The words were bald, but Regnault perfectly understood what was meant by them, as well as by the troubled consciousness of the black eyes raised to his. He laughed—shortly and bitterly.

'No, we don't lack brains, we French. All the same I tell you, in the whole of that room there are about half-a-dozen people,—oh, not so many!—not nearly so many!—who will ever make a mark, even for their own generation, who will ever strike anything out of nature that is worth having—wrestle with her to any purpose. Why? Because they have every sort of capacity—every sort of cleverness—and *no character*!'

David walked beside him in silence. He thought suddenly of Regnault's own picture—its strange cruelty and force, its craftsman's brilliance. And the recollection puzzled him.

Regnault, however, had spoken with passion, and as though out of the fulness of some sore and long-familiar pondering.

'You never saw anything like that in England,' he resumed quickly.

David hesitated.

'No, I never did. But I am a provincial, and I have seen nothing at all. Perhaps in London—'

'No, you would see nothing like it in London,' said Regnault decidedly. 'Bah! it is not that you are more virtuous than we are. Who believes such folly? But your vice is grosser, stupider. Lucky for you! You don't sacrifice to it the best young brain of the nation, as we are perpetually doing. Ah, *mon Dieu!*' he broke out in a kind of despair, 'this enigma of art!—of the artist! One flounders and blunders along. I have been floundering and blundering with the rest,—playing tricks—following this man and that— till suddenly—a door opens—and one sees the real world through for the first time!'

He stood still in his excitement, a smile of the most exquisite quality and sweetness dawning on his strong young face.

'And then,' he went on, beginning to walk again, and talking much more to the night than to his companion, 'one learns that the secret of life lies in *feeling*—in the heart, not in the head. And no more limits than before!—all is still open, divinely open. Range the whole world—see everything, learn everything—till at the end of years and years you may perhaps be found worthy to be called an artist! But let art have her ends, all the while, shining beyond the means she is toiling through—her ends of beauty or of power. To spend herself on the mere photography of the vile and the hideous! what waste—what sacrilege!'

They had reached the Place de la Concorde, which lay bathed in moonlight, the silver fountains plashing, the trees in the Champs-Elysées throwing their sharp yet delicate shadows on the intense whiteness of the ground, the buildings far away rising softly into the softest purest blue. Regnault stopped and looked round him with enchantment. As for David, he had no eyes save for his companion. His face was full of a quick responsive emotion. After an experience which had besmirched every ideal and bemocked every faith, the young Frenchman's talk had carried the lad once more into the full tide of poetry and romance. 'The secret of life lies in *feeling*, in the heart, not the head'—ah, *that* he understood! He tried to express his assent, his homage to the speaker; but neither he nor the artist understood very clearly what he was saying. Presently Regnault said in another tone:

'And they are such good fellows, many of them. Starving often—but nothing to propitiate the *bourgeois*, nothing to compromise the "dignity of art." A man will paint to please himself all day, paint, on a crust, something that won't and can't sell, that the world in fact would be mad to buy; then in the evening he will put his canvas to the wall, and paint sleeve-links or china to live. And so generous to each other: they will give each other all they have—food, clothes, money, knowledge. That man who gave that abominable thing about St. Francis—I know him, he has a little apartment near the Quai St.-Michel, and an invalid mother. He is a perfect angel to her. I could take off my hat to him whenever I think of it.'

His voice dropped again. Regnault was pacing along across the Place, his arms behind him, David at his side. When he resumed, it was once more in a tone of despondency.

'There is an ideal; but so twisted, so corrupted! What is wanted is not less intelligence but *more*—more knowledge, more experience—something beyond this fevering, brutalising Paris, which is all these men know. They have got the poison of the Boulevards in their blood, and it dulls their eye and hand. They want scattering to the wilderness; they want the wave of life to come and lift them past the mud they are dabbling in, with its hideous wrecks and *debris*, out and away to the great sea, to the infinite beyond of experience and feeling! you, too, feel with me?—you, too, see it like that? Ah! when one has seen and felt Italy—the East,—the South—lived heart to heart with a wild nature, or with the great embodied thought of the past,—lived at large, among great things, great sights, great emotions, then there comes purification! There is no other way out—no, none!'

So for another hour Regnault led the English boy up and down and along the quays, talking in the frankest openest way to this acquaintance of a night. It was as though he were wrestling his own way through his own life-problem. Very often David could hardly follow. The joys, the passions, the temptations of the artist, struggling with the life of thought and aspiration, the craving to know everything, to feel everything, at war with the hunger for a moral unity and a stainless self-respect—there was all this in his troubled, discursive talk, and there was besides the magic touch of genius, youth, and poetry.

'Well, this is strange!' he said at last, stopping at a point between the Louvre on the one hand and the Institute on the other, the moonlit river lying between.—' My friends come to me at Rome or at Tangiers, and they complain of me, "Regnault, you have grown morose, no one can get a word out of you"—and they go away wounded—I have seen it often. And it was always true. For months I have had no words. I have been in the dark, wrestling with my art and with this goading, torturing world, which the artist with his puny forces has somehow to tame and render. Then—the other day—ah! well, no matter!—but the dark broke, and there was light! and when I saw your face, your stranger's face, in that crowd to-night, listening to those things, it drew me. I wanted to say my say. I don't make excuses. Very likely we shall never meet again—but for this hour we have been friends. Good night!—good night! Look,—the dawn is coming!'

And he pointed to where, behind the towers of Notre-Dame, the first whiteness of the coming day was rising into the starry blue.

They shook hands.

'You go back to England soon?'

'In a—a—week or two.'

'Only believe this—we have things better worth seeing than "Les Trois Rats"—things that represent us better. That is what the foreigner is always doing; he spends his time in wondering at our monkey tricks; there is no nation can do them so well as we; and the great France—the undying France!—disappears in a splutter of *blague*!'

He leant over the parapet, forgetting his companion, his eyes fixed on the great cathedral, on the slender shaft of the Sainte Chapelle, on the sky filling with light.

Then suddenly he turned round, laid a quick hand on his companion's shoulder.

'If you ever feel inclined to write to me, the Ecole des Beaux-Arts will find me. Adieu.'

And drawing his coat round him in the chilliness of the dawn, he walked off quickly across the bridge.

David also hurried away, speeding along the deserted pavements till again he was in his own dark street. The dawn was growing from its first moment of mysterious beauty into a grey disillusioning light. But he felt no reaction. He crept up the squalid stairs to his room. It was heavy with the scent of the narcissus.

He took them, and stole along the passage to Elise's door. There were three steps outside it. He sat down on the lowest, putting his flowers beside him. There was something awful to him even in this nearness; he dare not have gone higher.

He sat there for long—his heart beating, beating. Every part of his French experience so far, whether by sympathy or recoil, had helped to bring him to this intoxication of sense and soul. Regnault had spoken of the 'great things' of life. Had he too come to understand them—thus?

At last he left his flowers there, kissing the step on which they were laid, and which her foot must touch. He could hardly sleep; the slight fragrance which clung to the old bearskin in which he wrapt himself helped to keep him restless; it was the faint heliotrope scent he had noticed in her room.

CHAPTER VI

'He loves me—he does really! Poor boy!'

The speaker was Elise Delaunay. She was sitting alone on the divan in her *atelier*, trying on a pair of old Pompadour shoes, with large faded rosettes and pink heels, which she had that moment routed out of a broker's shop in the Rue de Seine, on her way back from the Luxembourg with David. They made her feet look enchantingly small, and she was holding back her skirts that she might get a good look at them.

Her conviction of David's passion did not for some time lessen her interest in the shoes, but at last she kicked them off, and flung herself back on the divan, to think out the situation a little.

Yes, the English youth's adoration could no longer be ignored. It had become evident, even to her own acquaintances and comrades in the various galleries she was now haunting in this bye-time of the artistic year. Whenever she and he appeared together now, there were sly looks and smiles.

The scandal of it did not affect her in the least. She belonged to Bohemia, so apparently did he. She had been perfectly honest till now; but she had never let any convention stand in her way. All her conceptions of the relations between men and women were of an extremely free kind. Her mother's blood in her accounted both for a certain coldness and a certain personal refinement which both divided and protected her from a great many of her acquaintance, but through her father she had been acquainted for years with the type of life and *menage* which prevails among a certain section of the French artist class, and if the occasion were but strong enough she had no instincts inherited or acquired which would stand in the way of the gratification of passion.

On the contrary, her reasoned opinions so far as she had any were all in favour of *l'union libre*—that curious type of association which held the artist Theodore Rousseau for life to the woman who passed as his wife, and which obtains to a remarkable extent, with all those accompaniments of permanence, fidelity, and mutual service, which are commonly held to belong only to *l'union légale*, in one or two strata of French society. She was capable of sentiment; she had hidden veins of womanish weakness; but at the same time the little creature's prevailing temper was one of remarkable coolness and audacity. She judged for herself; she had read for herself, observed for herself. Such a temper had hitherto preserved her from adventures; but, upon occasion, it might as easily land her in one. She was at once a daughter of art and a daughter of the people, with a cross strain of gentle breeding and intellectual versatility thrown in, which made her more interesting and more individual than the rest of her class.

'We are a pair of Romantics out of date, you and I,' she had said once to David, half mocking, half in earnest, and the phrase fitted the relation and position of the pair very nearly. In spite of the enormous difference of their habits and training they had at bottom similar tastes—the same capacity for the excitements of art and imagination, the same shrinking from the coarse and ugly sides of the life amid which they moved, the same cravings for novelty and experience.

David went no more to the 'Trois Rats,' and when, in obedience to Lenain's recommendation, he had bought and begun to read a novel of the Goncourts, he threw it from him in a disgust beyond expression. *Her* talk, meanwhile, was in some respects of the freest; she would discuss subjects impossible to the English girl of the same class; she asked very few questions as to the people she mixed with; and he was, by now, perfectly acquainted with her view, that on the whole marriage was for the *bourgeois*, and had few attractions for people who were capable of penetrating deeper into the rich growths of life. But there was no *personal* taint or license in what she said; and she herself could be always happily divided from her topics. Their Bohemia was canopied with illusions, but the illusions on the whole were those of poetry.

Were all David's illusions hers, however? *Love!* She thought of it, half laughing, as she lay on the divan. She knew nothing about it—she was for *art*. Yet what a brow, what eyes, what a gait—like a young Achilles!

She sprang up to look at a sketch of him, dashed off the day before, which was on the easel. Yes, it was like. There was the quick ardent air, the southern colour, the clustering black hair, the young parting of the lips. The invitation of the eyes was irresistible—she smiled into them—the little pale face flushing.

But at the same moment her attention was caught by a sketch pinned against the wall just behind the easel.

'Ah! my cousin, my good cousin!' she said, with a little mocking twist of the mouth; 'how strange that you have not been here all this time—never once! There was something said, I remember, about a visit to Bordeaux about now. Ah! well—*tant mieux*—for you would be rather jealous, my cousin!'

Then she sat down with her hands on her knees, very serious. How long since they met? A week. How long till the temporary closing of the Salon and the voting of the rewards? A fortnight. Well, should it go on till then? Yes or no? As soon as she knew her fate—or at any rate if she got her *mention*—she would go back to work. She had two subjects in her mind; she would work at home, and Taranne had promised to come and advise her. Then she would have no time for handsome English boys. But till then?

She took an anemone from a bunch David had brought her, and began to pluck off the petals, alternating 'yes' and 'no.' The last petal fell to 'yes.'

'I should have done just the same if it had been "no,"' she said, laughing. '*Allons,* he amuses me, and I do him no harm. When I go back to work he can do his business. He has done none yet. He will forget me and make some money.'

She paced up and down the studio thinking again. She was conscious of some remorse for her part in sending the Englishman's sister to the Cervins. The matter had never been mentioned again between her and David; yet she knew instinctively that he was often ill at ease. The girl was perpetually in Montjoie's studio, and surrounded in public places by a crew of his friends. Madame Cervin was constantly in attendance no doubt, but if it came to a struggle she would have no power with the English girl, whose obstinacy was in proportion to her ignorance.

Elise had herself once stopped Madame Cervin on the stairs, and said some frank things of the sculptor, in order to quiet an uncomfortable conscience.

'Ah! you do not like Monsieur Montjoie?' said the other, looking hard at her.

Elise coloured, then she recovered herself.

'All the world knows that Monsieur Montjoie has no scruples, madame,' she cried angrily. 'You know it yourself. It is a shame. That girl understands nothing.'

Madame Cervin laughed.

'Certainly she understands everything that she pleases, mademoiselle. But if there is any anxiety, let her brother come and look after her. He can take her where she wants to go. I should be glad indeed. I am as tired as a dog. Since she came it is one *tapage* from morning till night.'

And Elise retired, discomfited before those small malicious eyes. Since David's adoration for the girl artist in No. 27 had become more or less public property, Madame Cervin, who had seen from the beginning that Louie was a burden on her brother, had decidedly the best of the situation.

'Has she lent Montjoie money?'

Elise meditated. The little *bourgeoise* had a curious weakness for posing as the patron of the various artists in the house. 'Very possible! and she looks on the Maenad as the only way of getting it back? She would sell her soul for a napoleon—I always knew that. *Canaille*, all of them!'

And the meditation ended in the impatient conclusion that neither she nor the brother had any responsibility. After all, any decent girl, French or English, could soon see for herself what manner of man was Jules Montjoie! And now for the 'private view' of a certain artistic club to which she had promised to take her English acquaintance. All the members of the club were young—of the new rebellious school of *'plein air'*—the afternoon promised to be amusing.

So the companionship of these two went on, and David passed from one golden day to another. How she lectured him, the little, vain, imperious thing; and how meek he was with her, how different from his Manchester self! The woman's cleverness filled the field. The man, wholly preoccupied with other things, did not care to produce himself, and in the first ardour of his new devotion kept all the self-assertive elements of his own nature in the background, caring for nothing but to watch her eyes as she talked, to have her voice in his ears, to keep her happy and content in his company.

Yet she was not taken in. With other people he must be proud, argumentative, self-willed—that she was sure of; but her conviction only made her realise her power over him with the more pleasure. His naive respect for her own fragmentary knowledge, his unbounded admiration for her talent, his quick sympathy for all she did and was, these things, little by little, tended to excite, to preoccupy her.

Especially was she bent upon his artistic education. She carried him hither and thither, to the Louvre, the Luxembourg, the Salon, insisting with a feverish eloquence and invention that he should worship all that she worshipped—no matter if he did not understand!—let him worship all the same—till he had learnt his new alphabet with a smiling docility, and caught her very tricks of phrase. Especially were they haunters of the sculptures in the Louvre, where, because of the difficulty of it, she piqued herself most especially on knowledge, and could convict him most triumphantly of a barbarian ignorance. Up and down they wandered, and she gave him eyes, whether for Artemis, or Aphrodite, or Apollo, or still more for the significant and troubling art of the Renaissance, French and Italian. She would flit before him, perching here and there like a bird, and quivering through and through with a voluble enjoyment.

Then from these lingerings amid a world charged at every point with the elements of passion and feeling, they would turn into the open air, into the May sunshine, which seemed to David's northern eyes so lavish and inexhaustible, carrying with it inevitably the kindness of the gods! They would sit out of doors either in the greenwood paths of the Bois, where he could lie at her feet, and see nothing but her face and the thick young wood all round them, or in some corner of the Champs-Elysées, or the sun-beaten Quai de la Conference, where the hurrying life of the town brushed past them incessantly, yet without disturbing for a moment their absorption in or entertainment of each other.

Yet all through she maintained her mastery of the situation. She was a riddle to him often, poor boy! One moment she would lend herself in bewildering unexpected ways to his passion, the next she would allow him hardly the privileges of the barest acquaintance, hardly the carrying of her cloak, the touch of her hand. But she had no qualms. It was but to last another fortnight; the friendship soothed and beguiled for her these days of excited waiting; and a woman, when she is an artist and a Romantic, may at least sit, smoke, and chat with whomsoever she likes, provided it be a time of holiday, and she is not betraying her art.

Meanwhile the real vulgarity of her nature—its insatiable vanity, its reckless ambition—was masked from David mainly by the very jealousy and terror which her artist's life soon produced in him. He saw no sign of other lovers; she had many acquaintances but no intimates; and the sketch in her room had been carelessly explained to him as the portrait of her cousin. But the *atelier*, and the rivalries it represented:—after three days with her he had learnt that what had seemed to him the extravagance, the pose of her first talk with him, was in truth the earnest, the reality of her existence. She told him that since she was a tiny child she had dreamed of *fame*—dreamed of people turning in the streets when she passed—of a glory that should lift her above all the commonplaces of existence, and all the disadvantages of her own start in life.

'I am neither beautiful, nor rich, nor well-born; but if I have talent, what matter? Everyone will be at my feet. And if I have no talent—*grand Dieu!*—what is there left for me but to kill myself?'

And she would clasp her hands round her knees, and look at him with fierce, drawn brows, as though defying him to say a single syllable in favour of any meaner compromise with fate.

This fever of the artist and the *concurrent*—in a woman above all— how it bewildered him! He soon understood enough of it, however, to be desperately jealous of it, to realise something of the preliminary bar it placed between any lover and the girl's heart and life.

Above all was he jealous of her teachers. Taranne clearly could beat her down with a word, reduce her to tears with an unfavourable criticism; then he had but to hold up a finger, to say, 'Mademoiselle, you have worked well this week, your drawing shows improvement, I have hopes of you,' to bring her to his feet with delight and gratitude. It was a *monstrous* power, this power of the master with his pupil! How could women submit to it?

Yet his lover's instincts led him safely through many perils. He was infinitely complaisant towards all her artistic talk, all her gossip of the *atelier*. It seemed to him—but then his apprehension of this strange new world was naturally a somewhat confused one—that Elise was not normally on terms with any of her fellow students.

'If I don't get my *mention*,' she would say passionately, 'I tell you again it will be intrigue; it will be those creatures in the *atelier* who want to get rid of me—to finish with me. Ah! I will *crush* them all yet. And I have been good to them all—every one—I vow I have—even to that animal of a Breal, who is always robbing me of my place at the *concours*, and taking mean advantages. *Miserables!*'

And the tears would stand in her angry eyes; her whole delicate frame would throb with fierce feeling.

Gradually he learnt how to deal with these fits, even when they chilled him with a dread, a conviction he dared not analyse. He would so soothe and listen to her, so ply her with the praises of her gift, which came floated to him on the talk of those acquaintances of hers to whom she had introduced him, that her most deep-rooted irritations would give way for a time. The woman would reappear; she would yield to the charm of his admiring eyes, his stammered flatteries; her whole mood would break up, dissolve into eager softness, and she would fall into a childish plaintiveness, saying wild generous things even of her rivals, now there seemed to be no one under heaven to take their part, and at last, even, letting her little hand fall into those eager brown ones which lay in wait for it, letting it linger there— forgotten.

Especially was she touched in his favour by the way in which Regnault had singled him out. After he had given her the history of that midnight walk, he saw clearly that he had risen to a higher plane in her esteem. She had no heroes exactly; but she had certain artistic passions, certain romantic fancies, which seemed to touch deep fibres in her. Her admiration for

Regnault was one of these; but David soon understood that he had no cause whatever to be jealous of it. It was a matter purely of the mind and the imagination.

So the days passed—the hot lengthening days. Sometimes in the long afternoons they pushed far afield into the neighbourhood of Paris. The green wooded hills of Sevres and St. Cloud, the blue curves and reaches of the Seine, the flashing lights and figures, the pleasures of companionship, self-revelation, independence—the day was soon lost in these quick impressions, and at night they would come back in a fragrant moonlight, descending from their train into the noise and glitter of the streets, only to draw closer together—for surely on these crowded pavements David might claim her little arm in his for safety's sake—till at last they stood in the dark passage between his door and hers, and she would suddenly pelt him with a flower, spring up her small stairway, and lock her door behind her, before, in his emotion, he could find his voice or a farewell. Then he would make his way into his own den, and sit there in the dark, lost in a thronging host of thoughts and memories,—feeling life one vibrating delight.

At last one morning he awoke to the fact that only four days more remained before the date on which, according to their original plan, they were to go back to Manchester. He laughed aloud when the recollection first crossed his mind; then, having a moment to himself, he sat down and scrawled a few hasty words to John. Business detained him yet a while—would detain him a few weeks—let John manage as he pleased, his employer trusted everything to him—and money was enclosed. Then he wrote another hurried note to the bank where he had placed his six hundred pounds. Let them send him twenty pounds at once, in Bank of England notes. He felt himself a young king as he gave the order—king of this mean world and of its dross. All his business projects had vanished from his mind. He could barely have recalled them if he had tried. During the first days of his acquaintance with Elise he had spent a few spare hours in turning over the boxes on the quays, in talks with booksellers in the Rue de Seine or the Rue de Lille, in preliminary inquiries respecting some commissions he had undertaken. But now, every hour, every thought were hers. What did money matter, in the name of Heaven? Yet when his twenty pounds came, he changed his notes and pocketed his napoleons with a vast satisfaction. For they meant power, they meant opportunity; every one should be paid away against so many hours by her side, at her feet.

Meanwhile day after day he had reminded himself of Louie, and day after day he had forgotten her again, absolutely, altogether. Once or twice he met her on the stairs, started, remembered, and tried to question her as to what she was doing. But she was still angry with him for his interference on the day of the pose; and he could get very little out of her. Let him only leave her alone; she was not a school-child to be meddled with; that he would find out. As to Madame Cervin, she was a little fool, and her meanness in money matters was disgraceful; but she, Louie, could put up with her. One of these meetings took place on the day of his letters to the bank and to John. Louie asked him abruptly when he thought of returning. He flushed deeply, stammered, said he was inclined to stay longer, but of course she could be sent home. An escort could be found for her. She stared at him; then suddenly her black eyes sparkled, and she laughed so that the sound echoed up the dark stairs. David hotly inquired what she meant; but she ran up still laughing loudly, and he was left to digest her scornful amusement as best he could.

Not long after he found the Cervins' door open as he passed, and in the passage saw a group of people, mostly men; Montjoie in front, just lighting a cigar; Louie's black hat in the background. David hurried past; he loathed the sculptor's battered look, his insolent eye, his slow ambiguous manner; he still burnt with the anger and humiliation of his ineffectual descent on the man's domain. But Madame Cervin, catching sight of him from the back of the party, pursued him panting and breathless to his own door. Would monsieur please attend to her; he was so hard to get hold of; never, in fact, at home! Would he settle her little bill, and give her more money for current expenses? Mademoiselle Louie required to be kept amused—*mon Dieu!*— from morning to night! She had no objection, provided it were made worth her while. And how much longer did monsieur think of remaining in Paris?

David answered recklessly that he did not know, paid her bill for Louie's board and extras without looking at it, and gave her a napoleon in hand, wherewith she departed, her covetous eyes aglow, her mouth full of excited civilities.

She even hesitated a moment at the door and then came back to assure him that she was really all discretion with regard to his sister; no doubt monsieur had heard some unpleasant stories, for instance, of M. Montjoie; she could understand perfectly, that coming from such a quarter, they had affected monsieur's mind; but he would see that she could not make a sudden quarrel with one of her husband's old friends; Mademoiselle Louie (who was already her *cherie*) had taken a fancy to pose for this statue; it was surely better to indulge her than to rouse her self-will, but she could assure monsieur that she had looked after her as though it had been her own daughter.

David stood impatiently listening. In a few minutes he was to be with Elise at the corner of the Rue Lafitte. Of course it was all right!—and if it were not, he could not mend it. The woman was vulgar and grasping, but what reason was there to think anything else that was evil of her? Probably she had put up with Louie more easily than a woman of a higher type would have done. At any rate she was doing her best, and what more could be asked of him than he had done? Louie behaved outrageously in Manchester; he could not help it, either there or here. He had interfered again and again, and had always been a fool for his pains. Let her choose for herself. A number of old and long-hidden exasperations seemed now to emerge whenever he thought of his sister.

Five minutes later he was in the Rue Lafitte.

It was Elise's caprice that they should always meet in this way, out of doors; at the corner of their own street; on the steps of the Madeleine; beneath the Vendome Column; in front of a particular bonbon shop; or beside the third tree from the Place de la Concorde in the northern alley of the Tuileries Gardens. He had been only once inside her studio since the first evening of their acquaintance.

His mind was full of excitement, for the Salon had been closed since the day before; and the awards of the jury would be informally known, at least in some cases, by the evening. Elise's excitement since the critical hours began had been pitiful to see. As he stood waiting he gave his whole heart to her and her ambitions, flinging away from him with a passionate impatience every other interest, every other thought.

When she came she looked tired and white. 'I can't go to galleries, and I can't paint,' she said, shortly. 'What shall we do?'

Her little black hat was drawn forward, but through the dainty veil he could see the red spot on either cheek. Her hands were pushed deep into the pockets of her light grey jacket, recalling the energetic attitude in which she had stood over Louie on the occasion of their first meeting. He guessed at once that she had not slept, and that she was beside herself with anxiety. How to manage her?—how to console her? He felt himself so young and raw; yet already his passion had awakened in him a hundred new and delicate perceptions.

'Look at the weather!' he said to her. 'Come out of town! let us make for the Gare St. Lazare, and spend the day at St. Germain.'

She hesitated.

'Taranne will write to me directly he knows—directly! He might write any time this evening. No, no!—I can't go! I must be on the spot.'

'He can't write *before* the evening. You said yourself before seven nothing could be known. We will get back in ample time, I swear.'

They were standing in the shade of a shop awning, and he was looking down at her, eagerly, persuasively. She had a debate with herself, then with a despairing gesture of the hands, she turned abruptly—

'Well then—to the station!'

When they had started, she lay back in the empty carriage he had found for her, and shut her eyes. The air was oppressive, for the day before had been showery, and the heat this morning was a damp heat which relaxed the whole being. But before the train moved, she felt a current of coolness, and hastily looking up she saw that David had possessed himself of the cheap fan which had been lying on her lap, and was fanning her with his gaze fixed upon her, a gaze which haunted her as her eyelids fell again.

Suddenly she fell into an inward perplexity, an inward impatience on the subject of her companion, and her relation to him. It had been all very well till yesterday! But now the artistic and professional situation had become so strained, so intense, she could hardly give him a thought. His presence there, and its tacit demands upon her, tried her nerves. Her mind was full of a hundred *miseres d'atelier*, of imaginary enemies and intrigues; one minute she was all hope, the next all fear; and she turned sick when she thought of Taranne's letter.

What had she been entangling herself for? she whose whole life and soul belonged to art and ambition! This comradeship, begun as a caprice, an adventure, was becoming too serious. It must end!—end probably to-day, as she had all along determined. Then, as she framed the thought, she became conscious of a shrinking, a difficulty, which enraged and frightened her.

She sat up abruptly and threw back her veil.

David made a little exclamation as he dropped the fan.

'Yes!' she said, looking at him with a little frown, 'yes—what did you say?'

Then she saw that his whole face was working with emotion.

'I wish you would have stayed like that,' he said, in a voice which trembled.

'Why?'

'Because—because it was so sweet!'

She gave a little start, and a sudden red sprang into her cheek.

His heart leapt. He had never seen her blush for any word of his before.

'I prefer the air itself,' she said, bending forward and looking away from him out of the open window at the villas they were passing.

Yet, all the while, as the country houses succeeded each other and her eyes followed them, she saw not their fragrant, flowery gardens, but the dark face and tall young form opposite. He was handsomer even than when she had seen him first—handsomer far than her portrait of him. Was it the daily commerce with new forms of art and intelligence which Paris and her companionship had brought him?—or simply the added care which a man in love instinctively takes of the little details of his dress and social conduct?—which had given him this look of greater maturity, greater distinction? Her heart fluttered a little—then she fell back on the thought of Taranne's letter.

They emerged from the station at St. Germain into a fierce blaze of sun, which burned on the square red mass of the old chateau, and threw a blinding glare on the white roads.

'Quick! for the trees!' she said, and they both hurried over the open space which lay between them and the superb chestnut grove which borders the famous terrace. Once there all was well, and they could wander from alley to alley in a green shade, the white blossom-spikes shining in the sun overhead, and to their right the blue and purple plain, with the Seine winding and dimpling, the river polders with their cattle, and far away the dim heights of Montmartre just emerging behind the great mass of Mont Valerien, which blocked the way to Paris. Such lights and shades, such spring leaves, such dancing airs!

Elise drew a long breath, slipped off her jacket which he made a joy of carrying, and loosened the black lace at her throat which fell so prettily over the little pink cotton underneath.

Then she looked at her companion unsteadily. There was excitement in this light wind, this summer sun. Her great resolve to 'end it' began to look less clear to her. Nay, she stood still and smiled up into his face, a very siren of provocation and wild charm—the wind blowing a loose lock about her eyes.

'Is this better than England—than your Manchester?' she asked him scornfully, and he—traitor!—flinging out of his mind all the bounties of an English May, all his memories of the whitethorn and waving fern and foaming streams set in the deep purple breast of the Scout—vowed to her that nowhere else could there be spring or beauty or sunshine, but only here in France and at St. Germain.

At this she smiled and blushed—no woman could have helped the blush. In truth, his will, steadily bent on one end, while hers was distracted by half a dozen different impulses, was beginning to affect her in a troubling, paralysing way. For all her parade of a mature and cynical enlightenment, she was just twenty; it was such a May day as never was; and when once she had let herself relax towards him again, the inward ache of jealous ambition made this passionate worship beside her, irrelevant as it was, all the more soothing, all the more luring.

Still she felt that something must be done to stem the tide, and again she fell back upon luncheon. They had bought some provisions on their way to the station in Paris. He might subsist on scenery and aesthetics if he pleased—as for her, she was a common person with common needs, and must eat.

'Oh, not here!' he cried, 'why, this is all in public. Look at the nursemaids, and the boys playing, and the carriages on the terrace. Come on a little farther. You remember that open place with the thorns and the stream?—there we should be in peace.'

She did not know that she wanted to be in peace; but she gave way.

So they wandered on past the chestnuts into the tangled depths of the old forest. A path sunk in brambles and fern took them through beech wood to the little clearing David had in his mind. A tiny stream much choked by grass and last year's leaves ran along one side of it. A fallen log made a seat, and the beech trees spread their new green fans overhead, or flung them out to right and left around the little space, and for some distance in front, till the green sprays and the straight grey stems were lost on all sides in a brownish pinkish mist which betrayed a girdle of oaks not yet conquered by the summer.

She took her seat on the log, and he flung himself beside her. Out came the stores in his pockets, and once more they made themselves childishly merry over a scanty meal, which left them still hungry.

Then for an hour or two they sat lounging and chattering in the warm shade, while the gentle wind brought them every spring scent, every twitter of the birds, every swaying murmur of the forest. David lay on his back against the log, his eyes now plunging into the forest, now watching the curls of smoke from his pipe mounting against the background of green, or the moist fleecy clouds which seemed to be actually tangled in the tree-tops, now fixed as long as they dared on his companion's face. She was not beautiful? Let her say it! For she had the softest mouth which drooped like a child with a grievance when she was silent, and melted into the subtlest curves when she talked. She had, as a rule, no colour, but her clear paleness, as contrasted with the waves of her light-gold hair, seemed to him an exquisite beauty. The eyebrows had an oriental trick of mounting at the corners, but the effect, taken with the droop of the mouth, was to give the face in repose a certain charming look of delicate and plaintive surprise. Above all it was her smallness which entranced him; her feet and hands, her tiny waist, the *finesse* of her dress and movements. All the women he had ever seen, Lucy and Dora among them, served at this moment only to make a foil in his mind for this little Parisian beside him.

How she talked this afternoon! In her quick reaction towards him she was after all more the woman than she had ever been. She chattered of her forlorn childhood, of her mother's woes and her father's iniquities, using the frankest language about these last; then of herself and her troubles. He listened and laughed; his look as she poured herself out to him was in itself a caress. Moreover, unconsciously to both, their relation had changed somewhat. The edge of his first ignorance and shyness had rubbed off. He was no longer a mere slave at her feet. Rather a new and sweet equality seemed at last after all these days to have arisen between them; a bond more simple, more natural. Every now and then he caught his breath under the sense of a coming crisis; meanwhile the May day was a dream of joy, and life an intoxication.

But he controlled himself long, being indeed in desperate fear of breaking the spell which held her to him this heavenly afternoon. The hours slipped by; the air grew stiller and sultrier. Presently, just as the sun was sinking into the western wood, a woman, carrying a bundle and with a couple of children, crossed the glade. One child was on her arm; the other, whimpering with heat and fatigue, dragged wearily behind her, a dead weight on its mother's skirts. The woman looked worn out, and was scolding the crying child in a thin exasperated voice. When she came to the stream, she put down her bundle, and finding a seat by the water, she threw back her cotton bonnet and began to wipe her brow, with long breaths which were very near to groans. Then the child on her lap set up a shout of hunger, while the child behind her began to cry louder than before. The woman hastily raised the baby, unfastened her dress, and gave it the breast, so stifling its cries; then, first slapping the other child with angry vehemence, she groped in the bundle for a piece of sausage roll, and by dint of alternately shaking the culprit and stuffing the food into its poor open mouth, succeeded in reducing it to a chewing and sobbing silence. The mother herself was clearly at the last gasp, and when at length the children were quiet, as she turned her harshly outlined head so as to see who the other occupants of the glade might be, her look had in it the dull hostility of the hunted creature whose powers of self-defence are almost gone.

But she could not rest long. After ten minutes, at longest, she dragged herself up from the grass with another groan, and they all disappeared into the trees, one of the children crying again—a pitiable trio.

Elise had watched the group closely, and the sight seemed in some unexplained way to chill and irritate the girl.

'There is one of the drudges that men make,' she said bitterly, looking after the woman.

'Men?' he demurred; 'I suspect the husband is a drudge too.'

'Not he!' she cried. 'At least he has liberty, choice, comrades. He is not battered out of all pleasure, all individuality, that other human beings may have their way and be cooked for, and this wretched human race may last. The woman is always the victim, say what you like. But for *some* of us at least there is a way out!'

She looked at him defiantly.

A tremor swept through him under the suddenness of this jarring note. Then a delicious boldness did away with the tremor. He met her eyes straight.

'Yes—*love* can always find it,' he said under his breath—'or make it.'

She wavered an instant, then she made a rally.

'I know nothing about that,' she said scornfully; 'I was thinking of art. *Art* breaks all chains, or accepts none. The woman that has art is free, and she alone; for she has scaled the men's heaven and stolen their sacred fire.'

She clasped her hands tightly on her knee; her face was full of aggression.

David sat looking at her, trying to smile, but his heart sank within him.

He threw away his pipe, and laid his hand down against the log, not far from her, trying to smile, but his heart sank within him.

He threw away his pipe and laid his head down against the log, not far from her, drawing his hat over his eyes. So they sat in silence a little while, till he looked up and said, in a bright beseeching tone:

'Finish me that scene in *Hernani!*'

The day before, after a *matinee* of *Andromaque* at the Theatre-Francais, in a moment of rebellion and reaction against all things classical, they had both thrown themselves upon *Hernani*. She had read it aloud to him in a green corner of the Bois, having a faculty that way, and bidding him take it as a French lesson. He took it, of course, as a lesson in nothing but the art of making wild speeches to the woman one loves.

But now she demurred.

'It is not here.'

He produced it out of his pocket.

She shrugged her shoulders.

'I am not in the vein.'

'You said last week you were not in the vein,' he said, laughing tremulously, 'and you read me that scene from *Ruy Blas*, so that when we went to see Sarah Bernhardt in the evening I was disappointed!'

She smiled, not being able to help it, for all flattery was sweet to her.

'We must catch our train. I would never speak to you again if we were late!'

He held up his watch to her.

'An hour—it is, at the most, half an hour's walk.'

'Ah, *mon Dieu!*' she cried, clasping her hands. 'It is all over, the vote is given. Perhaps Taranne is writing to me now, at this moment!'

'Read—read! and forget it half an hour more.'

She caught up the book in a frenzy, and began to read, first carelessly and with unintelligible haste; but before a page was over, the artist had recaptured her, she had slackened, she had begun to interpret.

It was the scene in the third act where Hernani the outlaw, who has himself bidden his love, Dona Sol, marry her kinsman the old Duke, rather than link her fortunes to those of a ruined chief of banditti, comes in upon the marriage he has sanctioned, nay commanded. The bridegroom's wedding gifts are there on the table. He and Dona Sol are alone.

The scene begins with a speech of bitter irony from Hernani. His friends have been defeated and dispersed. He is alone in the world; a price is on his head; his lot is more black and hopeless than before. Yet his heart is bursting within him. He had bidden her, indeed, but how could she have obeyed! Traitress! false love! false heart!

He takes up the jewels one by one.

'*This necklace is brave work,—and the bracelet is rare—though not so rare as the woman who beneath a brow so pure can bear about with her a heart so vile! And what in exchange? A little love? Bah!—a mere trifle!... Great God! that one can betray like this—and feel no shame—and live!*'

For answer, Dona Sol goes proudly up to the wedding casket and, with a gesture matching his own, takes out the dagger from its lowest depth. 'You stop halfway!' she says to him calmly, and he understands. In an instant he

'I think not.'

And he turned away to his own door.

But she ran back to him and laid her hand on his arm. Her eyes were full of tears.

'Please, Monsieur David. We were good friends this morning. Be now and always my good friend!'

He shook his head again, but he let himself be led by her. Still holding him—torn between her quick remorse and her eagerness for Taranne's letter, she unlocked her door. One dart for the table. Yes! there it lay. She took it up; then her face blanched suddenly, and she came piteously up to David, who was standing just inside the closed door.

'Wish me luck, Monsieur David, wish me luck, as you did before!'

But he was silent, and she tore open the letter. '*Dieu!—mon Dieu!*'

It was a sound of ecstasy. Then she flung down the letter, and running up to David, she caught his arm again with both hands.

'*Triomphe! Triomphe!* I have got my *mention*, and the picture they skied is to be brought down to the line, and Taranne says I have done better than any other pupil of his of the same standing—that I have an extraordinary gift—that I must succeed, all the world says so—and two other members of the jury send me their compliments. Ah! Monsieur David'—in a tone of reproach—'be kind—be nice—congratulate me.'

And she drew back an arm's-length that she might look at him, her own face overflowing with exultant colour and life. Then she approached again, her mood changing.

'It is too *detestable* of you to stand there like a statue! ah! that it is! For I never deceived you, no, never. I said to you the first night—there is nothing else for me in the world but art—nothing! Do you hear? This falling in love spoils everything—*everything!* Be friends with me. You will be going back to England soon. Perhaps—perhaps'—her voice faltered—'I will take a week's more holiday—Taranne says I ought. But then I must go to work—and we will part friends—always friends—and respect and understand each other all our lives, *n'est-ce pas!*'

'Oh! let me go!' cried David fiercely, his loud strained voice startling them both, and flinging her hand away from him, he made for the door. But impulsively she threw herself against it, dismayed to find herself so near crying, and shaken with emotion from head to foot.

They stood absorbed in each other; she with her hands behind her on the door, and her hat tumbling back from her masses of loosened hair. And as she gazed she was fascinated; for there was a grand look about him in his misery—a look which was strange to her, and which was in fact the emergence of his rugged and Puritan race. But whatever it was it seized her, as all aspects of his personal beauty had done from the beginning. She held out her little white hands to him appealing.

'No! no!' he said roughly, trying to put her away,' never—never—friends! You may kill me—you shan't make a child of me any more. Oh! my God!' It was a cry of agony. 'A man can't go about with a girl in this way, if—if she is like you, and not—' His voice broke—he lost the thread of what he was saying, and drew his hand across his eyes before he broke out again. 'What—you thought I was just a raw cub, to be played with. Oh, I am too dull, I suppose, to understand! But I have grown under your hands anyway. I don't know myself—I should do you or myself a mischief if this went on, Let me go—and go home to-night!'

And again he made a threatening step forward. But when he came close to her he broke down.

'I would have worked for you so,' he said thickly. 'For your sake I would have given up my country. I would have made myself French altogether. It should have been marriage or no marriage as you pleased. You should have been free to go or stay. Only I would have laid myself down for you to walk over. I have some money. I would have settled here. I would have protected you. It is not right for a woman to be alone—anyone so young and so pretty. I thought you understood—that you must understand—that your heart was melting to me. I should have done your work no harm—I should have been your slave—you know that. That *cursed, cursed* art!'

He spoke with a low intense emphasis; then turning away he buried his face in his hands.

'David!'

He looked up startled. She was stepping towards him, a smile of ineffable charm floating as it were upon tears.

'I don't know what is the matter with me!' she said tremulously. 'There is trouble in it, I know.' It is the broken glass coming true. *Mais, Voyons! c'est plus fort que moi!* Do you care so much—would it break your heart—would you let me work—and never, *never* get in the way? Would you be content that art should come first and you second? I can promise you no more than that—not one little inch! *Would* you be content? Say!'

He ran to her with a cry. She let him put his arms round her, and a shiver of excitement ran through her.

'What does it mean?' she said breathlessly. 'One is so strong one moment—and the next—like this! Oh, why did you ever come?'

Then she burst into tears, hiding her eyes upon his breast.

'Oh! I have been so much alone! but I have got a heart somewhere all the same. If you will have it, you must take the consequences.'

Awed by the mingling of his silence with that painful throbbing beneath her cheek, she looked up. He stooped—and their young faces met.

CHAPTER VII

During the three weeks which had ended for David and Elise in this scene of passion, Louie had been deliberately going her own way, managing even in this unfamiliar *milieu* to extract from it almost all the excitement or amusement it was capable of yielding her. All the morning she dragged Madame Cervin about the Paris streets: in the afternoon she would sometimes pose for Montjoie, and sometimes not; he had to bring her bonbons and theatre tickets to bribe her, and learn new English wherewith to flatter her. Then in the evenings she made the Cervins take her to theatres and various entertainments more or less reputable, for which of course David paid. It seemed to Madame Cervin, as she sat staring beside them, that her laughs never fell in with the laughs of other people. But whether she understood or no, it amused her, and go she would.

A looker-on might have found the relations between Madame Cervin and her boarder puzzling at first sight. In reality they represented a compromise between considerations of finance and considerations of morals—as the wife of the *ancien prix de Rome* understood these last. For the ex-modiste was by no means without her virtues or her scruples. She had ugly manners and ideas on many points, but she had lived a decent life at any rate since her marriage with a man for whom she had an incomprehensible affection, heavily as he burdened and exploited her; and though she took all company pretty much as it came, she had a much keener sense now than in her youth of the practical advantages of good behaviour to a woman, and of the general reasonableness of the *bourgeois* point of view with regard to marriage and the family. Her youth had been stormy; her middle age tended to a certain conservative philosophy of common sense, and to the development of a rough and ready conscience.

Especially was she conscious of the difficulties of virtue. When Elise Delaunay, for instance, was being scandalously handled by the talkers in her stuffy *salon*, Madame Cervin sat silent. Not only had she her own reasons for being grateful to the little artist, but with the memory of her own long-past adventures behind her she was capable by now of a secret admiration for an unprotected and struggling girl who had hitherto held her head high, worked hard, and avoided lovers.

So that when the artist's wife undertook the charge of the good-looking English girl she had done it honestly, up to her lights, and she had fulfilled it honestly. She had in fact hardly let Louie Grieve out of her sight since her boarder was handed over to her.

These facts, however, represent only one side of the situation. Madame Cervin was now respectable. She had relinquished years before the *chasse* for personal excitement; she had replaced it by 'the *chasse* of the five-franc piece.' She loved her money passionately; but at the same time she loved power, gossip, and small flatteries. They distracted her, these last, from the depressing spectacle of her husband's gradual and inevitable decay. So that her life represented a balance between these various instincts. For some time past she had gathered about her a train of small artists, whom she mothered and patronised, and whose wild talk and pecuniary straits diversified the monotony of her own childless middle age. Montjoie, whose undoubted talent imposed upon a woman governed during all her later life by the traditions and the admirations of the artist world, had some time before established a hold upon her, partly dependent on a certain magnetism in the man, partly, as Elise had suspected, upon money relations. For the grasping little *bourgeoise* who would haggle for a morning over half a franc, and keep a lynx-eyed watch over the woman who came to do the weekly cleaning, lest the miserable creature should appropriate a crust or a cold potato, had a weak side for her artist friends who flattered and amused her. She would lend to them now and then out of her hoards; she had lent to Montjoie in the winter when, after months of wild dissipation, he was in dire straits and almost starving.

But having lent, the thought of her jeopardised money would throw her into agonies, and she would scheme perpetually to get it back. Like all the rest of Montjoie's creditors she was hanging on the Maenad, which promised indeed to be the *chef—d'œuvre* of an indisputable talent, could that talent only be kept to work. When the sculptor—whose curiosity had been originally roused by certain phrases of Barbier's in his preliminary letters to his nephew, phrases embellished by Dubois' habitual *fanfaronnade*—had first beheld the English girl, he had temporarily thrown up his work and was lounging about Paris in moody despair, to Madame Cervin's infinite disgust. But at sight of Louie his artist's zeal rekindled. Her wild nature, her half-human eye, the traces of Greek form in the dark features—these things fired and excited him.

'Get me that girl to sit,' he had said to Madame Cervin, 'and the Maenad will be sold in six weeks!'

And Madame Cervin, fully determined on the one hand that Montjoie should finish his statue and pay his debts, and on the other that the English girl should come to no harm from a man of notorious character, had first led up to the sittings, and then superintended them with the utmost vigilance. She meant no harm—the brother was a fool for his pains—but Montjoie should have his sitter. So she sat there, dragon-like, hour after hour, knitting away with her little fat hands, while Louie posed, and Montjoie worked; and groups of the sculptor's friends came in and out, providing the audience which excited the ambition of the man and the vanity of the girl.

So the days passed. At last there came a morning when Louie came out early from the Cervins' door, shut it behind her, and ran up the ladder-like stairs which led to David's room.

'David!'

Her voice was pitched in no amiable key, as she violently shook the handle of the door. But, call and shake as she might, there was no answer, and after a while she paused, feeling a certain bewilderment.

'It is ridiculous! He can't be out; it isn't half-past eight. It's just his tiresomeness.'

And she made another and still more vehement attempt, all to no purpose. Not a sound was to be heard from the room within. But as she was again standing irresolute, she heard a footstep behind her on the narrow stairs, and looking round saw the *concierge*, Madame Merichat. The woman's thin and sallow face—the face of a born pessimist—had a certain sinister flutter in it.

She held out a letter to the astonished Louie, saying at the same time with a disagreeable smile:

'What is the use of knocking the house down when there is no one there?'

'Where is he?' cried Louie, not understanding her, and looking at the letter with stupefaction.

The woman put it into her hand.

'No one came back last night,' she said with a shrug. 'Neither monsieur nor mademoiselle; and this morning I receive orders to send letters to "Barbizon, pres Fontainebleau."'

Louie tore open her letter. It was from David, and dated Barbizon. He would be there, it said, for nearly a month. If she could wait with Madame Cervin till he himself could take her home, well and good. But if that were disagreeable to her, let her communicate with him 'chez Madame Pyat,

Barbizon, Fontainebleau,' and he would write to Dora Lomax at once, and make arrangements for her to lodge there, till he returned to Manchester. Some one could easily be found to look after her on the homeward journey if Madame Cervin took her to the train. Meanwhile he enclosed the money for two weeks' *pension* and twenty francs for pocket money.

No other person was mentioned in the letter, and the writer offered neither explanation nor excuses.

Louie crushed the sheet in her hand, with an exclamation, her cheeks flaming.

'So they are amusing themselves at Fontainebleau?' inquired Madame Merichat, who had been leaning against the wall, twisting her apron and studying the English girl with her hard, malicious eyes. 'Oh! I don't complain; there was a letter for me too. Monsieur has paid all. But I regret for mademoiselle—if mademoiselle is surprised.'

She spoke to deaf ears.

Louie pushed past her, flew downstairs, and rang the Cervins' bell violently. Madame Cervin herself opened the door, and the girl threw herself upon her, dragged her into the *salon*, and then said with the look and tone of a fury:

'Read that!'

She held out the crumbled letter. Madame Cervin adjusted her spectacles with shaking hands.

'But it is in English!' she cried in despair.

Louie could not have beaten her for not understanding. But, herself trembling with excitement, she was forced to bring all the French words she knew to bear, and between them, somehow, piecemeal, Madame Cervin was brought to a vague understanding of the letter.

'Gone to Fontainebleau!' she cried, subsiding on to the sofa. 'But why, with whom?'

'Why, with that girl, that *creature—can't* you understand?' said Louie, pacing up and down.

'Ah, I will go and find out all about that!' said Madame Cervin, and hastily exchanging the blue cotton apron and jacket she wore in the mornings in the privacy of her own apartment for her walking dress, she whisked out to make inquiries.

Louie was left behind, striding from end to end of the little *salon*, brows knit, every feature and limb tense with excitement. As the meaning of her discovery grew plainer to her, as she realised what had happened, and what the bearing of it must be on herself and her own position, the tumult within her rose and rose. After that day in the Louvre her native shrewdness had of course very soon informed her of David's infatuation for the little artist. And when it became plain, not only to her, but to all Elise Delaunay's acquaintance, there was much laughter and gossip on the subject in the Cervins' apartment. It was soon discovered that Louie had taken a dislike, which, perhaps, from the beginning had been an intuitive jealousy, to Elise, and had, moreover, no inconvenient sensitiveness on her brother's account, which need prevent the discussion of his love affairs in her presence. So the discussion went freely on, and Louie only regretted that, do what she would to improve herself in French, she understood so little of it. But the tone towards Elise among Montjoie's set, especially from Montjoie himself, was clearly contemptuous and hostile; and Louie instinctively enjoyed the mud which she felt sure was being thrown.

Yet, incredible as it may seem, with all this knowledge on her part, all this amusement at her brother's expense, all this blackening of Elise's character, the possibility of such an event as had actually occurred had never entered the sister's calculations.

And the reason lay in the profound impression which one side of his character had made upon her during the five months they had been together. A complete stranger to the ferment of the lad's imagination, she had been a constant and chafed spectator of his daily life. The strong self-restraint of it had been one of the main barriers between them. She knew that she was always jarring upon him, and that he was always blaming her recklessness and self-indulgence. She hated his Spartan ways—his teetotalism, the small store he set by any personal comfort or luxury, his powers of long-continued work, his indifference to the pleasures and amusements of his age, so far as Manchester could provide them. They were a reflection upon her, and many a gibe she had flung out at him about them. But all the same these ways of his had left a mark upon her; they had rooted a certain conception of him in her mind. She knew perfectly well that Dora Lomax was in love with him, and what did he care? 'Not a ha'porth!' She had never seen him turn his head for any girl; and when he had shown himself sarcastic on the subject of her companions, she had cast about in vain for materials wherewith to retort.

And *now*! That he should fall in love with this French girl—that was natural enough; it had amused and pleased her to see him lose his head and make a fool of himself like other people; but that he should run away with her after a fortnight, without apparently a word of marrying her—leaving his sister in the lurch—

'*Hypocrite!*'

She clenched her hands as she walked. What was really surging in her was that feeling of *ownership* with regard to David which had played so large a part in their childhood, even when she had teased and plagued him most. She might worry and defy him; but no sooner did another woman appropriate him, threaten to terminate for good that hold of his sister upon him which had been so lately renewed, than she was flooded with jealous rage. David had escaped her—he was hers no longer—he was Elise Delaunay's! Nothing that she did could scandalise or make him angry any more. He had sent her money and washed his hands of her. As to his escorting her back to England in two or three weeks, that was just a lie! A man who takes such a plunge does not emerge so soon or so easily. No, she would have to go back by herself, leaving him to his intrigue. The very calmness and secretiveness of his letter was an insult. 'Mind your own business, little girl—go home to work—and be good! '—that was what it seemed to say to her. She set her teeth over it in her wild anger and pride.

At the same moment the outer door opened and Madame Cervin came bustling back again, bursting with news and indignation.

Oh, there was no doubt at all about it, they had gone off together! Madame Merichat had seen them come downstairs about noon the day before. He was carrying a black bag and a couple of parcels. She also was laden; and about halfway down the street, Madame Merichat, watching from her window, had seen them hail a cab, get into it, and drive away, the cab turning to the right when they reached the Boulevard.

Madame Cervin's wrath was loud, and stimulated moreover by personal alarm. One moment, remembering the scene in Montjoie's studio, she cried out, like the sister, on the brother's hypocrisy; the next she reminded her boarder that there was two weeks' *pension* owing.

Louie smiled scornfully, drew out the notes from David's letter and flung them on the table. Then Madame Cervin softened, and took occasion to remember that condolence with the sister was at least as appropriate to the situation as abuse of the brother. She attempted some consolation, nay, even some caresses, but Louie very soon shook her off.

'Don't talk to me! don't kiss me!' she said impatiently.

And she swept out of the room, went to her own, and locked the door. Then she threw herself face downwards on her bed, and remained there for some time hardly moving. But with every minute that passed, as it seemed, the inward smart grew sharper. She had been hardly conscious of it, at first, this smart, in her rage and pride, but it was there.

At last she could bear it quietly no longer. She sprang up and looked about her. There, just inside the open press which held her wardrobe, were some soft white folds of stuff. Her eye gleamed: she ran to the cupboard and took out the Maenad's dress. During the last few days she had somewhat tired of the sittings—she had at any rate been capricious and tiresome about them; and Montjoie, who was more in earnest about this statue than he had been about any work for years, was at his wit's end, first to control his own temper, and next so to lure or drive his strange sitter as to manage her without offending her.

But to-day the dress recalled David—promised distraction and retaliation. She slipped off her tight gingham with hasty fingers, and in a few seconds she was transformed. The light folds floated about her as she walked impetuously up and down, studying every movement in the glass, intoxicated by the polished clearness and whiteness of her own neck and shoulders, the curves of her own grace and youth. Many a night, even after a long sitting, had she locked her door, made the gas flare, and sat absorbed before her mirror in this guise, throwing herself into one attitude after another, naively regretting that sculpture took so long, and that Montjoie could not fix them all. The ecstasy of self-worship in which the whole process issued was but the fruition of that childish habit which had wrought with childish things for the same end—with a couple of rushlights, an old sheet and primroses from the brook.

Her black abundant hair was still curled about her head. Well, she could pull it down in the studio—now for a wrap—and then no noise! She would slip downstairs so that madame should know nothing about it. She was tired of that woman always at her elbow. Let her go marketing and leave other people in peace.

But before she threw on her wrap she stood still a moment, her nostril quivering, expanding, one hand on her hip, the other swinging her Maenad's tambourine. She knew very little of this sculptor-man—she did not understand him; but he interested, to some extent overawed, her. He had poured out upon her the coarsest flatteries, yet she realised that he had not made love to her. Perhaps Madame Cervin had been in the way. Well, now for a surprise and a *tête-a-tête*! A dare-devil look—her mother's look—sprang into her eyes.

She opened the door, and listened. No one in the little passage, only a distant sound of rapid talking, which suggested to the girl that madame was at that moment enjoying the discussion of her boarder's affairs with monsieur, who was still in bed. She hurried on a waterproof which covered her almost from top to toe. Then, holding up her draperies, she stole out, and on to the public stairs.

They were deserted, and running down them she turned to the right at the bottom and soon found herself at the high studio door.

As she raised her hand to the bell she flushed with passion.

'I'll let him see whether I'll go home whining to Dora, while he's amusing himself,' she said under her breath.

The door was opened to her by Montjoie himself, in his working blouse, a cigarette in his mouth. His hands and dress were daubed with clay, and he had the brutal look of a man in the blackest of tempers. But no sooner did he perceive Louie Grieve's stately figure in the passage than his expression changed.

'You—you here! and for a sitting?'

She nodded, smiling. Her look had an excitement which he perceived at once. His eye travelled to the white drapery and the beautiful bare arm emerging from the cloak; then he looked behind her for Madame Cervin.

No one—except this Maenad in a waterproof. Montjoie threw away his cigarette.

'*Entrez, entrez, mademoiselle!*' he said, bowing low to her. 'When the heavens are blackest, then they open. I was in a mind to wring the Maenad's neck three minutes ago. Come and save your portrait!'

He led her in through the ante-room into the large outer studio. There stood the Maenad on her revolving stand, and there was the raised platform for the model. A heap of clay was to one side, and water was dripping from the statue on to the floor. The studio light had a clear evenness; and, after the heat outside, the coolness of the great bare room was refreshing.

They stood and looked at the statue together, Louie still in her cloak. Montjoie pointed out to her that he was at work on the shoulders and the left arm, and was driven mad by the difficulties of the pose. '*Tonnerre de Dieu!* when I heard you knock, I felt like a murderer; I rushed out to let fly at someone. And there was my Maenad on the mat!—all by herself, too, without that little piece of ugliness from upstairs behind her. I little thought this day—this cursed day—was to turn out so. I thought you were tired of the poor sculptor—that you had deserted him for good and all. Ah! *déesse— je vous salue!*'

He drew back from her, scanning her from head to foot, a new tone in his voice, a new boldness in his deep-set eyes—eyes which were already old. Louie stood instinctively shrinking, yet smiling, understanding something of what he said, guessing more.

There was a bull-necked strength about the man, with his dark, square, weather-beaten head, and black eyebrows, which made her afraid, in spite of the smooth and deprecating manner in which he generally spoke to women. But her fear of him was not unpleasant to her. She liked him; she would have liked above all to quarrel with him; she felt that he was her match, He stepped forward, touched her arm, and took a tone of command.

'Quick, mademoiselle, with that cloak!'

She mounted the steps, threw off her cloak, and fell into her attitude without an instant's hesitation. Montjoie, putting his hands over his eyes to look at her, exclaimed under his breath.

It was perfectly true that, libertine as he was, he had so far felt no inclination whatever to make love to the English girl. Nor was the effect merely the result of Madame Cervin's vigilance. Personally, for all her extraordinary beauty, his new model left him cold. Originally he had been a man of the most complex artistic instincts, the most delicate and varied perceptions. They and his craftsman's skill were all foundering now in a sea of evil living. But occasionally they were active still, and they had served him for the instant detection of that common egotistical paste of which Louie Grieve was made. He would have liked to chain her to his model's platform, to make her the slave of his fevered degenerating art. But she had no thrill for him. While he was working from her his mind was often running on some little *grisette* or other, who had not half Louie Grieve's physical perfection, but who had charm, provocation, wit—all that makes the natural heritage of the French woman, of whatever class. At the same time it had been an irritation and an absurdity to him that, under Madame Cervin's eye, he had been compelled to treat her with the ceremonies due to *une jeune fille honnete*. For he had at once detected the girl's reckless temper. From what social stratum did she come—she and the brother? In her, at least, there was some wild blood! When he sounded Madame Cervin, however, she, with her incurable habit of vain mendacity, had only put her lodger in a light which Montjoie felt certain was a false one.

But this morning! Never had she been so superb, so inspiring! All the vindictive passion, all the rage with David that was surging within her, did but give the more daring and decision to her attitude, and a wilder power to her look. Moreover, the boldness of her unaccompanied visit to him provoked and challenged him. He looked at her irresolutely; then with an effort he turned to his statue and fell to work. The touch of the clay, the reaction from past despondency prevailed; before half an hour was over he was more enamoured of his task than he had ever yet been, and more fiercely bent on success. Insensibly as the time passed, his tone with her became more and more short, brusque, imperious. Once or twice he made some rough alteration in the pose, with the overbearing haste of a man who can hardly bear to leave the work under his hands even for an instant. When he first assumed this manner Louie opened her great eyes. Then it seemed to please her. She felt no regret whatever for the smooth voice; the more dictatorial he became the better she liked it, and the more submissive she was.

This went on for about a couple of hours—an orgie of work on his side, of excited persistence on hers. Her rival in the clay grew in life and daring under her eyes, rousing in her, whenever she was allowed to rest a minute and look, a new intoxication with herself. They hardly talked. He was too much absorbed in what he was doing; and she also was either bent upon her task, or choked by wild gusts of jealous and revengeful thought. Every now and then as she stood there, in her attitude of eager listening, the wall of the studio would fade before her eyes, and she would see nothing but a torturing vision of David at Fontainebleau, wrapt up in 'that creature,' and only remembering his sister to rejoice that he had shaken her off. *Ah!* How could she sufficiently avenge herself! how could she throw all his canting counsels to the winds with most emphasis and effect!

At last a curious thing happened. Was it mere nervous reaction after such a strain of will and passion, or was it the sudden emergence of something in the sister which was also common to the brother—a certain tragic susceptibility, the capacity for a wild melancholy? For, in an instant, while she was thinking vaguely of Madame Cervin and her money affairs, *despair* seized her—shuddering, measureless despair—rushing in upon her, and sweeping away everything else before it. She tottered under it, fighting down the clutch of it as long as she could. It had no words, it was like a physical agony. All that was clear to her for one lurid moment was that she would like to kill herself.

The studio swam before her, and she dropped into the chair behind her.

Montjoie gave a protesting cry.

'Twenty minutes more!—*Courage!*'

Then, as she made no answer, he went up to her and put a violent hand on her shoulder—beside himself.

'You *shall* not be tired, I tell you. Look up! look at me!'

Under the stimulus of his master's tone she slowly recovered herself— her great black eyes lifted. He gazed into them steadily; his voice sank.

'You belong to me,' he said with breathless rapidity. 'Do you understand? What is the matter with you? What are those tears?'

A cry of nature broke from her.

'My brother has left me—with that girl!'

She breathed out the words into the ears of the man stooping towards her. His great brow lifted—he gave a little laugh. Then eagerly, triumphantly, he seized her again by the arms. '*A la bonne heure*! Then it is plainer still. You belong to me and I to you. In that statue we live and die together. Another hour, and it will be a masterpiece. Come! one more!'

She drank in his tone of mad excitement as though it were wine, and it revived her. The strange grip upon her heart relaxed; the nightmare was dashed aside. Her colour came back, and, pushing him proudly away from her, she resumed her pose without a word.

CHAPTER VIII

'Do you know, sir, that that good woman has brought in the soup for the second time? I can see her fidgeting about the table through the window. If we go on like this, she will depart and leave us to wait on ourselves. Then see if you get any soup out of *me*.'

David, for all answer, put his arm close round the speaker. She threw herself back against him, smiling into his face. But neither could see the other, for it was nearly dark, and through the acacia trees above them the stars glimmered in the warm sky. To their left, across a small grass-plat, was a tiny thatched house buried under a great vine which embowered it all from top to base, and overhung by trees which drooped on to the roof, and swept the windows with their branches. Through a lower window, opening on to the gravel path, could be seen a small bare room, with a paper of coarse brown and blue pattern, brightly illuminated by a paraffin lamp, which also threw a square of light far out into the garden. The lamp stood on a table which was spread for a meal, and a stout woman, in a white cap and blue cotton apron, could be seen moving beside it.

'Come in!' said Elise, springing to her feet, and laying a compelling hand on her companion. 'Get it over! The moon is waiting for us out there!'

And she pointed to where, beyond the roofs of the neighbouring houses, rose the dark fringe of trees which marked the edge of the forest.

They went in, hand in hand, and sat opposite each other at the little rickety table, while the peasant woman from whom they had taken the house waited upon them. The day before, after looking at the *auberge*, and finding it full of artists come down to look for spring subjects in the forest, they had wandered on searching for something less public, more poetical. And they had stumbled upon this tiny overgrown house in its tangled garden. The woman to whom it belonged had let it for the season, but till the beginning of her 'let' there was a month; and, after much persuasion, she had consented to allow the strangers to hire it and her services as *bonne*, by the week, for a sum more congruous with the old and primitive days of Barbizon than with the later claims of the little place to fashion and fame. As the lovers stood together in the *salon*, exclaiming with delight at its bare floor, its low ceiling, its old bureau, its hard sofa with the Empire legs, and the dilapidated sphinxes on the arms, the owner of the house looked them up and down, from the door, with comprehending eyes. Barbizon had known adventures like this before!

But she might think what she liked; it mattered nothing to her lodgers. To 'a pair of romantics out of date,' the queer overgrown place she owned was perfection, and they took possession of it in a dream of excitement and joy. From the top loft, still bare and echoing, where the highly respectable summer tenants were to put up the cots of their children, to the outside den which served for a kitchen, whence a wooden ladder led to a recess among the rafters, occupied by Madame Pyat as a bedroom; from the masses of Virginia creeper on the thatched roof to the thicket of acacias and roses on the front grass-plat, and the high flowery wall which shut them off from the curious eyes of the street, it was all, in the lovers' feeling, the predestined setting for such an idyll as theirs.

And if this was so in the hot mornings and afternoons, how much more in the heavenly evenings and nights, when the forest lay whispering and murmuring under the moonlight, and they, wandering together arm in arm under the gaunt and twisted oaks of the Bas Breau, or among the limestone blocks which strew the heights of this strange woodland, felt themselves part of the world about them, dissolved into its quivering harmonious life, shades among its shadows!

On this particular evening, after the hurried and homely meal, David brought Elise's large black hat, and the lace scarf which had bewitched him at St. Germain—oh, the joy of handling such things in this familiar, sacrilegious way!—and they strolled out into the long uneven street beyond their garden wall, on their way to the forest. The old inn to the left was in a clatter. Two *diligences* had just arrived, and the horses were drooping and panting at the door. A maidservant was lighting guests across the belittered courtyard with a flaring candle. There was a red glimpse of the kitchen with its brass and copper pans, and on the bench outside the gateway sat a silent trio of artists, who had worked well and dined abundantly, and were now enjoying their last smoke before the sleep, to which they were already nodding, should overtake them. The two lovers stepped quickly past, making with all haste for that leafy mystery beyond cleft by the retreating whiteness of the Fontainebleau road—into which the village melted on either side.

Such moonlight! All the tones of the street, its white and greys, the reddish brown of the roofs, were to be discerned under it; and outside in the forest it was a phantasmagoria, an intoxication. The little paths they were soon threading, paths strewn with limestone dust, wound like white threads among the rocks and through the blackness of the firs. They climbed them hand in hand, and soon they were on a height looking over a great hollow of the forest to the plain beyond, as it were a vast cup overflowing with moonlight and melting into a silver sky. The width of the heavens, the dim immensity of the earth, drove them close together in a delicious silence. The girl put the warmth of her lover's arm between her and the overpowering greatness of a too august nature. The man, on the other hand, rising in this to that higher stature which was truly his, felt himself carried out into nature on the wave of his own boundless emotion. That cold Deism he had held so loosely broke into passion. The humblest phrases of worship, of entreaty, swept across the brain.

'Could one ever have guessed,' he asked her, his words stumbling and broken, 'that such happiness was possible?'

She shook her head, smiling at him.

'Yes, certainly!—if one has read poems and novels. Nothing to me is ever *more* than I expect,—generally less.'

Then she broke off hesitating, and hid her face against his breast. A pang smote him. He cried out in the old commonplaces that he was not worthy, that she must tire of him, that there was nothing in him to hold, to satisfy her.

'And three weeks ago,' she said, interrupting him, 'we had never heard each other's names. Strange—life is strange! Well, now,' and she quickly drew herself away from him, and holding him by both hands lightly swung his arms backwards and forwards, 'this can't last for ever, you know. In the first place—we shall die.' and throwing herself back, she pulled against him childishly, a spray of ivy he had wound round her hat drooping with fantastic shadows over her face and neck.

'Do you know what you are like?' he asked her, evading what she had said, while his eyes devoured her.

'No!'

'You are like that picture in the Louvre,—Da Vinci's St. John, that you say should be a Bacchus.'

'Which means that you find me a queer,—heathenish,—sort of creature?' she said, still laughing and swaying. 'So I am. Take care! Well now, a truce to love-making! I am tired of being meek and charming—this night excites me. Come and see the oaks in the Bas Breau.'

And running down the rocky path before them she led him in and out through twisted leafy ways, till at last they stood among the blasted giants of the forest, the oaks of the Bas Breau. In the emboldening daylight, David, with certain English wood scenes in his mind, would swear the famous trees of Fontainebleau had neither size nor age to speak of. But at night they laid their avenging spell upon him. They stood so finely on the broken ground, each of them with a kingly space about him; there was so wild a fantasy in their gnarled and broken limbs; and under the night their scanty crowns of leaf, from which the sap was yearly ebbing, had so lofty a remoteness.

They found a rocky seat in front of a certain leafless monster, which had been struck by lightning in a winter storm years before, and rent from top to bottom. The bare trunk with its torn branches yawning stood out against the rest, a black and melancholy shape, preaching desolation. But Elise studied it coolly.

'I know that tree by heart,' she declared. 'Corot, Rousseau, Diaz—it has served them all. I could draw it with my eyes shut.'

Then with the mention of drawing she began to twist her fingers restlessly.

'I wonder what the *concours* was to-day,' she said. 'Now that I am away that Breal girl will carry off everything. There will be no bearing her—she was never second till I came.'

David took a very scornful view of this contingency. 'When you go back you will beat them all again; let them have their few weeks' respite! You told me yesterday you had forgotten the *atelier.*'

'Did I?' she said with a strange little sigh. 'It wasn't true—I haven't.'

With a sudden whim she pulled off his broad hat and threw it down. Reaching forward she took his head between her hands, and arranged his black curls about his brow in a way to suit her. Then, still holding him, she drew back with her head on one side to look at him. The moon above them, now at its full zenith of brightness, threw the whole massive face into strong relief, and her own look melted into delight.

'There is no model in Paris,' she declared, 'with so fine a head.' Then with another sigh she dropped her hold, and propping her chin on her hands, she stared straight before her in silence.

'Do you imagine you are *the first?*' she asked him presently, with a queer abruptness.

There was a pause.

'You told me so,' he said, at last, his voice quivering; 'don't deceive me—there is no fun in it—I believe it all!'

She laughed, and did not answer for a moment. He put out his covetous arms and would have drawn her to him, but she withdrew herself.

'What did I tell you? I don't remember. In the first place there was a cousin—there is always a cousin!'

He stared at her, his face flushing, and asked her slowly what she meant.

'You have seen his portrait in my room,' she said coolly.

He racked his brains.

'Oh! that portrait on the wall,' he burst out at last, in vain trying for a tone as self-possessed as her own,' that man with a short beard?'

She nodded.

'Oh, he is not bad at all, my cousin. He is the son of that uncle and aunt I told you of. Only while they were rusting in the Gironde, he was at Paris learning to be a doctor, and enlarging his mind by coming to see me every week. When they came up to town to put in a claim to me, *they* thought me a lump of wickedness, as I told you; I made their hair stand on end. But Guillaume knew a good deal more about me; and *he* was not scandalised at all; oh dear, no. He used to come every Saturday and sit in a corner while I painted—a long lanky creature, rather good looking, but with spectacles— he has ruined his eyes with reading. Oh, he would have married me any day, and let his relations shriek as they please; so don't suppose, Monsieur David, that I have had no chances of respectability, or that my life began with you!' She threw him a curious look.

'Why do you talk about him?' cried David, beside himself. 'What is your cousin to either of us?'

'I shall talk of what I like,' she said wilfully, clasping her hands round her knees with the gesture of an obstinate child.

David stared away into the black shadow of the oaks, marvelling at himself? at the strength of that sudden smart within him, that half-frenzied restlessness and dread which some of her lightest sayings had the power to awaken in him.

Then he repented him, and turning, bent his head over the little hands and kissed them passionately. She did not move or speak. He came close to her, trying to decipher her face in the moonlight. For the first time since that night in the studio there was a film of sudden tears in the wide grey eyes. He caught her in his arms and demanded why.

'You quarrel with me and dictate to me,' she cried, wrestling with herself, choked by some inexplicable emotion, 'when I have given you everything? when I am alone in the world with you? at your mercy? I who have been so proud, have held my head so high!'

He bent over her, pouring into her ear all the words that passion could find or forge. Her sudden attack upon him, poor fellow, seemed to him neither unjust nor extravagant. She *had* given him everything, and who and what was he that she should have thrown him so much as a look!

Gradually her mysterious irritation died away. The gentleness of the summer night, the serenity of the moonlight, the sea-like murmur of the forest, these things sank little by little into their hearts, and in the calm they made, youth and love spoke again, siren voices, with the old magic. And when at last they loitered home, they moved in a trance of feeling which wanted no words. The moon dropped slowly into the western trees; midnight chimes came to them from the villages which ring the forest; and a playing wind sprang up about them, cooling the girl's hot cheeks, and freshening the verdurous ways through which they passed.

But in the years which came after, whenever David allowed his mind to dwell for a short shuddering instant on these days at Fontainebleau, it often occurred to him to wonder whether during their wild dream he had ever for one hour been truly happy. At the height of their passion had there been any of that exquisite give and take between them which may mark the simplest love of the rudest lovers, but which is in its essence moral, a thing not of the senses but of the soul? There is nothing else which is vital to love. Without it passion dies into space like the flaming corona of the sun. With it, the humblest hearts may 'bear it out even to the edge of doom.'

There can be no question that after the storm of feeling, excitement, pity, which had swept her into his arms, he gained upon her vagrant fancy for a time day by day. Seen close, his social simplicity, his delicately tempered youth had the effect of great refinement. He had in him much of the peasant nature, but so modified by fine perception and wide-ranging emotion, that what had been coarseness in his ancestors was in him only a certain rich savour and fulness of being. His mere sympathetic, sensitive instinct had developed in him all the essentials of good manners, and books, poetry, observation had done the rest.

So that in the little matters of daily contact he touched and charmed her unexpectedly. He threw no veil whatever over his tradesman's circumstances, and enjoyed trying to make her understand what had been the conditions and prospects of his Manchester life. He had always, indeed, conceived his bookseller's profession with a certain dignity; and he was secretly proud, with a natural conceit, of the efforts and ability which had brought him so rapidly to the front. How oddly the Manchester names and facts sounded in the forest air! She would sit with her little head on one side listening; but privately he suspected that she understood very little of it; that she accepted him and his resources very much in the vague with the *insouciance* of Bohemia.

He himself, however, was by no means without plans for the future. In the first flush of his triumphant passion he had won from her the promise of a month alone with him, in or near Fontainebleau—her own suggestion—after which she was to go back in earnest to her painting, and he was to return to Manchester and make arrangements for their future life together. Louie must be provided for, and after that his ideas about himself were already tolerably clear. In one of his free intervals, during his first days in Paris, he had had a long conversation one evening with the owner of an important bookshop on the Quai St.-Michel. The man badly wanted an English clerk with English connections. David made certain of the opening, should he choose to apply for it. And if not there, then somewhere else. With the consciousness of capital, experience, and brains, to justify him, he had no fears. Meanwhile, John should keep on the Manchester shop, and he, David, would go over two or three times a year to stock-take and make up accounts. John was as honest as the day, and had already learnt much.

But although his old self had so far reasserted itself; although the contriving activity of the brain was all still there, ready to be brought to bear on this new life when it was wanted; Elise could never mistake him, or the true character of this crisis of his youth. The self-surrender of passion had transformed, developed him to an amazing extent, and it found its natural language. As she grew deeper and deeper into the boy's heart, and as the cloud of diffidence which had enwrapped him since he came to Paris gave way, so that even in this brilliant France he ventured at last to express his feelings and ideas, the poet and thinker in him grew before her eyes. She felt a new consideration, a new intellectual respect for him.

But above all his tenderness, his womanish consideration and sweetness amazed her. She had been hotly wooed now and then, but with no one, not even 'the cousin,' had she ever been on terms of real intimacy. And for the rest she had lived a rough-and-tumble, independent life, defending herself first of all against the big boys of the farm, then against her father, or her comrades in the *atelier*, or her Bohemian suitors. The ingenuity of service David showed in shielding and waiting upon her bewildered her—had, for a time, a profound effect upon her.

And yet!—all the while—what jars and terrors from the very beginning! He seemed often to be groping in the dark with her. Whole tracts of her thought and experience were mysteries to him, and grew but little plainer with their new relation. Little as he knew or would have admitted it, the gulf of nationality yawned deep between them. And those artistic ambitions of hers—as soon as they re-emerged on the other side of the first intoxication of passion—they were as much of a jealousy and a dread to him as before. His soul was as alive as it had ever been to the threat and peril of them.

Their relation itself, too—to her, perhaps, secretly a guarantee—was to him a perpetual restlessness. *L'union libre* as the French artist understands it was not in his social tradition, whatever might be his literary assimilation of French ideas. He might passionately adopt and defend it, because it was her will; none the less was he, at the bottom of his heart, both ashamed and afraid because of it. From the very beginning he had let her know that she had only to say the word and he was ready to marry her instantly. But she put him aside with an impatient wave of her little hand, a nervous, defiant look in her grey eyes. Yet one day, when in the little village shop of Barbizon, a woman standing beside Elise at the counter looked her insolently over from head to foot, and took no notice of a question addressed to her on the subject of one of the forest routes, the girl felt and unexpected pang of resentment and shame.

One afternoon, in a lonely part of the forest, she strained her foot by treading on a loose stone among the rocks. Tired with long rambling and jarred by the shock she sank down, looking white and ready to cry. Pain generally crushed and demoralized her. She was capable, indeed, of setting the body at defiance on occasion; but, as a rule, she had no physical fortitude, and did not pretend to it.

David was much perplexed. So far as he knew, they were not near any of the huts which are dotted over the forest and provide the tourist with *consommations* and carved articles. There was no water wherewith to revive her or to bandage the foot, for Fontainebleau has no streams. All he could do was to carry her. And this he did, with the utmost skill, and with a leaping thrill of tenderness which made itself felt by the little elfish creature in the clasp of his arms, and in the happy leaning of his dark cheek to hers, as she held him round the neck.

'Paul and Virginia!' she said to him, laughing. "*He bore her in his arms!*"—all heroes do it—in reality, most women would break the hero's back. 'Confess *I* am even lighter than you thought!'

'As light as Venus' doves,' he swore to her. 'Bid me carry you to Paris and see.'

'Paris!' At the mention of it she fell silent, and the corners of her mouth drooped into gravity. But he strode happily on, perceiving nothing.

Then when they got home, she limping through the village, he put on the airs of a surgeon, ran across to the grocer, who kept a tiny *pharmacie* in one corner of his miscellaneous shop, and conferred with him to such effect that the injured limb was soon lotioned and bandaged in a manner which made David inordinately proud of himself. Once, as he was examining his handiwork, it occurred to him that it was Mr. Ancrum who had taught him to use his fingers neatly. *Mr. Ancrum!* At the thought of his name the young man felt an inward shrinking, as though from contact with a cold and alien order of things. How hard to realise, indeed, that the same world contained Manchester with its factories and chapels, and this perfumed forest, this little overgrown house!

Afterwards, as he sat beside her, reading, as quiet as a mouse, so that she might sleep if the tumble-down Empire sofa did but woo her that way, she suddenly put up her arm and drew him down to her.

'Who taught you all this—this tenderness?' she said to him, in a curious wistful tone, as though her question were the outcome of a long reverie. 'Was it your mother?'

David started. He had never spoken to her or to anyone of his mother, and he could not bring himself to do so now.

'My mother died when I was five years old,' he said reluctantly. 'Why don't you go to sleep, little restless thing? Is the bandage right?'

'Quite. I can imagine,' she said presently in a low tone, letting him go, 'I can imagine one might grow so dependent on all this cherishing, so horribly dependent!'

'Well, and why not?' he said, taking up her hand and kissing it. 'What are we made for, but to be your bondslaves?'

She drew her hand away, and let it fall beside her with an impatient sigh. The poor boy looked at her with frightened eyes. Then some quick instinct came to the rescue, and his expression changed completely.

'I have thought it all out,' he began, speaking with a brisk, business-like air, 'what I shall do at Manchester, and when I get back here.'

And he hung over her, chattering and laughing about his plans. What did she say to a garret and a studio somewhere near the Quai St.-Michel, in the Quartier Latin, rooms whence they might catch a glimpse of the Seine and Notre-Dame, where she would be within easy reach of Taranne's studio, and the Luxembourg, and the Ecole des Beaux-Arts, and the Louvre rooms where after their day's work they might meet, shut out the world and let in heaven—a home consecrate at once to art and love?

The quick bright words flowed without a check; his eye shone as though it caught the light of the future. But she lay turned away from him, silent, till at last she stopped him with a restless gesture.

'Don't—don't talk like that! As soon as one dares to reckon on Him—*le bon Dieu* strikes—just to let one know one's place. And don't drive me mad about my art! You saw me try to draw this morning; you might be quiet about it, I think, *par pitié!* If I ever had any talent—which is not likely, or I should have had some notices of my pictures by this time—it is all dead and done for.'

And turning quite away from him, she buried her face in the cushion.

'Look here,' he said to her, smiling and stooping, 'shall I tell you something? I forgot it till now.'

She shook her head, but he went on:

You remember this morning while I was waiting for you, I went into the inn to ask about the way to the Gorges d'Affremont. I had your painting things with me. I didn't know whether you wanted them or not, and I laid them down on the table in the *cour*, while I went in to speak to madame. Well, when I came out, there were a couple of artists there, those men who have been here all the time painting, and they had undone the strap and were looking at the sketch—you know, that bit of beechwood with the rain coming on. I rushed at them. But they only grinned, and one of them, the young man with the fair moustache, sent you his compliments. You must have, he said, "very remarkable dispositions indeed." Perhaps I looked as if I knew that before! Whose pupil were you? I told him, and he said I was to tell you to stick to Taranne. You were one of the *peintres de temperament*, and it was they especially who must learn their grammar, and learn it from the classics; and the other man, the old bear who never speaks to anybody, nodded and looked at the sketch again, and said it was "amusing—not bad at all," and you might make something of it for the next Salon.'

Cunning David! By this time Elise had her arm round his neck, and was devouring his face with her keen eyes. Everything was shaken off—the pain of her foot, melancholy, fatigue—and all the horizons of the soul were bright again. She had a new idea!—what if she were to combine his portrait with the beechwood sketch, and make something large and important of it? He had the head of a poet—the forest was in its most poetical moment. Why not pose him at the foot of the great beech to the left, give him a book dropping from his hand, and call it 'Reverie'?

For the rest of the day she talked or sketched incessantly. She would hardly be persuaded to give her bandaged foot the afternoon's rest, and by eight o'clock next morning they were off to the forest, she limping along with a stick.

Two or three days of perfect bliss followed. The picture promised excellently. Elise was in the most hopeful mood, alert and merry as a bird. And when they were driven home by hunger, the work still went on. For they had turned their top attic into a studio, and here as long as the light lasted she toiled on, wrestling with the head and the difficulties of the figure. But she was determined to make it substantially a picture *en plein air*. Her mind was full of all the daring conceptions and ideals which were then emerging in art, as in literature, from the decline of Romanticism. The passion for light, for truth, was, she declared, penetrating, and revolutionising the whole artistic world. Delacroix had a studio to the south; she also would 'bedare the sun.'

At the end of the third day she threw herself on him in a passion of gratitude and delight, lifting her soft mouth to be kissed.

'*Embrasse-moi! Embrasse-moi! Blague a part,—je commence a me sentir artiste!*'

And they wandered about their little garden till past midnight, hand close in hand. She could talk of nothing but her picture, and he, feeling himself doubly necessary and delightful to her, overflowed with happiness and praise.

But next day things went less well. She was torn, overcome by the difficulties of her task. Working now in the forest, now at home, the lights and values had suffered. The general tone had neither an indoor nor an outdoor truth. She must repaint certain parts, work only out of doors. Then all the torments of the outdoor painter began: wind, which put her in a nervous fever, and rain, which, after the long spell of fine weather, began to come down on them, and drive them into shelter.

Soon she was in despair. She had been too ambitious. The landscape should have been the principal thing, the figure only indicated, a suggestion in the middle distance. She had carried it too far; it fought with its surroundings; the picture had no unity, no repose. Oh, for some advice! How could one pull such a thing through without help? In three minutes Taranne would tell her what was wrong.

In twenty-four hours more she had fretted herself ill. The picture was there in the corner, turned to the wall; he could only just prevent her from driving her palette-knife through it. And she was sitting on the edge of the sofa, silent, a book on her knee, her hands hanging beside her, and her feverish eyes wandering—wandering round the room, if only they might escape from David, might avoid seeing him—or so he believed. Horrible! It was borne in upon him that in this moment of despair he was little more to her than the witness, the occasion, of her discomfiture.

Oh! his heart was sore. But he could do nothing. Caresses, encouragements, reproaches, were alike useless. For some time she would make no further attempts at drawing; nor would she be wooed and comforted. She held him passively at arm's length, and he could make nothing of her. It was the middle of their third week; still almost the half left of this month she had promised him. And already it was clear to him that he and love had lost their first hold, and that she was consumed with the unspoken wish to go back to Paris, and the *atelier*. Ah, no!—*no!* With a fierce yet dumb tenacity he held her to her bargain. Those weeks were his; they represented his only hope for the future; she *should* not have them back.

But he, too, fell into melancholy and silence, and on the afternoon when this change in him first showed itself she was, for a time, touched, ashamed. A few pale smiles returned for him, and in the evening, as he was sitting by the open window, a newspaper on his knee, staring into vacancy, she came up to him, knelt beside him, and drew his half-reluctant arm about her. Neither said anything, but gradually her presence there, on his breast, thrilled through all his veins, filled his heart to bursting. The paper slid away; he put both arms about her, and bowed his head on hers. She put up her small hand, and felt the tears on his cheek. Then a still stronger repentance woke up in her.

'*Pauvre enfant!*' she said, pushing herself away from him, and tremulously drying his eyes. 'Poor Monsieur David—I make you very unhappy! But I warned you—oh, I *warned* you! What evil star made you fall in love with me?'

In answer he found such plaintive and passionate things to say to her that she was fairly melted, and in the end there was an effusion on both sides, which seemed to bring back their golden hours. But at bottom, David's sensitive instinct, do what he would to silence it, told him, in truth, that all was changed. He was no longer the happy and triumphant lover. He was the beggar, living upon her alms.

CHAPTER IX

Next morning David went across to the village shop to buy some daily necessaries, and found a few newspapers lying on the counter. He bought a *Debats*, seeing that there was a long critique of the Salon in it, and hurried home with it to Elise. She tore it open and rushed through the article, putting him aside that he might not look over her. Her face blanched as she read, and at the end she flung the paper from her, and tottering to a chair sat there motionless, staring straight before her. David, beside himself with alarm, and finding caresses of no avail, took up the paper from the floor.

'Let it alone!' she said to him with a sudden imperious gesture. 'There is a whole paragraph about Breal—her fortune is made. *La voilà lancée—arrivée!* And of me, not a line, not a mention! Three or four pupils of Taranne—all beginners—but *my* name—nowhere! Ah, but no—it is too much!'

Her little foot beat the ground, a hurricane was rising within her.

David tried to laugh the matter off. 'The man who wrote the wretched thing had been hurried—was an idiot, clearly, and what did one man's opinion matter, even if it were paid for at so much a column?'

'*Mais, tais-toi, donc!*' she cried at last, turning upon him in a fury. '*Can't* you see that everything for an artist—especially a woman—depends on the *protections* she gets at the beginning? How can a girl—helpless—without friends—make her way by herself? Some one must hold out a hand, and for me it seems there is no one—no one!'

The outburst seemed to his common sense to imply the most grotesque oblivion of her success in the Salon, of Taranne's kindness—the most grotesque sensitiveness to a few casual lines of print. But it wrung his heart to see her agitation, her pale face, the handkerchief she was twisting to shreds in her restless hands. He came to plead with her—his passion lending him eloquence. Let her but trust herself and her gift. She had the praise of those she revered to go upon. How should the carelessness of a single critic affect her? *Imbéciles!*—they would be all with her, at her feet, some day. Let her despise them then and now! But his extravagances only made her impatient.

'Nonsense!' she said, drawing her hand away from him; 'I am not made of such superfine stuff—I never pretended to be! Do you think I should be content to be an unknown genius? *Never!*—I must have my fame counted out to me in good current coin, that all the world may hear and see. It may be vulgar—I don't care! it is so. *Ah, mon Dieu!*' and she began to pace the room with wild steps, 'and it is my fault—my fault! If I were there on the spot, I should be remembered—they would have to reckon with me—I could keep my claim in sight. But I have thrown away everything—wasted everything—*everything!*'

He stood with his back to the window, motionless, his hand on the table, stooping a little forward, looking at her with a passion of reproach and misery; it only angered her; she lost all self-control, and in one mad moment she avenged on his poor heart all the wounds and vexations of her vanity. *Why* had he ever persuaded her? *Why* had he brought her away and hung a fresh burden on her life which she could never bear? Why had he done her this irreparable injury—taken all simplicity and directness of aim from her—weakened her energies at their source? Her only *milieu* was art, and he had made her desert it; her only power was the painter's power, and it was crippled, the fresh spring of it was gone. It was because she felt on her the weight of a responsibility, and a claim she was not made for. She was not made for love—for love at least as he understood it. And he had her word, and would hold her to it. It was madness for both of them. It was stifling—killing her!

Then she sank on a chair, in a passion of desperate tears. Suddenly, as she sat there, she heard a movement, and looking up she saw David at the door. He turned upon her for an instant, with a dignity so tragic, so true, and yet so young, that she was perforce touched, arrested. She held out a trembling hand, made a little cry. But he closed the door softly, and was gone. She half raised herself, then fell back again.

'If he had beaten me,' she said to herself with a strange smile, 'I could have loved him. *Mais!*'

She was all day alone. When he came back it was already evening; the stars shone in the June sky, but the sunset light was still in the street and on the upper windows of the little house. As he opened the garden gate and shut it behind him, he saw the gleam of a lamp behind the acacia, and a light figure beside it. He stood a moment wrestling with himself, for he was wearied out, and felt as if he could bear no more. Then he moved slowly on.

Elise was sitting beside the lamp, her head bent over something dark upon her lap. She had not heard the gate open, and she did not hear his steps upon the grass. He came closer, and saw, to his amazement, that she was busy with a coat of his—an old coat, in the sleeve of which he had torn a great rent the day before, while he was dragging her and himself through some underwood in the forest. She—who loathed all womanly arts, who had often boasted to him that she hardly knew how to use a needle!

In moving nearer, he brushed against the shrubs, and she heard him. She turned her head, smiling. In the mingled light she looked like a little white ghost, she was so pale and her eyes so heavy. When she saw him, she raised her finger with a childish, aggrieved air, and put it to her lips, rubbing it softly against them.

'It does prick so!' she said plaintively.

He came to sit beside her, his chest heaving.

'Why do you do that—for me?'

She shrugged her shoulders and worked on without speaking. Presently she laid down her needle and surveyed him.

'Where have you been all day? Have you eaten nothing, poor friend?'

He tried to remember.

'I think not; I have been in the forest.'

A little quiver ran over her face; she pulled at her needle violently and broke the thread.

'Finished!' she said, throwing down the coat and springing up. 'Don't tell your tailor who did it! I am for perfection in all things—*abas l'amateur!* Come in, it is supper-time past. I will go and hurry Madame Pyat. *Tu dois avoir une faim de loup.'*

He shook his head, smiling sadly.

'I tell you, you are hungry, you shall be hungry!' she cried, suddenly flinging her arm round his neck, and nestling her fair head against his shoulder. Her voice was half a sob.

'Oh, so I am!—so I am!' he said, with a wild emphasis, and would have caught her to him. But she slipped away and ran before him to the house, turning at the window with the sweetest, frankest gesture to bid him follow.

They passed the evening close together, she on a stool leaning against his knee, he reading aloud Alfred de Musset's *Nuit de Mai*. At one moment she was all absorbed in the verse, carried away by it; great battle-cry that it is! calling the artist from the miseries of his own petty fate to the lordship of life and nature as a whole; the next she had snatched the book out of his hands and was correcting his accent, bidding him speak after her, put his lips so. Never had she been so charming. It was the coaxing charm of the softened child that cannot show its penitence enough. Every now and then she fell to pouting because she could not move him to gaiety. But in reality his sad and passive gentleness, the mask of feelings which would otherwise have been altogether beyond his control, served him with her better than any gaiety could have done.

Gaiety! it seemed to him his heart was broken.

At night, after a troubled sleep, he suddenly woke, and sprang up in an agony. *Gone!* was she gone already? For that was what her sweet ways meant. Ah, he had known it all along!

Where was she? His wild eyes for a second or two saw nothing but the landscape of his desolate dream. Then gradually the familiar forms of the room emerged from the gloom, and there—against the further wall—she lay, so still, so white, so gracious! Her childish arm, bare to the elbow, was thrown round her head, her soft waves of hair made a confusion on the pillow. After her long day of emotion she was sleeping profoundly. Whatever cruel secret her heart might hold, she was there still, his yet, for a few hours and days. He was persuaded in his own mind that her penitence had been the mere fruit of a compromise with herself, their month had still eight days to run, then—*adieu!* Art and liberty should reclaim their own. Meanwhile why torment the poor boy, who must any way take it hardly?

He lay there for long, raised upon his arm, his haggard look fixed on the sleeping form which by-and-by the dawn illuminated. His life was concentrated in that form, that light breath. He thought with repulsion and loathing of all that had befallen him before he saw her—with anguish and terror of those days and nights to come when he should have lost her. For in the deep stillness of the rising day there fell on him the strangest certainty of this loss. That gift of tragic prescience which was in his blood had stirred in him—he knew his fate. Perhaps the gift itself was but the fruit of a rare power of self-vision, self-appraisement. He saw and cursed his own timid and ignorant youth. How could he ever have hoped to hold a creature of such complex needs and passions? In the pale dawn he sounded the very depths of self-contempt.

But when the day was up and Elise was chattering and flitting about the house as usual without a word of discord or parting, how was it possible to avoid reaction, the re-birth of hope? She talked of painting again, and that alone, after these long days of sullen alienation from her art, was enough to bring the brightness back to their little *menage* and to dull that strange second sight of David's. He helped her to set her palette, to choose a new canvas; he packed her charcoals, he beguiled some cold meat and bread out of Madame, and then before the heat they set out together for the Bas Breau.

Just as they started he searched his pockets for a knife of hers which was missing, and thrusting his hand into a breast pocket which he seldom used, he brought out some papers at which he stared in bewilderment.

Then a shock went through him; for there was Mr. Gurney's letter, the letter in which the cheque for 600 *pounds* had been enclosed, and there was also that faded scrap of Sandy's writing which contained the father's last injunction to his son. As he held the papers he remembered—what he had forgotten for weeks—that on the morning of his leaving Manchester he had put them carefully into this breast pocket, not liking to leave things so interesting to him behind him, out of his reach. Never had he given a thought to them since! He looked down at them, half ashamed, and his eye caught the words:—'*I lay it on him now I'm dying to look after her. She's not like other children; she'll want it. Let him see her married to a decent man, and give her what's honestly hers. I trust it to him. That little lad—*' and then came the fold of the sheet.

'I have found the knife,' cried Elise from the gate. 'Be quick!'

He pushed the papers back and joined her. The day was already hot, and they hurried along the burning street into the shade of the forest. Once in the Bas Breau Elise was not long in finding a subject, fell upon a promising one indeed almost at once, and was soon at work. This time there were to be no figures, unless indeed it might be a dim pair of woodcutters in the middle distance, and the whole picture was to be an impressionist dream of early summer, finished entirely out of doors, as rapidly and cleanly as possible. David lay on the ground under the blasted oak and watched her, as she sat on her camp-stool, bending forward, looking now up, now down, using her charcoal in bold energetic strokes, her lip compressed, her brow knit over some point of composition. The little figure in its pink cotton was so daintily pretty, so full of interest and wilful charm, it might well have filled a lover's eye and chained his thoughts. But David was restless and at times absent.

'Tell me what you know of that man Montjoie?' he asked her at last, abruptly. 'I know you disliked him.'

She paused, astonished.

'Why do you ask? Dislike—I *detest and despise* him. I told you so.'

'But what do you know of him?' he persisted.

'No good!' she said quickly, going back to her work. Then a light broke upon her, and she turned on her stool, her two hands on her knees.

'*Tiens!*—you are thinking of your sister. You have had news of her?'

A conscious half-remorseful look rose into her face.

'No, I have had no news. I ought to have had a letter. I wrote, you remember, that first day here. Perhaps Louie has gone home already,' he said, with constraint. 'Tell me anyway what you know.'

'Oh, he!—well, there is only one word for him—he is a *brute* I' said Elise, drawing vigorously, her colour rising. 'Any woman will tell you that. Oh, he has plenty of talent,—he might be anything. Carpeaux took him up at one time, got him commissions. Five or six years ago there was quite a noise about him for two or three Salons. Then people began to drop him. I believe he was the most mean, ungrateful animal towards those who had been kind to him. He drinks besides—he is over head and ears in debt, always wanting money, borrowing here and there, then locking his door for weeks, making believe to be out of town—only going out at night. As for his ways with women'—she shrugged her shoulders—'Was your sister still sitting to him when we left, or was it at an end? Hasn't your sister been sitting to him for his statue?'

She paused again and studied him with her shrewd, bright eyes.

He coloured angrily.

'I believe so—I tried to stop it—it was no use.'

She laughed out.

'No—I imagine she does what she wants to do. Well, we all do, *mon ami!* After all'—and she shrugged her shoulders again— 'I suppose she can do what I did?'

''What *you* did!'

She went on drawing in sharp deliberate strokes; her breath came fast.

'He met me on the stairs one night—it was just after I had taken the *atelier*. I knew no one in the house—I was quite defenceless there. He insulted me—I had a little walking-stick in my hand, my cousin had given me—I struck him with it across the face twice, three times—if you look close you will see the mark. You may imagine he tells fine stories of me when he gets the chance. *Oh! je m'en fiche!*'

The scorn of the last gesture was unmeasured.

'*Canaille!*' said David, between his teeth. 'If you had told me this!'

Her expression changed and softened.

'You asked me no questions after that quarrel we had in the Louvre,' she said, excusing herself. 'You will understand it is not a reminiscence one is exactly proud of; I did speak to Madame Cervin once—'

David said nothing, but sat staring before him into the far vistas of the wood. It seemed strange that so great a smart and fear as had possessed him since yesterday, should allow of any lesser smart within or near it. Yet that scrap of tremulous writing weighed heavy. *Where* was Louie; why had she not written? So far he had turned impatiently away from the thought of her, reiterating that he had done his best, that she had chosen her own path. Now in this fragrant quiet of the forest the quick vision of some irretrievable wreck presented itself to him; he thought of Mr. Ancrum—of John—and a cold shudder ran through him. In it spoke the conscience of a lifetime.

Elise meanwhile laid aside her charcoal, began to dash in some paint, drew back presently to look at it from a distance, and then, glancing aside, suddenly threw down her brushes, and ran up to David.

She sat down beside him, and with a coaxing, childish gesture, drew his arm about her.

'Tu me fais pitie, mon ami!' she said, looking up into his face. 'Is it your sister? Go and find her—I will wait for you.'

He turned upon her, his black eyes all passion, his lips struggling with speech.

'My place is here,' he said. 'My life is here!'

Then, as she was silent, not knowing in her agitation what to say, he broke out:

'What was in your mind yesterday, Elise? what is there to-day? There is something—something I *will* know.'

She was frightened by his look. Never did fear and grief speak more plainly from a human face. The great deep within had broken up.

'I was sorry,' she said, trembling, 'sorry to have hurt you. I wanted to make up.'

He flung her hand away from him with an impatient gesture.

'There was more than that!' he said violently; 'will you be like all the rest—betray me without a sign?'

'David!'

She bit her lip proudly. Then the tears welled up into her grey eyes, and she looked round at him—hesitated—began and stopped again—then broke into irrevocable confession.

'David!—Monsieur David!—how can it go on? *Voyons*—I said to myself yesterday—I am torturing him and myself—I cannot make him happy—it is not in me—not in my destiny. It must end—it must,—it *must*, for both our sakes. But then first,—first—'

'Be quiet!' he said, laying an iron hand on her arm. 'I knew it all.'

And he turned away from her, covering his face.

This time she made no attempt to caress him. She clasped her hands round her knees and remained quite still, gazing—yet seeing nothing—into the green depths which five minutes before had been to her a torturing ecstasy of colour and light. The tears which had been gathering fell, the delicate lip quivered.

Struck by her silence at last, he looked up—watched her a moment— then he dragged himself up to her and knelt beside her.

'Have I made you so miserable?' he said, under his breath.

'It is—it is—the irreparableness of it all,' she answered, half sobbing. 'No undoing it ever, and how a woman glides into it, how lightly, knowing so little!—thinking herself so wise! And if she has deceived herself, if she is not made for love, if she has given herself for so little—for an illusion—for a dream that breaks and must break—how dare the *man* reproach her, after all?'

She raised her burning eyes to him. The resentment in them seemed to be more than individual, it was the resentment of the woman, of her sex.

She stabbed him to the heart by what she said—by what she left unsaid. He took her little cold hand, put it to his lips—tried to speak.

'Don't,' she said, drawing it away and hiding her face on her knees. 'Don't say anything. It is not you, it is God and Nature that I accuse.'

Strange, bitter word!—word of revolt! He lay on his face beside her for many minutes afterwards, tasting the bitterness of it, revolving those other words she had said—*'an illusion—a dream that breaks—must break.'* Then he made a last effort. He came close to her, laid his arm timidly round her shoulders, bent his cheek to hers.

'Elise, listen to me a little. You say the debt is on my side—that is true— true—a thousand times true! I only ask you, *implore* you, to let me pay it. Let it be as you please—on what terms you please—servant or lover. All I pray for is to pay that debt, with my life, my heart.'

She shook her head softly, her face still hidden.

'When I am with you,' she said, as though the words were wrung out of her, 'I must be a woman. You agitate me, you divide my mind, and my force goes. There are both capacities in me, and one destroys the other. And I want—I *want* my art!'

She threw back her head with a superb gesture. But he did not flinch.

'You shall have it,' he said passionately, 'have it abundantly. Do you think I want to keep you for ever loitering here? Do you think I don't know what ambition and will mean? that I am only fit for kissing?'

He stopped almost with a smile, thinking of that harsh struggle to know and to have, in which his youth had been so far consumed night and day. Then words rushed upon him again, and he went on with a growing power and freedom.

'I never looked at a woman till I saw you!—never had a whim, a caprice. I have eaten my heart out with the struggle first for bread, then for knowledge. But when you came across me, then the world was all made new, and I became a new creature, your creature.'

He touched her face with a quick, tender hand, laid it against his breast, and spoke so, bending piteously down to her, within reach of her quivering mouth, her moist eyes:—

'Tell me this, Elise—answer me this! How can there be great art, great knowledge, only from the brain,—without passion, without experience? You and I have been *living* what Musset, what Hugo, what Shakespeare wrote,' and he struck the little volume of Musset beside him. 'Is not that worth a summer month? not worth the artist's while? But it is nearly gone. You can't wonder that I count the moments of it like a miser! I have had a *hard* life, and this has transfigured it. Whatever happens now in time or eternity, this month is to the good—for me and for you, Elise! —yes, for you, too! But when it is over,—see if I hold you back! We will work together— climb—wrestle, together. And on what terms you please,—mind that,— only dictate them. I deny your "illusion," your "dream that breaks." You *have* been happy! I dare to tell you so. But part now,—shirk our common destiny,—and you will indeed have given all for nothing, while I—'

His voice sank. She shook her head again, but as she drew herself gently away she was stabbed by the haggardness of the countenance, the pleading pathos of the eyes. His gust of speech had shaken her too—revealed new points in him. She bent forward quickly and laid her soft lips to his, for one light swift moment.

'Poor boy!' she murmured, 'poor poet!'

'Ah, that was enough!' he said, the colour flooding his cheeks.' That healed—that made all good. Will you hide nothing from me, Elise—will you promise?'

'Anything,' she said with a curious accent, 'anything—if you will but let me paint.'

He sprang up, and put her things in order for her. They stood looking at the sketch, neither seeing much of it.

'I must have some more cobalt,' she said wearily, 'Look, my tube is nearly done.'

Yes, that was certain. He must get some more for her. Where could it be got? No nearer than Fontainebleau, alas! where there was a shop which provided all the artists of the neighbourhood. He was eagerly ready to go—it would take him no time.

'It will take you between two and three hours, sir, in this heat. But oh, I am so tired, I will just creep into the fern there while you are away, and go to sleep. Give me that book and that shawl.'

He made a place for her between the spurs of a great oak-root, tearing the brambles away. She nestled into it, with a sigh of satisfaction. 'Divine! Take your food—I want nothing but the air and sleep. *Adieu, adieu!*'

He stood gazing down upon her, his face all tender lingering and remorse. How white she was, how fragile, how shaken by this storm of feeling he had forced upon her! How could he leave her?

But she waved him away impatiently, and he went at last, going first back to the village to fetch his purse which was not in his pocket.

As he came out of their little garden gate, turning again towards the forest which he must cross in order to get to Fontainebleau, he became aware of a group of men standing in front of the inn. Two of them were the landscape artists already slightly known to him, who saluted him as he came near. The other was a tall fine-looking man, with longish grizzled hair, a dark commanding eye, the rosette of the Legion of Honour at his buttonhole, and a general look of irritable power. He wore a wide straw hat and holland overcoat, and beside him on the bench lay some artist's paraphernalia.

All three eyed David as he passed, and he was no sooner a few yards away than they were looking after him and talking, the new-comer asking questions, the others replying.

'Oh, it is she!' said the stranger impatiently, throwing away his cigar. 'Auguste's description leaves me no doubt of it, and the woman at the house in the Rue Chantal where I had the caprice to inquire one day, when she had been three weeks away, told me they were here. It is annoying. Something might have been made of her. Now it is finished. A handsome lad all the same!—of a rare type. *Non!—je me suis trompé—en devenant femme, elle n'a pas cesse d'être artiste!*'

The others laughed. Then they all took up their various equipments, and strolled off smoking to the forest. The man from Paris was engaged upon a large historical canvas representing an incident in the life of Diane de Poitiers. The incident had Diane's forest for a setting, but his trees did not satisfy him, he had come down to make a few fresh studies on the spot.

David walked his four miles to Fontainebleau, bought his cobalt, and set his face homewards about three o'clock. When he was halfway home, he turned aside into a tangle of young beech wood, parted the branches, and found a shady corner where he could rest and think. The sun was very hot, the high road was scorched by it. But it was not heat or fatigue that had made him pause.

So far he had walked in a tumult of conflicting ideas, emotions, terrors, torn now by this memory, now by that—his mind traversed by one project after another. But now that he was so near to meeting her again, though he pined for her, he suddenly and pitifully felt the need for some greater firmness of mind and will. Let him pause and think! Where *was* he with her?—what were his real, tangible hopes and fears? Life and death depended for him on these days—these few vanishing days. And he was like one of the last year's leaves before him, whirled helpless and will-less in the dust-storm of the road!

He had sat there an unnoticed time when the sound of some heavy carriage approaching roused him. From his green covert he could see all that passed, and instinctively he looked up. It was the Barbizon *diligence* going in to meet the five o'clock train at Fontainebleau, a train which in these lengthening days very often brought guests to the inn. The *correspondance* had been only begun during the last week, and to the dwellers at Barbizon the afternoon *diligence* had still the interest of novelty. With the perception of habit David noticed that there was no one outside; but though the rough blinds were most of them drawn down he thought he perceived some one inside—a lady. Strange that anyone should prefer the stifling *interieur* who could mount beside the driver with a parasol!

The omnibus clattered past, and with the renewal of the woodland silence his mind plunged heavily once more into the agonised balancing of hope and fear. But in the end he sprang up with a renewed alertness of eye and step.

Despair? Impossible!—so long as one had one's love still in one's arms—could still plead one's cause, hand to hand, lip to lip. He strode homewards—running sometimes—the phrases of a new and richer eloquence crowding to his lips.

About a mile from Barbizon, the path to the Bas Breau diverges to the right. He sped along it, leaping the brambles in his path. Soon he was on the edge of the great avenue itself, looking across it for that spot of colour among the green made by her light dress.

But there was no dress, and as he came up to the tree where he had left her, he saw to his stupefaction that there was no one there—nothing, no sign of her but the bracken and brambles he had beaten down for her some three hours before, and the trodden grass where her easel had been. Something showed on the ground. He stooped and noticed the empty cobalt-tube of the morning.

Of course she had grown tired of waiting and had gone home. But a great terror seized him. He turned and ran along the path they had traversed in the morning making for the road; past the inn which seemed to have been struck to sleep by the sun, past Millet's studio on the left, to the little overgrown door in the brick wall.

No one in the garden, no one in the little *salon*, no one upstairs; Madame Pyat was away for the day, nursing a daughter-in-law. In all the house and garden there was not a sound or sign of life but the cat asleep on the stone step of the kitchen, and the bees humming in the acacias.

'Elise!' he called, inside and out, knowing already, poor fellow, in his wild despair that there could be no answer—that all was over.

But there was an answer. Elise was no untaught heroine. She played her part through. There was her letter, propped up against the gilt clock on the sham marble *cheminee*.

He found it and tore it open.

'You will curse me, but after a time you will forgive. I *could* not go on. Taranne found me in the forest, just half an hour after you left me. I looked up and saw him coming across the grass. He did not see me at first, he was looking about for a subject. I would have escaped, but there was no way. Then at last he saw me. He did not attack me, he did not persuade me, he only took for granted it was all over,—my Art! I must know best, of course; but he was sorry, for I had a gift. Had I seen the notice of my portrait in the "Temps," or the little mention in the "Figaro"? Oh, yes, Breal had been very successful, and deserved to be. It was a brave soul, devoted to art, and art had rewarded her.

'Then I showed him my sketch, trembling—to stop his talk—every word he said stabbed me. And he shrugged his shoulders quickly; then, as though recollecting himself, he put on a civil face all in a moment, and paid me compliments. To an amateur he is always civil. I was all white and shaking by this time. He turned to go away, and then I broke down. I burst into tears—I said I was coming back to the *atelier*—what did he mean by taking such a cruel, such an insolent tone with me? He would not be moved from his polite manner. He said he was glad to hear it; mademoiselle would be welcome; but just as though we were complete strangers. *He* who has befriended me, and taught me, and scolded me since I was fourteen! I could not bear it. I caught him by the arm. I told him he *should* tell me all he thought. Had I really talent?—a future?

'Then he broke out in a torrent—he made me afraid of him—yet I adored him! He said I had more talent than any other pupil he had ever had; that I had been his hope and interest for six years; that he had taught me for nothing—befriended me—worked for me, behind the scenes, at the Salon; and all because he knew that I must rise, must win myself a name, that when I had got the necessary technique I should make one of the poetical impressionist painters, who are in the movement, who sway the public taste. But I must give *all* myself—my days and nights—my thoughts, and brain, and nerves. Other people might have adventures and paint the better. Not I,—I was too highly strung—for me it was ruin. "*C'est un maitre sevire—l'Art,*" he said, looking like a god. "*Avec celui-là on ne transige pas. Ah! Dieu, je le connais, moi!*" I don't know what he meant; but there has been a tragedy in his life; all the world knows that.

'Then suddenly he took another tone, called me *pauvre enfant*, and apologised. Why should I be disturbed? I had chosen for my own happiness, no doubt. What was fame or the high steeps of art compared even with an *amour de jeunesse*? He had seen you, he said,—*une tête superbe—des epaules de lion!* I was a woman; a young handsome lover was worth more to me, naturally, than the drudgeries of art. A few years hence, when the pulse was calmer, it might have been all very well. Well! I must forgive him; he was my old friend. Then he wrung my hand, and left me.

'Oh, David, David, I must go! I *must*. My life is imprisoned here with you—it beats its bars. Why did I ever let you persuade me—move me? And I should let you do it again. When you are there I am weak. I am no cruel adventuress, I can't look at you and torture you. But what I feel for you is not love—no, no, it is not, poor boy! Who was it said "A love which can be tamed is no love"? But in three days—a week—mine had grown tame—it had no fears left. I am older than you, not in years, *mais dans l'âme*—there is what parts us.

'Oh! I must go—and you must not try to find me. I shall be quite safe, but with people you know nothing about. I shall write to Madame Pyat for my things. You need have no trouble.

'Very likely I shall pass you on the way, for if I hurry I can catch the *diligence*. But you will not see me. Oh, David, I put my arms round you! I press my face against you. I ask you to forgive me, to forget me, to work out your own life as I work out mine. It will soon be a dream—this little house—these summer days! I have kissed the chair you sat in last night, the book you read to me. *C'est déjà fini! Adieu! adieu!'*

He sat for long in a sort of stupor. Then that maddening thought seized him, stung him into life, that she had actually passed him, that he had seen her, not knowing. That little indistinct figure in the *interieur*, that was she.

He sprang up, in a blind anguish. Pursuit! the *diligence* was slow, the trains doubtful, he might overtake her yet. He dashed into the street, and into the Fontainebleau road. After he had run nearly a mile, he plunged into a path which he believed was a short cut. It led through a young and dense oak wood. He rushed on, seeing nothing, bruising himself and stumbling. At last a projecting branch struck him violently on the temple. He staggered, put up a feeble hand, sank on the grass against a trunk, and fainted.

CHAPTER X

It was between five and six o'clock in the morning. In the Tuileries Gardens flowers, grass, and trees were drenched in dew, the great shadow of the Palace spread grey and cool over terraces and slopes, while beyond the young sun had already shaken off all cumbering mists, and was pouring from a cloudless sky over the river with its barges and swimming-baths, over the bridges and the quays, and the vast courts and facades of the Louvre. Yet among the trees the air was still exquisitely fresh, the sun still a friend to be welcomed. The light morning wind swept the open, deserted spaces of the Gardens, playing merrily with the dust, the leaves, the fountains. Meanwhile on all sides the stir of the city was beginning, mounting slowly and steadily like a swelling tone.

On a bench under one of the trees in the Champs-Elysées sat a young man asleep. He had thrown himself against the back of the bench, his cheek resting on the iron, one hand on his knee. It was David Grieve; the lad's look showed that his misery was still with him, even in sleep.

He was dreaming, letting fall here and there a troubled and disconnected word. In his dream he was far from Paris—walking after his sheep among the heathery slopes of the Scout, climbing towards the grey smithy among the old mill-stones, watching the Red Brook slide by over its long, shallow steps of orange grit, and the Downfall oozing and trickling among its tumbled blocks. Who was that hanging so high above the ravine on that treacherous stone that rocked with the least touch? Louie—mad girl!—come back. Ah! too late—the stone rocks, falls; he leaps from block to block, only to see the light dress disappear into the stony gulf below. He cries—struggles—wakes.

He sat up, wrestling with himself, trying to clear his torpid brain. Where was he? His dream-self was still roaming the Scout; his outer eye was bewildered by these alleys, these orange-trees, these statues—that distant arch.

Then the hideous, undefined cloud that was on him took shape. Elise had left him. And Louie, too, was gone—he knew not where, save that it was to ruin. When he had arrived the night before at the house in the Rue Chantal, Madame Merichat could tell him nothing of Mademoiselle Delaunay, who had not been heard of. Then he asked, his voice dying in his throat before the woman's hard and cynical stare—the stare of one who found the chief savour of life in the misfortunes of her kind—he asked for his sister and the Cervins. The Cervins were staying at Sevres with relations, and were expected home again in a day or two; Mademoiselle Louie?—well, Mademoiselle Louie was not with them. Had she gone back to England? *Mais non!* A trunk of hers was still in the Cervins' vestibule. Did Madame Merichat know anything about her? the lad asked, forcing himself to it, his blanched face turned away. Then the woman shrugged her shoulders and spoke out.

If he really must know, she thought there was no doubt at all that where Monsieur Montjoie was, Mademoiselle Louie was too. Monsieur Montjoie had paid the arrears of his rent to the *proprietaire*, somehow or other, and had then made a midnight flitting of it so as to escape other creditors who were tired of waiting for his statue to be finished. He had got a furniture van there at night, and he and the driver and her husband between them had packed most of the things from the studio, and M. Montjoie had gone off in the van about one o'clock in the morning. But of course she did not know his address! she said so half-a-dozen times a day to the persons who called, and it was as true as gospel. Why, indeed, should M. Montjoie let her or anyone else know, that he could help? He had gone into hiding to keep honest people out of their money—that was what it meant.

Well, and the same evening Mademoiselle Louie also disappeared. Madame Cervin had been in a great way, but she and mademoiselle had already quarrelled violently, and madame declared that she had no fault in the matter and that no one could be held responsible for the doings of such a minx. She believed that madame had written to monsieur. Monsieur had never received it? Ah, well, that was not surprising! No one could ever read madame's writing, though it made her temper very bad to tell her so.

Could he have Madame Cervin's address? Certainly. She wrote it out for him. As to his old room?—no, he could not go back to it.

Monsieur Dubois had lately come back, with some money apparently, for he had paid his *loyer* just as the landlord was going to turn him out. But he was not at home.

Then she looked her questioner up and down, with a cool, inhuman curiosity working in her small eyes. So M'selle Elise had thrown him over already? That was sharp work! As for the rest of her news, her pessimism was interested in observing his demeanour under it. Certainly he did not seem to take it gaily; but what else did he expect with his sister?—'*Je vous demande!*'

The young man dropped his head and went out, shrinking together into the darkness. She called her husband to the door, and the two peered after him into the lamp-lit street, dissecting him, his mistress, and his sister with knifelike tongues.

David went away and walked up and down the streets, the quays, the bridges, hour after hour, feeling no fatigue, till suddenly, just as the dawn was coming on, he sank heavily on to the seat in the Champs-Elysées. The slip with Madame Cervin's address on it dropped unheeded from his relaxing hand. His nervous strength was gone, and he had to sit and bear his anguish without the relief of frenzied motion.

Now, after his hour's sleep, he was somewhat revived, ready to start again—to search again; but where? whither? *Somewhere* in this vast, sun-wrapped Paris was Elise, waking, perhaps, at this moment and thinking of him with a smile and a tear. He *would* find her, come what would; he could not live without her!

Then into his wild passion of loss and desire there slipped again that cold, creeping thought of Louie—ruined, body and soul—ruined in this base and dangerous Paris, while he still carried in his breast that little scrap of scrawled paper! And why? Because he had flung her to the wolves without a thought, that he and Elise might travel to their goal unchecked. '*My God!*'

The sense of some one near him made him look up. He saw a girl stopping near the seat whom in his frenzy he for an instant took for Louie. There was the same bold, defiant carriage, the same black hair and eyes. He half rose, with a cry.

The girl gave a quick, coarse laugh. She had been hurrying across the Avenue towards the nearest bridge when she saw him; now she came up to him with a hideous jest. David saw her face full, caught the ghastly suggestions of it—its vice, its look of mortal illness wrecking and blurring the cheap prettiness it had once possessed, and beneath all else the fierceness of the hunted creature. His whole being rose in repulsion; he waved her away, and she went, still laughing. But his guilty mind went with her, making of her infamy the prophecy and foretaste of another's.

He hurried on again, and again had to rest for faintness' sake, while the furies returned upon him. It seemed as though every passer-by were there only to scourge and torture him; or, rather, out of the moving spectacle of human life which began to flow past him with constantly increasing fulness, that strange selective poet-sense of his chose out the figures and incidents which bore upon his own story and worked into his own drama, passing by the rest. A group of persons presently attracted him who had just come apparently from the Rive Gauche, and were making for the Rue

Royale. They consisted of a man, a woman, and a child. The child was a tiny creature in a preposterous feathered hat as large as itself. It had just been put down to walk by its father, and was dragging contentedly at its mother's hand, sucking a crust. The man had a bag of tools on his shoulder and was clearly an artisan going to work. His wife's face was turned to him and they were talking fast, lingering a little in the sunshine like people who had a few minutes to spare and were enjoying them. The man had the blanched, unwholesome look of the city workman who lives a sedentary life in foul air, and was, moreover, undersized and noways attractive, save perhaps for the keen amused eyes with which he was listening to his wife's chatter. The great bell of Notre-Dame chimed in the distance. The man straightened himself at once, adjusted his bag of tools, and hurried off, nodding to his wife.

She looked after him a minute, then turned and came slowly along the alley towards the bench where David sat, idly watching her. The heat was growing steadily, the child was heavy on her hand, and she was again clearly on the way to motherhood. The seat invited her, and she came up to it.

She sat down, panting, and eyed her neighbour askance, detecting at once how handsome he was, and how unshorn and haggard. Before he knew where he was, or how it had begun, they were talking. She had no shyness of any sort, and, as it seemed to him, a motherly, half-contemptuous indulgence for his sex, as such, which fitted oddly with her young looks. Very soon she was asking him the most direct questions, which he had to parry as best he could. She made out at once that he was a foreigner and in the book trade, and then she let him know by a passing expression or two that naturally she understood why he was lounging there in that plight at that hour in the morning. He had been keeping gay company, of course, and had but just emerged from some nocturnal orgie or other. And then she shrugged her strong shoulders with a light, pitiful air, as though marvelling once more for the thousandth time over the stupidity of men who would commit these idiocies, would waste their money and health in them, say what women would.

Presently he discovered that she was giving him advice of different kinds, counselling him above all to find a good wife who would work and save his wages for him. A decent marriage was in truth an economy, though young men would never believe it.

David could only stare at her in return for her counsels. The difference between his place at that moment in the human comedy and hers was too great to be explained; it called only for silence or a stammering commonplace or two. Yet for a few moments the neighbourhood of her and her child was pleasant to him. She had a good comely head, which was bare under the sun, a little shawl crossed upon her ample bust, and a market-basket on her arm. The child was playing in the fine gravel at her feet, pausing every now and then to study her mother's eye with a furtive gravity, while the hat fell back and made a still more fantastic combination than before with the pensive little face.

Presently, tired of her play, she came to stand by her mother's knee, laying her head against it.

'*Mon petit ange! que tu es gentille!*' said the mother in a low, rapid voice, pressing her hand on the child's cheek. Then, turning back to David, she chattered on about the profit and loss of married life. All that she said was steeped in prose—in the prose especially of sous and francs; she talked of rents, of the price of food, of the state of wages in her husband's trade. Yet every here and there came an exquisite word, a flash. It seemed that she had been very ill with her first child. She did not mince matters much even with this young man, and David gathered that she had not only been near dying, but that her illness had made a moral epoch in her life. She was laid by for three months; work was slack for her husband; her own earnings, for she was a skilled embroideress working for a great linen-shop in the Rue Vivienne, were no longer forthcoming. Would her husband put up with it, with the worries of the baby, and the *menage*, and the sick wife, and that sharp pinch of want into the bargain, from which during two years she had completely protected him?

'I cried one day,' she said simply; 'I said to him, "You're just sick of it, ain't you? Well, I'm going to die. Go and shift for yourself, and take the baby to the *Enfants Trouves. Alors—*"'

She paused, her homely face gently lit up from within. 'He is not a man of words—Jules. He told me to be quiet, called me *petite sotte*. "Haven't you slaved for two years?" he said. "Well, then, lie still, can't you?—*faut bien que chacun prenne son tour!*"'

She broke off, smiling and shaking her head. Then glancing round upon her companion again, she resumed her motherly sermon. That was the good of being married; that there was some one to share the bad times with, as well as the good.

'But perhaps,' she inquired briskly, 'you don't believe in being married? You are for *l'union libre?*'

She spoke like one touching on a long familiar question—as much a question indeed of daily life and of her class as those other matters of wages and food she had been discussing.

A slow and painful red mounted into the Englishman's cheek.

'I don't know,' he said stupidly. 'And you?'

'No, no!' she said emphatically, twice, nodding her head. 'Oh, I was brought up that way. My father was a Red—an Anarchist—a great man among them; he died last year. He said that liberty was everything. It made him mad when any of his friends accepted *l'union légale*—for him it was a treason. He never married my mother, though he was faithful to her all his life. But for me—' she paused, shaking her head slowly. 'Well, I had an elder sister—that says everything. *Faut pas en parler;* it makes melancholy, and one must keep up one's spirits when one is like this. It is three years since she died; she was my father's favourite. When they buried her—she died in the hospital—I sat down and thought a little. It was abominable what she had suffered, and I said to myself, "Why?"'

The child swayed backward against her knee, so absorbed was it in its thumb and the sky, and would have fallen but that she caught it with her housewife's hand, being throughout mindful of its slightest movement.

'"Why?" I said. She was a good creature—a bit foolish perhaps, but she would have worked the shoes off her feet to please anybody. And they had treated her—but like a dog! It bursts one's heart to think of it, and I said to myself,—*le mariage c'est la justice!* it is nothing but that. It is not what the priests say—oh! not at all. But it strikes me like that—*c'est la justice*; it is nothing but that!'

And she looked at him with the bright fixed eyes of one whose thoughts are beyond their own expressing. He interrupted her, wondering at the harsh rapidity of his own voice. 'But if it is the woman who will be free?—who will have no bond?'

Her expression changed, became shrewd, inquisitive, personal.

'Well, then!' she said with a shrug, and paused. 'It is because one is ignorant, you see, or one is bad—*on peut toujours être une coquine!* And one forgets—one thinks one can be always young, and love is all pleasure—and it is not true! one get old—and there is the child—and one may die of it.'

She spoke with the utmost simplicity, yet with a certain intensity. Evidently she had a natural pride in her philosophy of life, as though in a possession of one's own earning and elaborating. She had probably expressed it often before in much the same terms, and with the same verbal hitches and gaps.

The young fellow beside her rose hastily, and bade her good morning. She looked mildly surprised at such an abrupt departure, but she was not offended.

'Good day, citizen,' she said, nodding to him. 'I disturb you?'

He muttered something and strode away.

How much time had that wasted of his irrevocable day that was to set him on Elise's track once more! The first post had been delivered by this time. Elise must either return to her studio or remove her possessions; anyhow, sooner or later the Merichats must have information. And if they were forbidden to speak, well, then they must be bribed.

That made him think of money, and in a sudden panic he turned aside into a small street and examined his pockets. Nearly four napoleons left, after allowing for his debt to Madame Pyat, which must be payed that day. Even in his sick, stunned state of the evening before, when he was at last staggering on again, after his fall, to the Fontainebleau station, he had remembered to stop a Barbizon man whom he came across and give him a pencilled message for the deserted madame. He had sent her the Tue Chantal address, there would be a letter from her this morning. And he must put her on the watch, too—Elise could not escape him long.

But he must have more money. He looked out for a stationer's shop, went in and wrote a letter to John, which he posted at the next post-office.

It was an incoherent scrawl, telling the lad to change the cheque he enclosed in Bank of England notes and send them to the Rue Chantal, care of Madame Merichat. He was not to expect him back just yet, and was to say to any friend who might inquire that he was still detained.

That letter, with the momentary contact it involved with his Manchester life, brought down upon him again the thought of Louie. But this time he flung it from him with a fierce impatience. His brain, indeed, was incapable of dealing with it. Remorse? rescue? there would be time enough for that by-and-by. Meanwhile—to find Elise!

And for a week he spent the energies of every thought and every moment on this mad pursuit. Of these days of nightmare he could afterwards remember but a few detached incidents here and there. He recollected patrols up and down the Rue Chantal; talks with Madame Merichat; the gleam in her eyes as he slipped his profitless bribes into her hand; visits to Taranne's *atelier*, where the *concierge* at last grew suspicious and reported the matter within; and finally an interview with the artist himself, from which the English youth emerged no nearer to his end than before, and crushed under the humiliation of the great man's advice. He could vaguely recall the long pacings of the Louvre; the fixed scrutiny of face after face; vain chases; ignominious retreats; and all the wretched stages of that slow descent into a bottomless despair! At last there was a letter—the long-expected letter to Madame Merichat, directing the removal of Mademoiselle Delaunay's possessions from the Rue Chantal. It was written by a certain M. Pimodan, who did not give his address, but who declared himself authorised by Mademoiselle Delaunay to remove her effects, and named a day when he would himself superintend the process and produce his credentials. David passed the time after the arrival of this letter in a state of excitement which left him hardly master of his actions. He had a room at the top of a wretched little hotel close to the Nord station, but he hardly ate or slept. The noises of Paris were agony to him night and day; he lived in a perpetual nausea of mind and body, hardly able at times to distinguish between the images of the brain and the impressions coming from without.

Before the day came, a note was brought to him from the Rue Chantal. It was from M. Pimodan, and requested an interview.

'I should be glad to see you on Mademoiselle Delaunay's behalf. Will you meet me in the Garden of the Luxembourg in front of the central pavilion, at three o'clock to-morrow?

'GUSTAVE PIMODAN.'

Before the hour came David was already pacing up and down the blazing gravel in front of the Palace. When M. Pimodan came the Englishman in an instant recognised the cousin—the lanky fellow with the spectacles, who had injured his eyes by reading.

As soon as he had established this identification—and the two men had hardly exchanged half-a-dozen sentences before the flashing inward argument was complete—a feeling of enmity arose in his mind, so intense that he could hardly keep himself still, could hardly bring his attention to bear on what he or his companion was saying. He had been brought so low that, with anyone else, he must have broken into appeals and entreaties. With this man—No!

As for M. Pimodan, the first sight of the young Englishman had apparently wrought in him also some degree of nervous shock; for the hand which held his cane fidgeted as he walked. He had the air of a person, too, who had lately gone through mental struggle; the red rims of the eyes under their large spectacles might be due either to chronic weakness or to recent sleeplessness.

But however these things might be, he took a perfectly mild tone, in which David's sick and irritable sense instantly detected the note of various offensive superiorities—the superiority of class and the superiority of age to begin with. He said in the first place that he was Mademoiselle Delaunay's relative, and that she had commissioned him to act for her in this very delicate matter. She was well aware—had been aware from the first day—that she was watched, and that M. Grieve was moving heaven and earth to discover her whereabouts. She did not, however, intend to be discovered; let him take that for granted. In her view all was over—their relation was irrevocably at an end. She wished now to devote herself wholly and entirely to her art, without disturbance or distraction from any other quarter whatever. Might he, under these circumstances, give M. Grieve the advice of a man of the world, and counsel him to regard the matter in the same light?

David walked blindly on, playing with his watch-chain. In the name of God whom and what was this fellow talking about? At the end of ten minutes' discourse on M. Pimodan's part, and of a few rare monosyllables on his own, he said, straightening his young figure with a nervous tremor:

'What you say is perfectly useless—I shall find her.'

Then a sudden angry light leapt into the cousin's eyes.

'You will *not* find her!' he said, drawing a sharp breath. 'It shows how little you know her, after all—compared with—those who—No matter! Oh, you can persecute and annoy her! No one doubts that. You can stand between her and all that she now cares to live for—her art. But you can do nothing else; and you will not be allowed to do that long, for she is not alone, as you seem to think. She will be protected. There are resources, and we shall employ them!'

The cousin had gone beyond his commission. David guessed as much. He did not believe that Elise had set this man on to threaten him. What a fool! But he merely said with a sarcastic dryness, endeavouring the while to steady his parched lips and his eyelids swollen with weariness.

'*A la bonne heure!*—employ them. Well, sir, you know, I believe, where Mademoiselle Delaunay is. I wish to know. You will not inform me. I therefore pursue my own way, and it is useless for me to detain you any longer.'

'Know where she is!' cried the other, a triumphant flash passing across his sallow student's face; 'I have but just parted from her.'

But he stopped. As a physician, he was accustomed to notice the changes of physiognomy. Instinctively he put some feet of distance between himself and his companion. Was it agony or rage he saw?

But David recovered himself by a strong effort.

'Go and tell her, then, that I shall find her,' he said with a shaking voice. 'I have many things to say to her yet.'

'Absurd!' cried the other angrily. 'Very well, sir, we know what to expect. It only remains for us to take measures accordingly.'

And drawing himself up he walked quickly away, looking back every now and then to see whether he were followed or no.

'Supposing I did track him,' thought David vaguely, 'what would he do? Summon one of the various *gardiens* in sight?'

He had, however, no such intention. What could it have ended in but a street scuffle? Patience! and he would find Elise for himself in spite of that prater.

Meanwhile he descended the terrace, and threw himself, worn out, upon the first seat, to collect his thoughts again.

Oh, this summer beauty:—this festal moment of the great city! Palace and Garden lay under the full June sun. The clipped trees on the terraces, statues, alleys, and groves slept in the luminous dancing air. All the normal stir and movement of the Garden seemed to have passed to-day into the leaping and intermingling curves of the fountains; the few figures passing and repassing hardly disturbed the general impression of heat and solitude.

For hours David sat there, head down, his eyes on the gravel, his hands tightly clasped between his knees. When he rose at last it was to hurry down the Rue de Seine and take the nearest bridge and street northwards to the Quartier Montmartre. He had been dreaming too long! and yet so great by now was his confusion of mind that he was no nearer a fresh plan of operations than when the cousin left him.

When he arrived at Madame Merichat's *loge* it was to find that no new development had occurred. Elise's possessions were still untouched; neither she nor M. Pimodan had given any further sign. The *concierge*, however, gave him a letter which had just arrived for him. Seeing that it bore the Manchester postmark, he thrust it into his pocket unread.

When he entered the evil-smelling passage of his hotel, a *garcon* emerged from the restaurant, dived into the *salle de lecture*, and came out with an envelope, which he gave to the Englishman. It had been left by a messenger five minutes before monsieur arrived. David took it, a singing in his ears; mounted to the first landing, where the gas burnt at midday, and read it.

'Gustave tells me you would not listen to him. Do you want to make me curse our meeting? Be a man and leave me to myself! While I know that you are on the watch I shall keep away from Paris—*voilà, tout*. I shall eat my heart out, — I shall begin to hate you, —you will have chosen it so. Only understand this: I will *never* see you again, for both our sakes, if I can help it. Believe what I say—believe that what parts us is a fate stronger than either of us, and go! Oh! you men talk of love—and at bottom you are all selfish and cruel. Do you want to break me more than I am already broken? Set me free!—will you kill both my youth and my art together?'

He carefully refolded the letter and put it into its envelope. Then he turned and went downstairs again towards the street. But the same frowsy waiter who had given him his letter was on the watch for him. In the morning monsieur had commanded some dinner. Would he take it now?

The man's tone was sulky. David understood that he was not considered a profitable customer of the hotel—that, considering his queer ways, late hours, and small spendings, they would probably be glad to be rid of him. With a curious submission and shrinking he followed the man into the stifling restaurant and sat down at one of the tables.

Here some food was brought to him, which he tried to eat. But in the midst of it he was seized with so great a loathing, that he suddenly rose, so violently as to upset a plate of bread beside him, and make a waiter spring forward to save the table itself. He pushed his way to the glass-door into the street, totally unconscious of the stir his behaviour was causing among the stout women in bonnets and the red-faced men with napkins tucked under their chins who were dining near, fumbled at the handle, and tottered out.

'*Quel animal!*' said the enraged *dame du comptoir*, who had noticed the incident. 'Marie!'—this to the sickly girl who sat near with the books in front of her, 'enter that plate, and charge it high. To-morrow I shall raise the price of his room. One must really finish with him. *C'est un fou!*'

Meanwhile David, revived somewhat by the air, was already in the Boulevard, making for Opera and the Rue Royale. It was not yet seven, the Salon would be still open. The distances seemed to him interminable—the length of the Rue Royale, the expanse of the Place de la Concorde, the gay and crowded ways of the Champs-Elysée. But at last he was mounting the stairs and battling through the rooms at the top. He looked first at the larger picture which had gained her *mention honorable*. It was a study of factory girls at their work, unequal, impatient, but full of a warm inventive talent— full of *her*. He knew its history—the small difficulties and triumphs of it, the adventures she had gone through on behalf of it—by heart. That fair-haired girl in the corner was studied from herself; the tint of the hair, the curve of the cheek were exact. He strained his eyes to look, searching for this detail and that. His heart said farewell—that was the last, the nearest he should ever come to her on this earth! Next year? Ah, he would give much to see her pictures of next year, with these new perceptions she had created in him.

He stood a minute before the other picture, the portrait—a study from one of her comrades in the *atelier*—and then he wound his way again through the thronged and suffocating rooms, and out into the evening.

The excessive heat of the last few days was about to end in storm. A wide tempestuous heaven lay beyond the Arc de Triomphe; the red light struck down the great avenue and into the faces of those stepping westwards. The deep shade under the full-leafed trees—how thinly green they were still against the sky that day when she vanished from him beside the arch and their love began!—was full of loungers and of playing children; the carriages passed and repassed in the light. So it had been, the enchanting never-ending drama, before this spectator entered—so it would be when he had departed.

He turned southwards and found himself presently on the Quai de la Conference, hanging over the river in a quiet spot where few people passed.

His frenzy of will was gone, and his last hope with it. Elise had conquered. Her letter had brought him face to face with those realities which, during this week of madness, he had simply refused to see. He could pit himself against her no longer. When it came to the point he had not the nerve to enter upon a degrading and ignoble conflict, in which all that was to be won was her hatred or her fear. That, indeed, would be the last and worst ruin, for it would be the ruin, not of happiness or of hope, but of love itself, and memory.

He took out her letter and re-read it. Then he searched for some of the writing materials he had bought when he had written his last letter to Manchester, and, spreading a sheet on the parapet of the river wall, he wrote:

'Be content. I think now—I am sure—that we shall never meet again. From this moment you will be troubled with me no more. Only I tell you for the last time that you have done ill—irrevocably ill. For what you have slain in yourself and me is not love or happiness, but *life* itself—the life of life!'

Foolish, incoherent words, as they seemed to him, but he could find no better. Confusedly and darkly they expressed the cry, the inmost conviction of his being. He could come no nearer at any rate to that desolation at the heart of him.

But now what next? Manchester?—the resumption and expansion of his bookseller's life—the renewal of his old friendships—the pursuit of money and of knowledge?

No. That is all done. The paralysis of will is complete. He cannot drive himself home, back to the old paths. The disgust with life has sunk too deep—the physical and moral collapse of which he is conscious has gone too far.

'Wretched man that I am! who shall deliver me from the body of this death?'

There, deep in the fibre of memory lie these words, and others like them—the typical words of a religion which is still in some sense the ineradicable warp of his nature, as it had been for generations of his forefathers. His individual resources of speech, as it were, have been overpassed; he falls back upon the inherited, the traditional resources of his race.

He looked up. A last gleam was on the Invalides—on the topmost roof of the Corps Législatif; otherwise the opposite bank was already grey, the river lay in shade. But the upper air was still aglow with the wide flame and splendour of the sunset; and beneath, on the bridges and the water and the buildings, how clear and gracious was the twilight!

'Who shall deliver me?' *'Deliver thyself!'* One instant, and the intolerable pressure on this shrinking point of consciousness can be lightened, this hunger for sleep appeased! Nothing else is possible—no future is even conceivable. His life in flowering has exhausted and undone itself, so spendthrift has been the process.

So he took his resolve. Then, already calmed, he hung over the river, thinking, reviewing the past.

Six weeks—six weeks only!—yet nothing in his life before matters or counts by comparison. For this mood of deadly fatigue the remembrance of all the intellectual joys and conquests of the last few years has no savour whatever. Strange that the development of one relation of life—the relation of passion—should have been able so to absorb and squander the power of living! His fighting, enduring capacity, compared with that of other men, must be small indeed. He thinks of himself as a coward and a weakling. But neither the facts of the present nor the face of the future are altered thereby.

The relation of sex—in its different phases—as he sees the world at this moment, there is no other reality. The vile and hideous phase of it has been present to him from the first moment of his arrival in these Paris streets. He thinks of the pictures and songs at the 'Trois Rats' from which in the first delicacy and flush of passion he had shrunk with so deep a loathing; of the photographs and engravings in the shops and the books on the stalls; of some of those pictures he had passed, a few minutes before, in the Salon; of that girl's face in the Tuileries Gardens. The animal, the beast in human nature, never has it been so present to him before; for he has understood and realised it while loathing it, has been admitted by his own passion to those regions of human feeling where all that is most foul and all that is most beautiful are generated alike from the elemental forces of life. And because he had loved Elise so finely and yet so humanly, with a boy's freshness and a man's energy, this animalism of the great city had been to him a perpetual nightmare and horror. His whole heart had gone into Regnault's cry — into Regnault's protest. For his own enchanted island had seemed to him often in the days of his wooing to be but floating on the surface of a ghastly sea, whence emerged all conceivable shapes of ruin, mockery, terror, and disease. It was because of the tremulous adoration which filled him from the beginning that the vice of Paris had struck him in this tragical way. At another time it might have been indifferent to him, might even have engulfed him.

But he! — he had known the best of passion! He laid his head down on the wall, and lived Barbizon over again — day after day, night after night. Now for the first time there is a pause in the urging madness of his despair. All the pulses of his being slacken; he draws back as it were from his own fate, surveys it as a whole, separates himself from it. The various scenes of it succeed each other in memory, set always — incomparably set — in the spring green of the forest, or under a charmed moonlight, or amid the flowery detail of a closed garden. Her little figure flashes before him — he sees her gesture, her smile; he hears his own voice and hers; recalls the struggle to express, the poverty of words, the thrill of silence, and that perpetual and exquisite recurrence to the interpreting images of poetry and art. But no poet had imagined better, had divined more than they in those earliest hours had *lived*! So he had told her, so he insisted now with a desperate faith.

But, poor soul! even as he insists, the agony within rises, breaks up, overwhelms the picture. He lives again through the jars and frets of those few burning days, the growing mistrust of them, the sense of jealous terror and insecurity — and then through the anguish of desertion and loss. He writhes again under the wrenching apart of their half-fused lives — under this intolerable ache of his own wound.

This the best of passion! Why his whole soul is still athirst and ahungered. Not a single craving of it has been satisfied. What is killing him is the sense of a thwarted gift, a baffled faculty — the faculty of self-spending, self-surrender. This, the best?

Then the mind fell into a whirlwind of half-articulate debate, from the darkness of which emerged two scenes — fragments — set clear in a passing light of memory.

That workman and his wife standing together before the day's toil—the woman's contented smile as her look clung to the mean departing figure.

And far, far back in his boyish life—Margaret sitting beside 'Lias in the damp autumn dawn, spending on his dying weakness that exquisite, ineffable passion of tenderness, of pity.

Ah! from the very beginning he had been in love with loving. He drew the labouring breath of one who has staked his all for some long-coveted gain, and lost.

Well!—Mr. Ancrum may be right—the English Puritan may be right—'sin' and 'law' may have after all some of those mysterious meanings his young analysis had impetuously denied them—he and Elise may have been only dashing themselves against the hard facts of the world's order, while they seemed to be transcending the common lot and spurning the common ways. What matter now! A certain impatient defiance rises in his stricken soul. He has made shipwreck of this one poor opportunity of life—confessed! now let the God behind it punish, if God there be. *The rest is silence.* With Elise in his arms, he had grasped at immortality. Now a stubborn, everlasting 'Nay' possesses him. There is nothing beyond.

He gathered up his letter, folded it, and put it into the breast—pocket of his coat. But in doing so his fingers touched once more the ragged edges of a bit of frayed paper.

Louie!

Through all these half-sane days and nights he had never once thought of his sister. She had passed out of his life—she had played no part even in the nightmares of his dreams.

But now!—while that intense denial of any reality in the universe beyond and behind this masque of life and things was still vibrating through his deepest being, it was as though a hand gently drew aside a curtain, and there grew clear before him, slowly effacing from his eyes the whole grandiose spectacle of buildings, sky, and river, that scene of the past which had worked so potently both in his childish sense and in Reuben's maturer conscience—the bare room, the iron bed, the dying man, one child within his arm, the other a frightened baby beside him.

It was frightfully clear, clearer than it had ever been in any normal state of brain, and as his mind lingered on it, unconsciously shaping, deepening its own creation, the weird impression grew that the helpless figure amid the bedclothes rose on its elbow, opened its cavernous eyes, and looked at him face to face, at the son whose childish heart had beat against his father's to the last. The boy's tortured soul quailed afresh before the curse his own remorse called into those eyes.

He hung over the water pleading with the phantom—defending himself. Every now and then he found that he was speaking aloud; then he would look round with a quick, piteous terror to see whether he had been heard or no, the parched lips beginning to move again almost before his fear was soothed.

All his past returned upon him, with its obligations, its fetters of conscience and kinship, so slowly forged, so often resisted and forgotten, and yet so strong. The moment marked the first passing away of the philtre, but it brought no recovery with it.

'My God! my God! I tried, father—I tried. But she is lost, lost—as I am!'

Then a thought found entrance and developed. He walked up and down the quay, wrestling it out, returning slowly and with enormous difficulty, because of his physical state, to some of the normal estimates and relations of life.

At last he dragged himself off towards his hotel. He must have some sleep, or how could these hours that yet remained be lived through—his scheme carried out?

On the way he went into a shop still open on the boulevard. When he came out he thrust his purchase into his pocket, buttoned his coat over it, and pursued his way northwards with a brisker step.

CHAPTER XI

Two days afterwards David stood at the door of a house in the outskirts of the Auteuil district of Paris. The street had a half-finished, miscellaneous air; new buildings of the villa type were mixed up with old and dingy houses standing in gardens, which had been evidently overtaken by the advancing stream of Paris, having once enjoyed a considerable amount of country air and space.

It was at the garden gate of one of these older houses that David rang, looking about him the while at the mean irregular street and the ill-kept side-walks with their heaps of cinders and refuse.

A powerfully built woman appeared, scowling, in answer to the bell. At first she flatly refused the new-comer admission. But David was prepared. He set to work to convince her that he was not a Paris creditor, and, further, that he was well aware M. Montjoie was not at home, since he had passed him on the other side of the road, apparently hurrying to the railway station, only a few minutes before. He desired simply to see madame. At this the woman's expression changed somewhat. She showed, however, no immediate signs of letting him in, being clearly chosen and paid to be a watch-dog. Then David brusquely put his hand in his pocket. Somehow he must get this harridan out of the way at once! The same terror was upon him that had been upon him now for many days and nights—of losing command of himself, of being no more able to do what he had to do.

The creature studied him, put out a greedy palm, developed a smile still more repellent than her brutality, and let him in.

He found himself in a small, neglected garden; in front of him, to the right, a wretched, weather-stained house, bearing every mark of poverty and dilapidation, while to the left there stretched out from the house a long glass structure, also in miserable condition—a sculptor's studio, as he guessed.

His guide led him to the studio-door. Madame was there a few minutes ago. As they approached, David stopped.

'I will knock. You may go back to the house. I am madame's brother.'

She looked at him once more, reluctant. Then, in the clearer light of the garden, the likeness of the face to one she already knew struck her with amazement; she turned and went off, muttering.

David knocked at the door; there was a movement within, and it was cautiously opened.

'*Monsieur est sorti.*—You!'

The brother and sister were face to face.

David closed the door behind him, and Louie retreated slowly, her hands behind her, her tall figure drawing itself up, her face setting into a frowning scorn.

'*You!*—what are you here for? We have done with each other!'

For answer David went up to a stove which was feebly burning in the damp, cheerless place, put down his hat and stick, and bent over it, stretching out his hands to the warmth. A chair was beside it, and on the chair some scattered bits of silk and velvet, out of which Louie was apparently fashioning a hat.

She stood still, observing him. She was in a loose dress of some silky Oriental material, and on her black hair she wore a red close-fitting cap with a fringe of golden coins dropping lightly and richly round her superb head and face.

'What is the matter with you?' she asked him grimly, after a minute's silence.' She has left you—that's plain!'

The young man involuntarily threw back his head as though he had been struck, and a vivid colour rushed into his cheek. But he answered quickly:

'We need not discuss my affairs. I did not come here to speak of them. They are beyond mending. I came to see—before I go—whether there is anything I can do to help you.'

'Much obliged to you!' she cried, flinging herself down on the edge of a rough board platform, whereon stood a fresh and vigorous clay-study, for which she had just been posing, to judge from her dress. Beyond was the Maenad. And in the distance loomed a great block of marble, upon which masons had been working that afternoon.

'I am *greatly* obliged to you!' she repeated mockingly, taking the crouching attitude of an animal ready to attack. 'You are a pattern brother.'

Her glowing looks expressed the enmity and contempt she was at the moment too excited to put into words.

David drew his hand across his eyes with a long breath. How was he to get through it, this task of his, with this swollen, aching brain and these trembling limbs? Louie *must* let him speak; he bitterly felt his physical impotence to wrestle with her.

He went up to her slowly and sat down beside her. She drew away from him with a violent movement. But he laid his hand upon her knee—a shaking hand which his impatient will tried in vain to steady.

'Louie, look at me!' he commanded.

She did so unwillingly, but the proud repulsion of her lip did not relax.

'Well, I dare say you look pretty bad. Whose fault is it? everybody else but you knew what the creature was worth. Ask anybody!'

The lad's frame straightened and steadied. He took his hand from her knee.

'Say that kind of thing again,' he said calmly, 'and I walk straight out of that door, and you set eyes on me for the last time. That would be what you want, I dare say. All I wish to point out is, that you would be a great fool. I have not come here to-day to waste words, but to propose something to your advantage—your money-advantage,' he repeated deliberately, looking round the dismal building with its ill-mended gaps and rents, and its complete lack of the properties and appliances to which the humblest modern artist pretends. 'To judge from what I heard in Paris, and what I see, money is scarce here.'

His piteous sudden wish to soften her, to win a kind word from her, from anyone, had passed away. He was beginning to take command of her as in the old days.

'Well, maybe we are hard up,' she admitted slowly. 'People are such brutes and won't wait, and a sculptor has to pay out for a lot of things before he can make anything at all. But that statue will put it all right,' and she pointed behind her to the Maenad. 'It's me—it's the one you tried to put a stopper on.'

She looked at him darkly defiant. She was leaning back on one arm, her foot beating with the trick familiar to her. For reckless and evil splendour the figure was unsurpassable.

'When he sells that,' she went on, seeing that he did not answer, 'and he will sell it in a jiffy—it is the best he's ever done—there'll be heaps of money.'

David smiled.

'For a week perhaps. Then, if I understand this business aright—I have been doing my best, you perceive, to get information, and M. Montjoie seems to be better known than one supposed to half Paris—the game will begin again.'

'Never you mind,' she broke in, breathing quickly. 'Give me my money—the money that belongs to me—and let me alone.'

'On one condition,' he said quietly. 'That money, as you remember, is in my hands and at my disposal.'

'Ah! I supposed you would try to grab it!' she cried.

Even he was astonished at her violence—her insolence. The demon in her had never been so plain, the woman never so effaced. His heart dropped within him like lead, and his whole being shrank from her.

'Listen to me!' he said, seizing her strongly by the hand, while a light of wrath leapt into his changed and bloodshot eyes. 'This man will desert you; in a year's time he will have tired of you; what'll you do then?'

'Manage for myself, thank you! without any canting interference from you. I have had enough of that.'

'And fall again,' he said, releasing her, and speaking with a deliberate intensity; 'fall again—from infamy to infamy!'

She sprang up.

'Mind yourself!' she cried.

Miserable moment! As he looked at her he felt that that weapon of his old influence with her which, poor as it was, he had relied on in the last resort all his life, had broken in his hand. His own act had robbed it of all virtue. That pang of 'irreparableness' which had smitten Elise smote him now. All was undone—all was done!

He buried his face in his hands an instant. When he lifted it again, she was standing with her arms folded across her chest, leaning against an iron shaft which supported part of the roof.

'You had better go!' she said, still in a white heat. 'Why you ever came I don't know. If you won't give me that money, I shall get it somehow.'

Suddenly, as she spoke, everything—the situation, the subject of their talk, the past—seemed to be wiped out of David's brain. He stared round him helplessly. Why were they there—what had happened?

This blankness lasted a certain number of seconds. Then it passed away, and he painfully recovered his identity. But the experience was not new to him—it would recur—let him be quick.

This time a happier instinct served him. He, too, rose and went up to her.

'We are a pair of fools,' he said to her, half bitterly, half gently; 'we reproach and revile each other, and all the time I am come to give you not only what is yours, but all—all I have—that it may stand between you and—and worse ruin.'

'Ruin!' she said, throwing back her head and catching at the word; 'speak for yourself! If I am Montjoie's mistress, Elise Delaunay was yours. Don't preach. It won't go down.'

'I have no intention of preaching—don't alarm yourself,' he replied quietly, this time controlling himself without difficulty.'

'I have only this to say. On the day when you become Montjoie's wife, all our father's money—all the six hundred pounds Mr. Gurney paid over to me in January, shall be paid to you.'

She started, caught her breath, tried to brazen it out.

'What is this idiocy for?' she asked coldly. 'What does marrying matter to you?'

He sank down again on the chair by the stove, being, indeed, unable to stand.

'Perhaps I can't tell you,' he said, after a pause, shading his face from her with his hand; 'perhaps I could not make plain to myself what I feel. But this I know—that this man with whom you are living here is a man for whom nobody has a good word. I want to give you a hold over him. But first—stop a moment,'—he dropped his hand and looked up eagerly, 'will you leave him—leave him at once? I could arrange that.'

'Make your mind easy,' she said shortly; 'he suits me—I stay. I went with him, well, because I was dull—and because I wanted to make you smart for it, if you're keen to know!—but if you think I am anxious to go home, to be cried over by Dora and lectured by you, you're vastly mistaken. I can manage him! I have my hold on him—he knows very well what I am worth to him.'

She threw her head back superbly against the iron shaft, putting one arm round it and resting her hot cheek against it as though for coolness.

'Why should we argue?' he said sharply—after a wretched silence. 'I didn't come for that. If you won't leave him I have only this to say. On the day he marries you, if the evidence of the marriage is satisfactory to an

English lawyer I have discovered in Paris and whose address I will give you, six hundred pounds will be paid over to you. It is there now, in the lawyer's hands. If not, I go home, and the law does not compel me to hand you over one farthing.'

She was silent, and began to pace up and down.

'Montjoie despises marriage,' she said presently.

'Try whether he despises money too,' said David, and could not for the life of him keep the sarcastic note out of his voice.

She bit her lip.

'And when, if it is done, must this precious thing be settled?'

'If your marriage does not take place within a month, Mr. O'Kelly—I will leave you his address,' he put his hand into his pocket—'has orders to return the money—'

'To whom?' she inquired, struck by his sudden break.

'To me, of course,' he said slowly. 'Is it perfectly plain? do you understand? Now, then, listen. I have inquired what the law is—you will have to be married both at the mairie and by the chaplain at the British embassy.'

She stopped suddenly in her walk and confronted him.

'If I am married at all,' she said abruptly, 'I shall be married as a Catholic.'

'A Catholic!' David stared at her. She enjoyed his astonishment.

'Oh, I have had that in my mind for a long time,' she said scornfully. 'There is a priest at that church with the steps, you know, near that cemetery place on the hill, who is very much interested in me indeed. He speaks English. I used to go to confession. Madame Cervin told me all about it, and how to do it; I did it exact! Oh, if I am to be married, that will make it plain sailing enough. It was awkward—while—'

She broke off and sat down again beside him, pondering and smiling as he had seen her do in Manchester, when she had the prospect of a new dress or some amusement that excited her.

'How have you been able to think about such things?' he asked her, marvelling.

'Think about them! What was the good of that? It's the churches I like, and the priests. Now there *is* something to see in the Paris churches, like the Madeleine—worth a dozen St. Damian's, —you may tell Dora that. The flowers and the dresses and the music—they *are* something like. And the priests—'

She smiled again, little meditative smiles, as though she were recalling her experiences.

'Well, I don't know that there's much about them,' she said at last; 'they're queer, and they're awfully clever, and they want to manage you, of course.'

She stopped, quite unable to express herself any more fully. But it was evident that the traditional relation of the Catholic priest to his penitent had been to her a subject of curiosity and excitement—that she would gladly know more of it.

David could hardly believe his ears. He sat lost at first in the pure surprise of it, in the sense of Louie's unlikeness to any other human creature he had ever seen. Then a gleam of satisfaction arose. He had heard of the hold on women possessed by the Catholic Church, and maintained by her marvellous, and on the whole admirable, system of direction. For himself, he would have no priests of whatever Church. But his mind harboured none of the common Protestant rules and shibboleths. In God's name, let the priests get hold of this sister of his:—if they could—when he—

'Marry this man, then!' he said to her at last, breaking the silence abruptly,' and square it with the Church, if you want to.'

'Oh, indeed!' she said mockingly. 'So you have nothing to say against my turning Catholic? I should like to see Uncle Reuben's face.'

Her voice had the exultant mischief of a child. It was evident that her spirits were rising, that her mood towards her brother was becoming more amiable.

'Nothing,' he said dryly, replying to her question.

Then he got up and looked for his hat. She watched him askance. 'What are you going for? I could get you some tea. *He* won't be in for hours.'

'I have said what I had to say. These'—taking a paper from his pocket and laying it down, 'are all the directions, legal and other, that concern you, as to the marriage. I drew them up this morning, with Mr. O'Kelly. I have given you his address. You can communicate with him at any time.'

'I can write to you, I suppose?'

'Better write to him,' he said quietly, 'he has instructions. He seemed to me a good sort.'

'Where are you going?'

'Back to Paris, and then—home.'

She placed herself in his way, so that the sunny light of the late afternoon, coming mostly from behind her, left her face in shadow.

'What'll you do without that money?' she asked abruptly.

He paused, getting together his answer with difficulty.

'I have the stock, and there is something left of the sixty pounds Uncle Reuben brought. I shall do.'

'He'll muddle it all,' she said roughly. 'What's the good?'

And she folded her arms across her with the recklessness of one quite ready and eager, if need be, to fight her own battle, with her own weapons, in her own way.

'Get Mr. O'Kelly to keep it, if you can persuade him, and draw it by degrees. I'd have made a trust of it, if it had been enough; but it isn't. Twenty-four pounds a year: that's all you'd get, if we tied up the capital.'

She laughed. Evidently her acquaintance with Montjoie had enlarged her notions of money, which were precise and acute enough before.

'He spends that in a supper when he's in cash. I'll be curious to see whether, all in a lump, it'll be enough to make him marry me. Still, he is precious hard up: he don't stir out till dark, he's so afraid of meeting people.'

'That's my hope,' said David heavily, hardly knowing what he said. 'Good-bye.'

'Hope!' she re-echoed bitterly. 'What d'you want to tie me to him for, for good and all?'

And, turning away from him, she stared, frowning, through the dingy glass door in to the darkening garden. In her mind there was once more that strange uprising swell of reaction—of hatred of herself and life.

Why, indeed? David could not have answered her question. He only knew that there was a blind instinct in him driving him to this, as the best that remained open—the only *ainde* possible for what had been so vilely done by himself, by her, and by the man who had worked out her fall for a mere vicious whim. There was no word in any mouth, it seemed to him, of his being in love with her.

There were all sorts of whirling thoughts in his mind—fragments cast up by the waves of desolate experience he had been passing through—inarticulate cries of warning, judgment, pain. But he could put nothing into words.

'Good-bye, Louie!'

She turned and stood looking at him.

'What made you get ill?' she inquired, eyeing him.

His thirsty heart drank in the change of tone.

'I don't sleep,' he said hurriedly. 'It's the noise. The Nord station is never quiet. Well, mind you've got to bring that off. Keep the papers safe. Good-bye, for a long time'.

'I can come over when I want?' she said half sullenly.

'Yes,' he assented, 'but you won't want.'

He drew her by the hand with a solemn tremulous feeling, and kissed her on the cheek. He would have liked to give her their father's dying letter. It was there, in his coat-pocket. But he shrank from the emotion of it. No, he must go. He had done all he could.

She opened the door for him, and took him to the garden-gate in silence.

'When I'm married,' she said shortly, 'if ever I am—Lord knows! —you can tell Uncle Reuben and Dora?'

'Yes. Good-bye.'

The gate closed behind him. He went away, hurrying towards the Auteuil station.

When he landed again in the Paris streets, he stood irresolute.

'One more look,' he said to himself, 'one more.'

And he turned down the Rue Chantal. There was the familiar archway, and the light shining behind the porter's door. Was her room already stripped and bare, or was the broken glass—poor dumb prophet!—still there, against the wall?

He wandered on through the lamp-lit city and the crowded pavements. Elise—the wraith of her—went with him, hand in hand, ghost with ghost, amid this multitude of men. Sometimes, breaking from this dream-companionship, he would wake with terror to the perception of his true, his utter loneliness. He was not made to be alone, and the thought that nowhere in this great Paris was there a single human being to whose friendly eye or hand he might turn him in his need, swept across him from time to time, contracting the heart. Dora—Mr. Ancrum—if they knew, they would be sorry.

Then again indifference and blankness came upon him, and he could only move feebly on, seeing everything in a blur and mist. After these long days and nights of sleeplessness, semi-starvation, and terrible excitement, every nerve was sick, every organ out of gear. The lights of the Tuileries, the stately pile of the Louvre, under a gray driving sky.—There would be rain soon—ah, there it came! the great drops hissing along the pavement. He pushed on to the river, careless of the storm, soothed, indeed, by the cool dashes of rain in his face and eyes.

The Place de la Concorde seemed to him as day, so brilliant was the glare of its lamps. To the right, the fairyland of the Champs-Elysées, the trees tossing under the sudden blast; in front, the black trench of the river. On, on—let him see it all—gather it all into his accusing heart and brain, and then at a stroke blot out the inward and the outward vision, and 'cease upon the midnight with no pain'!

He walked till he could walk no more; then he sank on a dark seat on the Quai Saint-Michel, cursing himself. Had he no nerve left for the last act—was that what this delay, this fooling meant? Coward!

But not here! not in these streets—this publicity! Back—to this little noisome room. There lock the door, and make an end!

On the way northward, at the command of a sudden caprice, he sat outside a blazing cafe on the Boulevard and ordered absinthe, which he had never tasted. While he waited he looked round on the painted women, on the men escorting them, on the loungers with their newspapers and cigars, the shouting, supercilious waiters. But all the little odious details of the scene escaped him; he felt only the touchingness of his human comradeship, the yearning of a common life, bruised and wounded but still alive within him.

Then he drank the stuff they gave him, loathed it, paid and staggered on. When he reached his hotel he crept upstairs, dreading to meet any of the harsh-faced people who frowned as he passed them. He had done abject things these last three days to conciliate them—tipped the waiter, ordered food, not that he might eat it but that he might pay for it, bowed to the landlady—all to save the shrinking of his sore and quivering nerves. In vain! It seemed to him that since that last look from Elise as she nestled into the fern, there had been no kindness for him in human eyes—save, perhaps, from that woman with the child.

As he dragged himself up to his fourth floor, the stimulant he had taken began to work upon his starved senses. The key was in his door, he turned it and fell into his room, while the door, with the key still in it, swung to behind him. Guiding himself by the furniture, he reached the only chair the room possessed—an arm-chair of the commonest and cheapest hotel sort, which, because of the uncertainty of its legs, the *femme de chambre* had propped up against the bed. He sat down in it and his head fell back on the counterpane. There was much to do. He had to write to John about the sale of his stock and the payment of his debts. He had to put his father's letter into an envelope for Louie, to send all the papers and letters he had on him and a last message to Mr. Ancrum, and then to post these letters, so that nothing private might fall into the hands of the French police, who would, of course, open his bag.

While these thoughts were rising in him, a cloud came over the brain, bringing with it, as it seemed, the first moment of ease which had been his during this awful fortnight. Before he yielded himself to it he thrust his hand into his coat-pocket with a sudden vague anxiety to feel what was there. But even as he withdrew his fingers they relaxed; a black object came with them, and fell unheeded, first on his knee, then on to a coat lying on the floor between him and the window.

A quarter of an hour afterwards there was a stir and voices on the landing outside. Some one knocked at the door of No. 139. No answer. 'The key is in the door. *Ouvrez donc!'* cried the waiter, as he ran downstairs again to the restaurant, which was still crowded. The visitor opened the door and peeped in. Some quick words broke from him. He rushed in and up to the bed. But directly the heavy feverish breathing of the figure in the chair caught his ear his look of sudden horror relaxed, and he fell back, looking at the sleeping youth.

It was a piteous sight he saw! Exhaustion, helplessness, sorrow, physical injury, and moral defeat, were written in every line of the poor drawn face and shrunken form. The brow was furrowed, the breathing hard, the mouth dry and bloodless. Upon the mind of the new-comer, possessed as it was with the image of what David Grieve had been two short months before, the effect of the spectacle was presently overwhelming.

He fell on his knees beside the sleeper. But as he did so, he noticed the black thing on the floor, stooped to it, and took it up. That it should be a loaded revolver seemed to him at that moment the most natural thing in the world, little used as he personally was to such possessions. He looked at it carefully, took out the two cartridges it contained, put them into one pocket and the revolver into the other.

Then he laid his arm round the lad's neck.

'David!'

The young man woke directly and sat up, shaking with terror and excitement. He pushed his visitor from him, looking at him with defiance. Then he slipped his hand inside his coat and sprang up with a cry.

'David!—dear boy—dear fellow!'

The voice penetrated the lad's ear. He caught his visitor and dragged him forward to the light. It fell on the twisted face and wet eyes of Mr. Ancrum. So startling was the vision, so poignant were the associations which it set vibrating, that David stood staring and trembling, struck dumb.

'Oh, my poor lad! my poor lad! John wanted me to come yesterday, and I delayed. I was a selfish wretch. Now I will take you home.'

David fell again upon his chair, too feeble to speak, too feeble even to weep, the little remaining colour ebbing from his cheeks. The minister used all his strength, and laid him on the bed. Then he rang and made even the callous and haughty madame, who was presently summoned, listen to and obey him while he sent for brandy and a doctor, and let the air of the night into the stifling room.

CHAPTER XII

In two or three days the English doctor who was attending David strongly advised Mr. Ancrum to get his charge home. The fierce strain his youth had sustained acting through the nervous system had disordered almost every bodily function, and the collapse which followed Mr. Ancrum's appearance was severe. He would lie in his bed motionless and speechless, volunteered no confidence, and showed hardly any rallying power.

'Get him out of this furnace and that doghole of a room,' said the doctor. 'He has come to grief here somehow—that's plain. You won't make anything of him till you move him.'

When the lad was at last stretched on the deck of a Channel steamer speeding to the English coast, and the sea breeze had brought a faint touch of returning colour to his cheek, he asked the question he had never yet had the physical energy to ask.

'Why did you come, and how did you find me?'

Then it appeared that the old cashier at Heywood's bank, who had taken a friendly interest in the young bookseller since the opening of his account, had dropped a private word to John in the course of conversation, which had alarmed that youth not a little. His own last scrawl from David had puzzled and disquieted him, and he straightway marched off to Mr. Ancrum to consult. Whereupon the minister wrote cautiously and affectionately to David asking for some prompt and full explanation of things for his friends' sake. The letter was, as we know, never opened, and therefore never answered. Whereupon John's jealous misery on Louie's account and Mr. Ancrum's love for David had so worked that the minister had broken in upon his scanty savings and started for Paris at a few hours' notice. Once in the Rue Chantal he had come easily on David's track.

Naturally he had inquired after Louie as soon as David was in a condition to be questioned at all. The young man hesitated a moment, then he said resolutely, 'She is married,' and would say no more. Mr. Ancrum pressed the matter a little, but his patient merely shook his head, and the sight of him as he lay there on the pillow was soon enough to silence the minister.

On the evening before they left Paris he called for a telegraph form, wrote a message and paid the reply, but Mr. Ancrum saw nothing of either. When the reply arrived David crushed it in his hand with a strange look, half bitterness, half relief, and flung it behind a piece of furniture standing near.

Now, on the cool, wind-swept deck, he seemed more inclined to talk than he had been yet. He asked questions about John and the Lomaxes—he even inquired after Lucy, as to whom the minister who had lately improved an acquaintance with Dora and her father, begun through David, could only answer vaguely that he believed she was still in the south. But he volunteered nothing about his own affairs or the cause of the state in which Mr. Ancrum had found him.

Every now and then, indeed, as they stood together at the side of the vessel, David leaning heavily against it, his words would fail him altogether, and he would be left staring stupidly, the great black eyes widening, the lower lip falling—over the shifting brilliance of the sea.

Ancrum was almost sure too that in the darkness of their last night in Paris there had been, hour after hour, a sound of hard and stifled weeping, mingled with the noises from the street and from the station; and to-day the youth in the face was more quenched than ever, in spite of the signs of reviving health. There had been a woman in the case, of course: Louie might have misbehaved herself; but after all the world is so made that no sister can make a brother suffer as David had evidently suffered—and then there was the revolver! About this last, after one or two restless movements of search, which Mr. Ancrum interpreted, David had never asked, and the minister, timid man of peace that he was, had resold it before leaving.

Well, it was a problem, and it must be left to time. Meanwhile Mr. Ancrum was certainly astonished that *any* love affair should have had such a destructive volcanic power with the lad. For it was no mere raw and sensuous nature, no idle and morbid brain. One would have thought that so many different aptitudes and capacities would have kept each other in check.

As they neared Manchester, David grew plainly restless and ill at ease. He looked out sharply for the name of each succeeding town, half turning afterwards, as though to speak to his companion; but it was not till they were within ten minutes of the Central Station that he said—

'John will want to know about Louie. She is married,—as I told you,—to a French sculptor. I have handed over to her all my father's money—that is why I drew it out.'

Mr. Ancrum edged up closer to him—all ears—waiting for more. But there was nothing more.

'And you are satisfied?' he said at last.

David nodded and looked out of window intently.

'What is the man's name?'

David either did not or would not hear, and Mr. Ancrum let him alone. But the news was startling. So the boy had stripped himself, and must begin the world again as before! What had that minx been after?

Manchester again. David looked out eagerly from the cab, his hand trembling on his knee, beads of perspiration on his face.

They turned up the narrow street, and there in the distance to the right was the stall and the shop, and a figure on the steps. Mr. Ancrum had sent a card before them, and John was on the watch.

The instant the cab stopped, and before the driver could dismount, John had opened the door. Putting his head in he peered at the pair inside, and at the opposite seat, with his small short-sighted eyes.

'Where is she?' he said hoarsely, barring the way.

Mr. Ancrum looked at his companion. David had shrunk back into the corner, with a white hangdog look, and said nothing. The minister interposed.

'David will tell you all,' he said gently. 'First help me in with him, and the bags. He is a sick man.'

With a huge effort John controlled himself, and they got inside. Then he shut the shop door and put his back against it.

'Tell me where she is,' he repeated shortly.

'She is married,' David said in a low voice, but looking up from the chair on which he had sunk.' By now—she is married. I heard by telegram last night that all was arranged for to-day.'

The lad opposite made a sharp, inarticulate sound which startled the minister's ear. Then clutching the handle of the door, he resumed sharply—

'Who has she married?'

The assumption of the right to question was arrogance itself—strange in the dumb, retiring creature whom the minister had hitherto known only as David's slave and shadow!

'A French sculptor,' said David steadily, but propping his head and hand against the counter, so as to avoid John's stare—'a man called Montjoie.

I was a brute—I neglected her. She got into his hands. Then I sent for all my money to bribe him to marry her. And he has.'

'You—you *blackguard!*' cried John.

David straightened instinctively under the blow, and his eyes met John's for one fierce moment. Then Mr. Ancrum thought he would have fainted. The minister took rough hold of John by the shoulders.

'If you can't stay and hold your tongue,' he said, 'you must go. He is worn out with the journey, and I shall get him to bed. Here's some money: suppose you run to the house round the corner, in Prince's Street; ask if they've got some strong soup, and, if they have, hurry back with it. Come—look sharp. And—one moment—you've been sleeping here, I suppose? Well, I shall take your room for a bit, if that'll suit you. This fellow'll have to be looked after.'

The little lame creature spoke like one who meant to have his way. John took the coin, hesitated, and stumbled out.

For days afterwards there was silence between him and David, except for business directions. He avoided being in the shop with his employer, and would stand for hours on the step, ostensibly watching the stall, but in reality doing no business that he could help. Whenever Mr. Ancrum caught sight of him he was leaning against the wall, his hat slouched over his eyes, his hands in his pockets, utterly inert and listless, more like a log than a human being. Still he was no less stout, lumpish, and pink-faced than before. His fate might have all the tragic quality; nature had none the less inexorably endowed him with the externals of farce.

Meanwhile David dragged himself from his bed to the shop and set to work to pick up dropped threads. The customers, who had been formerly interested in him, discovered his return, and came in to inquire why he had been so long away, or, in the case of one or two, whether he had executed certain commissions in Paris. The explanation of illness, however, circulated from the first moment by Mr. Ancrum, and perforce adopted—though with an inward rage and rebellion—by David himself, was amply sufficient to cover his omissions and inattentions, and to ease his resumption of his old place. His appearance indeed was still ghastly. The skin of the face had the tightened, transparent look of weakness; the eyes, reddened and sunk, showed but little of their old splendour between the blue circles beneath and the heavy brows above; even the hair seemed to have lost its boyish curl, and fell in harsh, troublesome waves over the forehead, whence its owner was perpetually and impatiently thrusting it back. All the bony structure of the face had been emphasised at the expense of its young grace and bloom, and the new indications of moustache and beard did but add to its striking and painful black and white. And the whole impression of change was completed by the melancholy aloofness, the shrinking distrust with which eyes once overflowing with the frankness and eagerness of one of the most accessible of human souls now looked out upon the world.

'Was it fever?' said a young Owens College professor who had taken a lively interest from the beginning in the clever lad's venture. 'Upon my word! you do look pulled down. Paris may be the first city in the world—it is an insanitary hole all the same. So you never found time to inquire after those Moliere editions for me?'

David racked his brains. What was it he had been asked to do? He remembered half an hour's talk on one of those early days with a bookseller on the Quai Voltaire—was it about this commission? He could not recall.

'No, sir,' he said, stammering and flushing. 'I believe I did ask somewhere, but I can't remember.'

'It's very natural, very natural,' said the professor kindly. 'Never mind. I'll send you the particulars again, and you can keep your eyes open for me. And, look here, take your business easy for a while. You'll get on—you're sure to get on—if you only recover your health.'

David opened the door for him in silence.

The reawakening of his old life in him was strange and slow. When he first found himself back among his books and catalogues, his ledgers and business memoranda, he was bewildered and impatient. What did these elaborate notes, with their cabalistic signs and abbreviations—whether as to the needs of customers, or the whereabouts of books, or the history of prices—mean or matter? He was like a man who has lost a sense. Then the pressure of certain debts which should have been met out of the money in the bank first put some life into him. He looked into his financial situation and found it grave, though not desperate. All hope of a large and easy expansion of business was, of course, gone. The loss of his capital had reduced him to the daily shifts and small laborious accumulations with which he had begun. But this factor in his state was morally of more profit to him at the moment than any other. With such homely medicines nature and life can often do most for us.

Such was Ancrum's belief, and in consequence he showed a very remarkable wisdom during these early days of David's return.

'As far as I can judge, there has been a bad shake to the heart in more senses than one,' had been the dry remark of the Paris doctor; 'and as for nervous system, it's a mercy he's got any left. Take care of him, but for Heaven's sake don't make an invalid of him—that would be the finish.'

So that Ancrum offered no fussy opposition to the resumption of the young man's daily work, though at first it produced a constant battle with exhaustion and depression. But never day or night did the minister forget his charge. He saw that he ate and drank; he enforced a few common sense remedies for the nervous ills which the moral convulsion had left behind it, ills which the lad in his irritable humiliation would fain have hidden even from him; above all he knew how to say a word which kept Dora and Daddy and other friends away for a time, and how to stand between David and that choked and miserable John.

He had the strength of mind also to press for no confidence and to expect no thanks. He had little fear of any further attempts at suicide, though he would have found it difficult perhaps to explain why. But instinctively he felt that for all practical purposes David had been mad when he found him, and that he was mad no longer. He was wretched, and only a fraction of his mind was in Manchester and in his business—that was plain. But, in however imperfect a way, he was again master of himself; and the minister bided his time, putting his ultimate trust in one of the finest mental and physical constitutions he had ever known.

In about ten days David took up his hat one afternoon and, for the first time, ventured into the streets. On his return he was walking down Potter Street in a storm of wind and rain, when he ran against some one who was holding an umbrella right in front of her and battling with the weather. In his recoil he saw that it was Dora.

Dora too looked up, a sudden radiant pleasure in her face overflowing her soft eyes and lips.

'Oh, Mr. Grieve! And are you really better?'

'Yes,' he said briefly. 'May I walk with you a bit?'

'Oh no!—I don't believe you ought to be out in such weather. I'll just come the length of the street with you.'

And she turned and walked with him, chattering fast, and of course, from the point of view of an omniscience which could not have been hers, foolishly. Had he liked Paris?—what he saw of it at least before he had been ill?—and how long had he been ill? Why had he not let Mr. Ancrum or some one know sooner? And would he tell her more about Louie? She heard that she was married, but there was so much she, Dora, wanted to hear.

To his first scanty answers she paid in truth but small heed, for the joy of seeing him again was soon effaced by the painful impression of his altered aspect. The more she looked at him, the more her heart went out to him; her whole being became an effusion of pity and tenderness, and her simplest words, maidenly and self-restrained as she was, were in fact charged with something electric, ineffable. His suffering, his neighbourhood, her own sympathy—she was taken up, overwhelmed by these general impressions. Inferences, details escaped her.

But as she touched on the matter of Louie, and they were now at his own steps, he said to her hurriedly—

'Walk a little further, and I'll tell you. John's in there.'

She opened her eyes, not understanding, and then demurred a little on the ground of his health and the rain.

'Oh, I'm all right,' he said impatiently. 'Look here, will you walk to Chetham's Library? There'll be a quiet place there, in the reading room—sure to be—where we can talk.'

She assented, and very soon they were mounting the black oak stairs leading to this old corner of Manchester. At the top of the stairs they saw in the distance, at the end of the passage on to which open the readers' studies, each with its lining of folios and its oaken lattice, a librarian, who nodded to David, and took a look at Dora. Further on they stumbled over a small boy from the charity school who wished to lionise them over the whole building. But when he had been routed, they found the beautiful panelled and painted reading-room quite empty, and took possession of it in peace. David led the way to an oriel window he had become familiar with in the off-times of his first years at Manchester, and they seated themselves there with a low sloping desk between them, looking out on the wide rain-swept yard outside, the buildings of the grammar-school, and the black mass of the cathedral.

Manchester had never been more truly Manchester than on this dark July afternoon, with its low shapeless clouds, its darkness, wind, and pelting rain. David, staring out through the lozenge panes at the familiar gloom beyond, was suddenly carried by repulsion into the midst of a vision which was an agony—of a spring forest cut by threadlike paths; of a shadeless sun; of a white city steeped in charm, in gaiety.

Dora watched him timidly, new perceptions and alarms dawning in her.

'You were going to tell me about Louie,' she said.

He returned to himself, and abruptly turned with his back to the window, so that he saw the outer world no more.

'You heard that she was married?'

'Yes.'

'She has married a brute. It was partly my fault. I wanted to be rid of her; she got in my way. This man was in the same house; I left her to herself, and partly, I believe, to spite me, she went off with him. Then at the last when she wouldn't leave him I made her marry him. I bribed him to marry her. And he did. I had just enough money to make it worth his while. But he will ill-treat her; and she won't stay with him. She will go from bad to worse.'

Dora drew back, with her hand on the desk, staring at him with incredulous horror.

'But you were ill?' she stammered.

He shook his head.

'Never mind my being ill. I wanted you to know, because you were good to her, and I'm not going to be a hypocrite to you. Nobody else need know anything but that she's married, which is true. If I'd looked after her it mightn't have happened—perhaps. But I didn't look after her—I couldn't.'

His face, propped in his hands, was hidden from her. She was in a whirl of excitement and tragic impression—understanding something, divining more.

'Louie was always so self-willed,' she said trembling.

'Aye. That don't make it any better. You remember all I told you about her before? You know we didn't get on; she wasn't nice to me, and I didn't suit her, I suppose. But all this year, I don't know why, she's been on my mind from morning till night; I've always felt sure, somehow, that she would come to harm; and the worrying oneself about her—well! it has seemed *to grow into one's very bones.* '—He threw out the last words after a pause, in which he had seemed to search for some phrase wherewith to fit the energy of his feeling. 'I took her to Paris to keep her out of mischief. I had much rather have gone alone; but she would not ask you to take her in, and I couldn't leave her with John. Well, then, she got in my way—I told you—and I let her go to the dogs. There—it's done—*done!*'

He turned on his seat, one hand drumming the desk, while his eyes fixed themselves apparently on the portrait of Sir Humphry Chetham over the carved mantelpiece. His manner was hard and rapid; neither voice nor expression had any of the simplicity or directness of remorse.

Dora remained silent looking at him; her slender hands were pressed tight against either cheek; the tears rose slowly till they filled her grey eyes.

'It is very sad,' she said in a low voice.

There was a pause.

'Yes—it's sad. So are most things in this world, perhaps. All natural wants seem just to lead us to misery sooner or later. And who gave them to us—who put us here—with no choice but just to go on blundering from one muddle into another?'

Their eyes met. It was as though he had remembered her religion, and could not, in his bitterness, refrain from an indirect fling at it.

As for her, what he said was strange and repellent to her. But her forlorn passion, so long trampled on, cried within her; her pure heart was one prayer, one exquisite throb of pain and pity.

'Did some one deceive you?' she asked, so low that the words seemed just breathed into the air.

'No,—I deceived myself.'

Then as he looked at her an impulse of confession crossed his mind. Sympathy, sincerity, womanly sweetness, these things he had always associated with Dora Lomax. Instinctively he had chosen her for a friend long ago as soon as their first foolish spars were over.

But the impulse passed away. He thought of her severity, her religion, her middle-class canons and judgments, which perhaps were all the stricter because of Daddy's laxities. What common ground between her and his passion, between her and Elise? No! if he must speak—if, in the end, he proved too weak to forbear wholly from speech—let it be to ears more practised, and more human!

So he choked back his words, and Dora felt instinctively that he would tell her no more. Her consciousness of this was a mingled humiliation and relief; it wounded her to feel that she had so little command of him; yet she dreaded what he might say. Paris was a wicked place—so the world reported. Her imagination, sensitive, Christianised, ascetic, shrank from what he might have done. Perhaps the woman shrank too. Instead, she threw herself upon the thought, the bliss, that he was there again beside her, restored, rescued from the gulf, if gulf there had been.

He went back to the subject of Louie, and told her as much as a girl of Dora's kind could be told of what he himself knew of Louie's husband. In the course of his two days' search for them, which had included an interview with Madame Cervin, he had become tolerably well acquainted with Montjoie's public character and career. Incidentally parts of the story of Louie's behaviour came in, and for one who knew her as Dora did, her madness and wilfulness emerged, could be guessed at, little as the brother intended to excuse himself thereby. How, indeed, should he excuse himself? Louie's character was a fixed quantity to be reckoned on by all who had dealings with her. One might as well excuse oneself for letting a lunatic escape by the pretext of his lunacy. Dora perfectly understood his tone. Yet in her heart of hearts she forgave him—for she knew not what!—became his champion. There was a dry sharpness of self-judgment, a settled conviction of coming ill in all he said which wrung her heart. And how blanched he was by that unknown misery! How should she not pity, not forgive? It was the impotence of her own feeling to express itself that swelled her throat. And poor Lucy, too—ah! poor Lucy.

Suddenly, as he was speaking, he noticed his companion more closely, the shabbiness of the little black hat and jacket, the new lines round the eyes and mouth.

'*You* have not been well,' he said abruptly.' How has your father been going on?'

She started and tried to answer quietly. But her nerves had been shaken by their talk, and by that inward play of emotion which had gone on out of his sight. Quite unexpectedly she broke down, and covering her eyes with one hand, began to sob gently.

'I can't do anything with him now, poor father,' she said, when she could control herself. 'He won't listen to me at all. The debts are beginning to be dreadful, and the business is going down fast. I don't know what we shall do. And it all makes him worse—drives him to drink.'

David thought a minute, lifted out of himself for the first time.

'Shall I come to-night to see him?'

'Oh do!' she said eagerly; 'come about nine o'clock. I will tell him—perhaps that will keep him in.'

Then she went into more details than she had yet done; named the creditors who were pressing; told how her church-work, though she worked herself blind night and day, could do but little for them; how both the restaurant and the reading-room were emptying, and she could now get no servants to stay, but Sarah, because of her father's temper.

It seemed to him as he listened that the story, with its sickened hope and on-coming fate, was all in some strange way familiar; it or something like it was to have been expected; for him the strange and jarring thing now would have been to find a happy person. He was in that young morbid state when the mind hangs its own cloud over the universe.

But Dora got up to go, tying on her veil with shaking hands. She was so humbly grateful to him that he was sorry for her—that he could spare a thought from his own griefs for her.

As they went down the dark stairs together, he asked after Lucy. She was now staying with some relations at Wakely, a cotton town in the valley of the Irwell, Dora said; but she would probably go back to Hastings for the winter. It was now settled that she and her father could not get on; and the stepmother that was to be—Purcell, however, was taking his time—as determined not to be bothered with her.

David listened with a certain discomfort. 'It was what she did for me,' he thought, 'that set him against her for good and all. Old brute!'

Aloud he said: 'I wrote to her, you know, and sent her that book. She did write me a queer letter back—it was all dashes and splashes—about the street-preachings on the beach, and a blind man who sang hymns. I can't remember why she hated him so particularly!'

She answered his faint smile. Lucy was a child for both of them. Then he took her to the door of the Parlour, noticing, as he parted from her, how dingy and neglected the place looked.

Afterwards—directly he had left her—the weight of his pain which had been lightened for an hour descended upon him again, shutting the doors of the senses, leaving him alone within, face to face with the little figure which haunted him day and night. During the days since his return from Paris the faculty of projective imagination, which had endowed his childhood with a second world, and peopled it with the incidents and creatures of his books, had grown to an abnormal strength. Behind the stage on which he was now painfully gathering together the fragments of his old life, it created for him another, where, amid scenes richly set and lit with perpetual summer, he lived with Elise, walked with her, watched her, lay at her feet, quarrelled with her, forgave her. His drama did not depend on memory alone, or rather it was memory passing into creation. Within its bounds he was himself and not himself; his part was loftier than any he had ever played in reality; his eloquence was no longer tongue-tied—it flowed and penetrated. His love might be cruel, but he was on her level, nay, her master; he could reproach, wrestle with, command her; and at the end evoke the pardoning flight into each other's arms—confession—rapture.

Till suddenly, poor fool! a little bolt shot from the bow of memory— the image of a *diligence* rattling along a white road—or of black rain-beaten quays, with their lines of wavering lamps—or of a hideous upper room with blue rep furniture where one could neither move nor breathe—would strike his dream to fragments, and as it fell to ruins within him, his whole being would become one tumult of inarticulate cries—delirium—anguish—with which the self at the heart of all seemed to be wrestling for life.

It was so to-day after he left Dora. First the vision, the enchantment—then the agony, the sob of desolation which could hardly be kept down. He saw nothing in the streets. He walked on past the Exchange, where an unusual crowd was gathered, elbowing his way through it mechanically, but not in truth knowing that it was there.

When he reached the shop he ran past John, who was reading a newspaper, up to his room and locked the door.

About an hour afterwards Mr. Ancrum came in, all excitement, a batch of papers under his arm.

'It is going to be war, John! *War*—I tell you! and such a war. They'll be beaten, those braggarts, if there's justice in heaven. The streets are all full; I could hardly get here; everybody talking of how it will affect Manchester. Time enough to think about that! What a set of selfish beasts we all are! Where's David?'

'Come in an hour ago!' said John sullenly; 'he went upstairs.'

'Ah, he will have heard—the placards are all over the place.'

The minister went upstairs and knocked at David's door.

'David!'

'All right,' said a voice from inside.

'David, what do you think of the news?'

'What news?' after a pause.

'Why, the war, man! Haven't you seen the evening paper?'

No answer. The minister stood listening at the door. Then a tender look dawned in his odd grey face.

'David, look here, I'll push you the paper under the door. You're tired, I suppose—done yourself up with your walk?'

'I'll be down to supper,' said the voice from inside, shortly. 'Will you push in the paper?'

The minister descended, and sat by himself in the kitchen thinking. He was a wiser man now than when he had gone out, and not only as to that reply of the King of Prussia to the French ultimatum on the subject of the Hohenzollern candidature.

For he had met Barbier in the street. How to keep the voluble Frenchman from bombarding David in his shattered state had been one of Mr. Ancrum's most anxious occupations since his return. It had been done, but it had been difficult. For to whom did David owe his first reports of Paris if not to the old comrade who had sent him there, found him a lodging, and taught him to speak French so as not to disgrace himself and his country? However, Ancrum had found means to intercept Barbier's first visit, and had checkmated his attempts ever since. As a natural result, Barbier was extremely irritable. Illness—stuff! The lad had been getting into scrapes—that he would swear.

On this occasion, when Ancrum stumbled across him, he found Barbier, at first bubbling over with the war news; torn different ways; now abusing the Emperor for a cochon and a *fou*, prophesying unlimited disaster for France, and sneering at the ranting crowds on the boulevards; the next moment spouting the same anti-Prussian madness with which his whole unfortunate country was at the moment infected. In the midst of his gallop of talk, however, the old man suddenly stopped, took off his hat, and running one excited hand through his bristling tufts of grey hair pointed to Ancrum with the other.

'*Halte là!*' he said, 'I know what your young rascal has been after. I know, and I'll be bound you don't. Trust a lover for hoodwinking a priest. Come along here.'

And putting his arm through Ancrum's, he swept him away, repeating, as they walked, the substance of a letter from his precious nephew, in which the Barbizon episode as it appeared to the inhabitants of No. 7 Rue Chantal and to the students of Taranne's *atelier de femmes* was related, with every embellishment of witticism and *blague* that the imagination of a French *rapin* could suggest. Mademoiselle Delaunay was not yet restored, according to the writer, to the *atelier* which she adorned. '*On criait au scandale,*' mainly because she was such a clever little animal, and the others envied and hated her. She had removed to a studio near the Luxembourg, and Taranne was said to be teaching her privately. Meanwhile Dubois requested his dear uncle to supply him with information as to *l'autre*; it would be gratefully received by an appreciative circle. As for *la sœur de l'autre*, the dear uncle no doubt knew that she had migrated to the studio of Monsieur Montjoie, an artist whose little affairs in the *genre* had already, before her advent, attained a high degree of interest and variety. On a review of all the circumstances, the dear uncle would perhaps pardon the writer if he were less disposed than before to accept those estimable views of the superiority of the English *morale* to the French, which had been so ably impressed upon him during his visit to Manchester.

For after a very short stay at Brussels the nephew had boldly and suddenly pushed over to England, and had spent a fortnight in Barbier's lodgings reconnoitering his uncle. As to the uncle, Xavier had struck him, on closer inspection, as one of the most dissolute young reprobates he had ever beheld. He had preached to him like a father, holding up to him the image of his own absent favourite, David Grieve, as a brilliant illustration of what could be achieved even in this wicked world by morals and capacity. And in the intervals he had supplied the creature with money and amused himself with his *gaminerie* from morning till night. On their parting the uncle had with great frankness confessed to the nephew the general opinion he had formed of his character; all the same they were now embarked on a tolerably frequent correspondence; and Dubois' ultimate chance of obtaining his uncle's savings, on the *chasse* of which he had come to England, would have seemed to the cool observer by no means small.

'But now, look here,' said Barbier, taking off his spectacles to wipe away the 'merry tear' which dimmed them, after the recapitulation of Xavier's last letter, 'no more nonsense! I come and have it out with that young man. I sent him to Paris, and I'll know what he did there. *He's* not made of burnt sugar. Of course he's broken his heart—we all do. Serve him right.'

'It's easy to laugh,' said Ancrum dryly, 'only these young fellows have sometimes an uncomfortable way of vindicating their dignity by shooting themselves.'

Barbier started and looked interrogative.

'Now suppose you listen to me,' said the minister.

And the two men resumed their patrol of Albert Square while Ancrum described his rescue of David. The story was simply told but impressive. Barbier whistled, stared, and surrendered. Nay, he went to the other extreme. He loved the absurd, but he loved the romantic more. An hour before, David's adventures had been to him a subject of comic opera. As Ancrum talked, they took on 'the grand style,' and at the end he could no more have taken liberties with his old pupil than with the hero of the *Nuit de Mai*. He became excited, sympathetic, declamatory, tore open old sores, and Mr. Ancrum had great difficulty in getting rid of him.

So now the minister was sitting at home meditating. Through the atmosphere of mockery with which Dubois had invested the story he saw the outlines of it with some clearness.

CHAPTER XIII

In the midst of his meditations, however, the minister did not forget to send John out for David's supper, and when David appeared, white, haggard, and exhausted, it was to find himself thought for with a care like a woman's. The lad, being sick and irritable, showed more resentment than gratitude; pushed away his food, looking sombrely the while at the dry bread and tea which formed the minister's invariable evening meal as though to ask when he was to be allowed his rational freedom again to eat or fast as he pleased. He scarcely answered Ancrum's remarks about the war, and finally he got up heavily, saying he was going out.

'You ought to be in your bed,' said Ancrum, protesting almost for the first time, 'and it's there you will be—tied by the leg—if you don't take a decent care of yourself.'

David took no notice and went. He dragged himself to the German Athenaeum, of which he had become a member in the first flush of his inheritance. There were the telegrams from Paris, and an eager crowd reading and discussing them. As he pushed his way in at last and read, the whole scene rose before him as though he were there—the summer boulevards with their trees and kiosks, the moving crowds, the shouts, the 'Marseillaise'—the blind infectious madness of it all. And one short fortnight ago, what man in Europe could have guessed that such a day was already on the knees of the gods?

Afterwards, on the way to the Parlour, he talked to Elise about it, — placing her on the boulevards with the rest, and himself beside her to guard her from the throng. Hour by hour, this morbid gift of his, though it tortured him, provided an outlet for passion, saved him from numbness and despair.

When he got to Dora's sitting-room he found Daddy sitting there, smoking sombrely over the empty grate. He had expected a flood of questions, and had steeled himself to meet them. Nothing of the sort. The old man took very little notice of him and his travels. Considering the petulant advice with which Daddy had sent him off, David was astonished and, in the end, piqued. He recovered the tongue which he had lost for Ancrum, and was presently discussing the war like anybody else. Reminiscences of the talk amid which he had lived during those Paris weeks came back to them; and he repeated some of them which bore on the present action of Napoleon III and his ministry, with a touch of returning fluency. He was, in fact, playing for Daddy's attention.

Daddy watched him silently with a wild and furtive eye. At last, looking round to see whether Dora was there, and finding that she had gone out, he laid a lean long hand on David's knee.

'That'll do, Davy. Davy, why were you all that time away?'

The young man drew himself up suddenly, brought back to realities from this first brief moment of something like forgetfulness. He tried for his common excuse of illness; but it stuck in his throat.

'I can't tell you, Daddy,' he said at last, slowly. 'I might tell you lies, but I won't. It concerns myself alone.'

Daddy still bent forward, his peaked wizard's face peering at his companion.

'You've been in trouble, Davy?'

'Yes, Daddy. But if you ask me questions I shall go.'

He spoke with a sudden fierce resolution.

Daddy paid no attention. He threw himself back in his chair with a long breath.

'Bedad, and I knew it, Davy! But sorrow a bit o' pity will you get out o' me, my boy—sorrow a bit!'

He lay staring at his companion with a glittering hostile look.

'By the powers!' he said presently, 'to be a gossoon of twenty again and throubled about a woman!'

David sprang up.

'Well, Daddy, I'll bid you good night! I wanted to hear something about your own affairs, which don't seem to be flourishing. But I'll wait till Miss Dora's at home.'

'Sit down, sit down again!' cried Lomax angrily, catching him by the arm. 'I'll not meddle with you. Yes, we're in a bad way, a deuced bad way, if you listen to Dora. If it weren't for her I'd have walked myself off long ago and let the devil take the creditors.'

David sat down and tried to get at the truth. But Daddy turned restive, and now invited the traveller's talk he had before repelled. He fell into his own recollections of the Paris streets in '48, and his vanity enjoyed showing this slip of a fellow that old Lomax was well acquainted with France and French politics before he was born.

Presently Dora came in, saw that her father had been beguiled into foregoing his usual nocturnal amusements, and looked soft gratitude at David. But as for him, he had never realised so vividly the queer aloofness and slipperiness of Daddy's nature, nor the miserable insecurity of Dora's life. Such men were not meant to have women depending on them.

He went downstairs pondering what could be done for the old vagabond. Drink had indeed made ravages since he had seen him last. For Dora's sake the young man recalled with eagerness some statements and suggestions in a French treatise on 'L'Alcoolisme' he chanced to have been turning over among his foreign scientific stock. Dora, no doubt, had invoked the parson; he would endeavour to bring in the doctor. And there was a young one, a frequenter of the stall in Birmingham Street, not as yet overburdened with practice, who occurred to him as clever and likely to help.

Nor did he forget his purpose. The very next morning he got hold of the young man in question. Out came the French book, which contained the record of a famous Frenchman's experiments, and the two hung over it together in David's little back room, till the doctor's views of booksellers and their probable minds were somewhat enlarged, and David felt something of the old intellectual glow which these scientific problems of mind and matter had awakened in him during the winter. Then he walked his physician off to Daddy during the dinner hour and boldly introduced him as a friend. The young doctor, having been forewarned, treated the situation admirably, took up a jaunty and jesting tone, and, finally, putting morals entirely aside, invited Daddy to consider himself as a scientific case, and deal with himself as such for the benefit of knowledge.

Daddy was feeling ill and depressed; David struck him as an 'impudent varmint,' and the doctor as little better; but the lad's solicitude nevertheless flattered the old featherbrain, and in the end he fell into a burst of grandiloquent and self-excusing confidence. The doctor played him; prescribed; and when he and David left together it really seemed as though the old man from sheer curiosity about and interest in his own symptoms would probably make an attempt to follow the advice given him.

Dora came in while the three were still joking and discussing. Her face clouded as she listened, and when David and the doctor left she gave them a cool and shrinking good bye which puzzled David.

Daddy, however, after a little while, mended considerably, developed an enthusiasm for his self-appointed doctor, and, what was still better, a strong excitement about his own affairs. When it came to the stage of a loan for the meeting of the more pressing liabilities, of fresh and ingenious efforts to attract customers, and of a certain gleam of returning prosperity,

David's concern for his old friend very much dropped again. His former vivid interest in the human scene and the actors in it, as such, was not yet recovered; in these weeks weariness and lassitude overtook each reviving impulse and faculty in turn.

He was becoming more and more absorbed, too, by the news from France. Its first effect upon him was one of irritable repulsion. Barbier and Hugo had taught him to loathe the Empire; and had not he and she read *Les Chatiments* together, and mocked the Emperor's carriage as it passed them in the streets? The French telegrams in the English papers, with their accounts of the vapouring populace, the wild rhetoric in the Chamber, and the general outburst of *fanfaronnade*, seemed to make the French nation one with the Empire in its worst aspects, and, as we can all remember, set English teeth on edge. David devoured the papers day by day, and his antagonism grew, partly because, in spite of that strong gravitation of his mind towards things expansive, emotional, and rhetorical, the essential paste of him was not French but English—but mostly because of other and stronger reasons of which he was hardly conscious. During that fortnight of his agony in Paris all that sympathetic bond between the great city and himself which had been the source of so much pleasure and excitement to him during his early days with Elise had broken down. The glamour of happiness torn away, he had seen, beneath the Paris of his dream, a greedy brutal Paris from which his sick senses shrank in fear and loathing. The grace, the spell, was gone— he was alone and miserable!—and amid the gaiety, the materialism, the selfish vice of the place he had moved for days, an alien and an enemy, the love within him turning to hate.

So now his mortal pain revenged itself. They would be beaten—this depraved and enervated people!—and his feverish heart rejoiced. But Elise? His lips quivered. What did the war matter to her except so far as its inconveniences were concerned? What had *la patrie* any more than *l'amour* to do with art? He put the question to her in his wild evening walks. It angered him that as the weeks swept on, and the great thunderbolts began to fall—Wissembourg, Forbach, Worth—his imagination would sometimes show her to him agitated and in tears. No pity for him! why this sorrow for France? Absurd! let her go paint while the world loved and fought. In '48, while monarchy and republic were wrestling it out in the streets of Paris, was not the landscape painter Chintreuil quietly sketching all the time just outside one of the gates of the city? There was the artist for you.

Meanwhile the growing excitement of the war, heightened and poisoned by this reaction of his personality, combined with his painful efforts to recover his business to make him for a time more pale and gaunt than ever. Ancrum remonstrated in vain. He would go his way.

One evening—it was the day after Worth—he was striding blindly up the Oxford Road when he ran against a man at the corner of a side street. It was Barbier, coming out for the last news.

Barbier started, swore, caught him by the arm, then fell back in amazement.

'*C'est toi? bon Dieu!*'

David, who had hitherto avoided his old companion with the utmost ingenuity, began hurriedly to inquire whether he was going to look at the evening's telegram.

'Yes—no—what matter? You can tell me. David, my lad, Ancrum told me you had been ill, but—'

The old man slipped his arm through that of the youth and looked at him fixedly. His own face was all furrowed and drawn, the eyes red.

'*Oui; tu es change,*' he said at last with a sudden quivering breath, almost a sob, 'like everything,—like the world!'

And hanging down his head he drew the lad on, down the little street, towards his lodging.

'Come in! I'll ask no questions. Oh, come in! I have the French papers; for three hours I have been reading them alone. Come in or I shall go mad!'

And they discussed the war, the political prospect, and Barbier's French letters till nearly midnight. All the exile's nationality had revived, and so lost was he in weeping over France he had scarcely breath left wherewith to curse the Empire. In the presence of a grief so true, so poignant, wherein all the man's little tricks and absurdities had for the moment melted out of sight, David's own seared and bitter feeling could find no voice. He said not a word that could jar on his old friend. And Barbier, like a child, took his sympathy for granted and abused the 'heartless hypocritical' English press to him with a will.

The days rushed on. David read the English papers in town, then walked up late to Barbier's lodgings to read a French batch and talk. Gravelotte was over, the siege was approaching. In that strange inner life of his, David with Elise beside him looked on at the crashing trees in the Bois de Boulogne, at the long lines of carts laden with household stuff and fugitives from the *zone militaire* flocking into Paris, at the soldiers and horses camping in the Tuileries Gardens, at the distant smoke-clouds amid the woods of Issy and Meudon, as village after village flamed to ruins.

One night—it was a day or two after Sedan—in a corner of the Constitutionnel, he found a little paragraph:—

'M. Henri Regnault and M. Clairin, leaving their studio at Tangiers to the care of the French Consul, have returned to Paris to offer themselves for military service, from which, as holder of the *prix de Rome*, M. Regnault is legally exempt. To praise such an act would be to insult its authors. France— our bleeding France! —does but take stern note that her sons are faithful.'

David threw the paper down, made an excuse to Barbier, and went out. He could not talk to Barbier, to whom everything must be explained from the beginning, and his heart was full. He wandered out towards Fallowfield under a moon which gave beauty and magic even to these low, begrimed streets, these jarring, incongruous buildings, thinking of Regnault and that unforgotten night beside the Seine. The young artist's passage through the Louvre, the towering of his great head above the crowd in the 'Trois Rats,' and that outburst under the moonlight—everything, every tone, every detail, returned upon him.

'*The great France—the undying France—*'

And now for France—ah!—David divined the eagerness, the passion, with which it had been done. He was nearer to the artist than he had been two months before—nearer to all great and tragic things. His recognition of the fact had in it the start of a strange joy.

So moved was he, and in such complex ways, that as he thought of Regnault with that realising imagination which was his gift, the whole set of his feeling towards France and the war wavered and changed. The animosity, the drop of personal gall in his heart, disappeared, conjured by Regnault's look, by Regnault's act. The one heroic figure he had seen in France began now to stand to him for the nation. He walked home doing penance in his heart, passionately renewing the old love, the old homage, in this awful presence of a stricken people at bay.

And Elise came to him, in the moonlight, leaning upon him, with soft, approving eyes—

Ah! where was she—where—in this whirlwind of the national fate? where was her frail life hidden? was she still in this Paris, so soon to be 'begirt with armies'?

Four days later Barbier sent a note to Ancrum: 'Come and see me this afternoon at six o'clock. Say nothing to Grieve.'

A couple of hours afterwards Ancrum came slowly home to Birmingham Street, where he was still lodging. David had just put up the shop-shutters, John had departed, and his employer was about to retire to supper and his books in the back kitchen.

Ancrum went in and stood with his back to the fire which John had just made for the kettle and the minister's tea, when David came in with an armful of books and shut the door behind him. Ancrum let him put down his cargo, and then walked up to him.

'David,' he said, laying his hand with a timid gesture on the other's shoulder, 'Barbier has had some letters from Paris to-day—the last he will get probably—and among them a letter from his nephew.'

David started, turned sharp round, shaking off the hand.

'It contains some news which Barbier thinks you ought to know. Mademoiselle Elise Delaunay has married suddenly—married her cousin, Mr. Pimodan, a young doctor.'

The shock blanched every atom of colour from David's face. He tried wildly to control himself, to brave it out with a desperate 'Why not?' But speech failed him. He walked over to the mantelpiece and leant against it. The room swam with him, and the only impression of which for a moment or two he was conscious was that of the cheerful singing of the kettle.

'She would not leave Paris,' said Ancrum in a low voice, standing beside him. 'People tried to persuade her—nothing would induce her. Then this young man, who is said to have been in love with her for years, urged her to marry him—to accept his protection really, in view of all that might come. Dubois thinks she refused several times, but anyway two days ago they were married, civilly, with only the legal witnesses.'

David moved about the various things on the mantelpiece with restless fingers. Then he straightened himself.

'Is that all?' he asked, looking at the minister.

'All,' said Ancrum, who had, of course, no intention of repeating any of Dubois' playful embroideries on the facts. 'You will be glad, won't you, that she should have some one to protect her in such a strait?'—he added, after a minute's pause, his eyes on the fire.

'Yes,' said the other after a moment. 'Thank you. Won't you have your tea?'

Mr. Ancrum swallowed his emotion, and they sat down to table in silence. David played with some food, took one thing up after another, laid it down, and at last sprang up and seized his hat.

'Going out again?' asked the minister, trembling, he knew not why.

The lad muttered something. Instinctively the little lame fellow, who was closest to the door, rushed to it and threw himself against it.

'David, don't—don't go out alone—let me go with you!'

'I want to go out alone,' said David, his lips shaking. 'Why do you interfere with me?'

'Because—' and the short figure drew itself up, the minister's voice took a stern deep note, 'because when a man has once contemplated the sin of self-murder, those about him have no right to behave as though he were still like other innocent and happy people!'

David stood silent a moment, every limb trembling. Then his mouth set, and he made a step forward, one arm raised.

'Oh, yes!' cried Ancrum, 'you may fling me out of the way. My weakness and deformity are no match for you. Do, if you have the heart! Do you think I don't know that I rescued you from despair—that I drew you out of the very jaws of death? Do you think I don't guess that the news I have just given you wither the heart in your breast? You imagine, I suppose, that because I am deformed and a Sunday-school teacher, because I think something of religion, and can't read your French books, I cannot enter into what a *man* is and feels. Try me! When you were a little boy in my class, *my* life was already crushed in me—my tragedy was over. I have come close to passion and to sin; I'm not afraid of yours! You are alive here to-night, David Grieve, because I went to look for you on the mountains—lost sheep that you were—and found you, by God's mercy. You never thanked me—I knew you couldn't. Instead of your thanks I demand your confidence, here—now. Break down this silence between us. Tell me what you have done to bring your life to this pass. You have no father—I speak in his place and I *deserve* that you should trust and listen to me!'

David looked at him with amazement—at the worn misshapen head thrown haughtily back—at the arms folded across the chest. Then his pride gave way, and that intolerable smart within could no longer hide itself. His soul melted within him; tears began to rain over his cheeks. He tottered to the fire and sat down, instinctively spreading his hands to the blaze, that word 'father' echoing in his ears; and by midnight Mr. Ancrum knew all the story, or as much of it as man could to tell to man.

From this night of confession and of storm there emerged at least one result—the beginnings of a true and profitable bond between David and Ancrum. Hitherto there had been expenditure of interest and affection on the minister's side, and a certain responsiveness and friendly susceptibility on David's; but no true understanding and contact, mind with mind. But in these agitated hours of such talk as belongs only to the rare crises of life, not only did Ancrum gain an insight into David's inmost nature, with all its rich, unripe store of feelings and powers, deeper than any he had possessed before, but David, breaking through the crusts of association, getting beyond and beneath the Sunday-school teacher and minister, came for the first time upon the real man in his friend, apart from trappings—cast off the old sense of pupilage, and found a brother instead of a monitor.

There came a moment when Ancrum, laying his hand on David's knee, told his own story in a few bare sentences, each of them, as it were, lightning on a dark background, revealing some few things with a ghastly plainness, only to let silence and mystery close again upon the whole. And there came another moment when the little minister, carried out of himself, fell into incoherent sentences, full of obscurity, yet often full of beauty, in which for the first time David came near to the living voice of religion speaking in its purest, intensest note. Christ was the burden of it all; the religion of pain, sacrifice, immortality; the religion of chastity and self-repression.

'Life goes from test to test, David; it's like any other business—the more you know the more's put on you. And this test of the man with the woman— there's no other cuts so deep. Aye, it parts the sheep from the goats. A man's failed in it—lost his footing—rolled into hell, before he knows where he is. "On this stone if a man fall"—I often put those words to it—there's all meanings in Scripture. Yes, you've stumbled, David—stumbled badly, but not more. There's mercy in it! You must rise again—you can. Accept yourself; accept the sin even; bear with yourself and go forward. That's what the Church says. Nothing can be undone, but break your pride, do penance, and all can be forgiven.

'But you don't admit the sin? A man has a right to the satisfaction of his own instincts. You asked a free consent and got it. What is law but a convention for miserable people who don't know how to love? Who was injured?

'David, that's the question of a fool. Were you and she the first man and woman in the world that ever loved? That's always the way; each man imagines the matter is still for his deciding, and he can no more decide it than he can tamper with the fact that fire burns or water drowns. All these centuries the human animal has fought with the human soul. And step by step the soul has registered her victories. She has won them only by feeling for the law and finding it—uncovering, bringing into light, the firm rocks beneath her feet. And on these rocks she rears her landmarks—marriage, the family, the State, the Church. Neglect them, and you sink into the quagmire from which the soul of the race has been for generations struggling to save you. Dispute them! overthrow them—yes, if you can! You have about as much chance with them as you have with the other facts and laws amid which you live—physical or chemical or biological.

'I speak after the manner of men. If I were to speak after the manner of a Christian, I should say other things. I should ask how a man *dare* pluck from the Lord's hand, for his own wild and reckless use, a soul and body for which He died; how he, the Lord's bondsman, *dare* steal his joy, carrying it off by himself into the wilderness, like an animal his prey, instead of asking it at the hands, and under the blessing, of his Master; how he *dare*—a man under orders, and member of the Lord's body—forget the whole in his greed for the one—eternity in his thirst for the present.'

'But no matter. Christ is nothing to you, nor Scripture, nor the Church—'

The minister broke off abruptly, his lined face working with emotion and prayer. David said nothing. In this stage of the conversation—the stage, as it were, of judgment and estimate—he could take no part. The time for it with him had not yet come. He had exhausted all his force in the attempt to explain himself—an attempt which began in fragmentary question and answer, and ended on his part in the rush of a confidence, an 'Apologia,' representing, in truth, that first reflex action of the mind upon experience, whence healing and spiritual growth were ultimately to issue. But for the moment he could carry the process no farther. He sat crouched over the flickering fire, saying nothing, letting Ancrum soliloquise as he pleased. His mind surged to and fro, indeed, as Ancrum talked between the poles of repulsion and response. His nature was not as Ancrum's, and every now and then the quick critical intellect flashed through his misery, detecting an assumption, probing an hypothesis. But in general his *feeling* gave way more and more. That moral sensitiveness in him which in its special nature was a special inheritance, the outcome of a long individualist development under the conditions of English Protestantism, made him from the first the natural prey of Ancrum's spiritual passion. As soon as a true contact between them was set up, David began to feel the religious temper and life in Ancrum draw him like a magnet. Not the forms of the thing, but the thing itself. In it, or something like it, as he listened, his heart suspected, for the first time, the only possible refuge from the agony of passion, the only possible escape from this fever of desire, jealousy, and love, in which he was consumed.

At the end he let Ancrum lead him up to bed and give him the bromide the Paris doctor had prescribed. When Ancrum softly put his head in, half an hour later, he was heavily asleep. Ancrum's face gleamed; he stole into the room carrying a rug and a pillow; and when David woke in the morning it was to see the twisted form of the little minister stretched still and soldierlike beside him on the floor.

CHAPTER XIV

From that waking David rose and went about his work another man. As he moved about in the shop or in the streets, he was conscious of a gulf between his present self and his self of yesterday, which he could hardly explain. Simply the whole atmosphere and temperature of the soul was other, was different. He could have almost supposed that some process had gone on within him during the unconsciousness of sleep, of which he was now feeling the results; which had carried him on, without his knowing it, to a point in the highroad of life, far removed from that point where he had stood when his talk with Ancrum began. That world of enervating illusion, that 'kind of ghastly dreaminess, 'as John Sterling called it, in which since his return he had lived with Elise, was gone, he knew not how—swept away like a cloud from the brain, a mist from the eyes. The sense of catastrophe, of things irrevocable and irreparable, the premature ageing of the whole man, remained-only the fever and the restlessness were past. Memory, indeed, was not affected. In some sort the scenes of his French experience would be throughout his life a permanent element in consciousness; but the persons concerned in them were dead-creatures of the past. He himself had been painfully re-born, and Pimodan's wife had no present personal existence for him. He turned himself deliberately to his old life, and took up the interests of it again one by one, but, as he soon discovered, with an insight, a power, a comprehension which had never yet been his. A moral and spiritual life destined to a rich development practically began for him with this winter— this awful winter of the agony of France.

His thoughts were often occupied now with Louie, but in a saner way. He could no longer, without morbidness, take on himself the whole responsibility of her miserable marriage. Human beings after all are what they make themselves. But the sense of his own share in it, and the perception of what her future life was likely to be, made him steadily accept beforehand the claims upon him which she was sure to press.

He had written to her early in September, when the siege was imminent, offering her money to bring her to England, and the protection of his roof during the rest of the war. And by a still later post than that which brought the news of Elise's marriage arrived a scrawl from Louie, written from a country town near Toulouse, whither she and Montjoie had retreated—apparently the sculptor's native place.

The letter was full of complaints—complaints of the war, which was being mismanaged by a set of rogues and fools who deserved stringing to the nearest tree; complaints of her husband, who was a good-for-nothing brute; and complaints of her own health. She was expecting her confinement in the spring; if she got through it—which was not likely, considering the way in which she was treated—she should please herself about staying with such a man. *He* should not keep her for a day if she wanted to go. Meanwhile David might send her any money he could spare. There was not much of the six hundred left—*that* she could tell him; and she could not even screw enough for baby-clothes out of her husband. Very likely there would not be enough to pay for a nurse when her time came. Well, then she would be out of it—and a good job too.

She wished to be remembered to Dora; and Dora was especially to be told again that she needn't suppose St. Damian's was a patch on the real Catholic churches, because it wasn't. She—Louie—had been at the Midnight Mass in Toulouse Cathedral on Christmas Eve. That was something like. And down in the crypt they had a 'Bethlehem'—the sweetest thing you ever saw. There were the shepherds, and the wise men, and the angels—dolls, of course, but their dresses were splendid, and the little Jesus was dressed in white satin, embroidered with gold—*old* embroidery, tell Dora.

To this David had replied at once, sending money he could ill spare, and telling her to keep him informed of her whereabouts.

But the months passed on, and no more news arrived. He wrote again *via* Bordeaux, but with no result, and could only wait patiently till that eagle's grip, in which all French life was stifled, should be loosened.

Meanwhile his relation to another human being, whose life had been affected by the French episode, passed into a fresh phase. Two days after the news of Elise's marriage had reached him, he and John had just shut up the shop, and the young master was hanging over the counter under the gas, heavily conning a not very satisfactory business account.

John came in, took his hat and stick from a corner, and threw David a gruff 'good night.'

Something in the tone struck David's sore nerves like a blow. He turned abruptly—

'Look here, John! I can't stand this kind of thing much longer. Hadn't we better part? You've learnt a lot here, and I'll see you get a good place. You—you rub it in too long!'

John stood still, his big rough hands beginning to shake, his pink cheeks turning a painful crimson.

'You—you never said a word to me!' he flung out at last, incoherently, resentfully.

'Said a word to you? What do you mean? I told you the truth, and I would have told you more, if you hadn't turned against me as though I had been the devil himself. Do you suppose you are the only person who came to grief because of that French time? *Good God!*'

The last words came out with a low exasperation. The young man leant against the counter, looking at his assistant with bitter, indignant eyes.

John first shrank from them, then his own were drawn to meet them. Even his slow perceptions, thus challenged, realised something of the truth. He gave way—as David might have made him give way long before, if his own misery had not made him painfully avoid any fresh shock of speech.

'Well!' said John, slowly, with a mighty effort; 'I'll not lay it agen you any more. I'll say that. But if you want to get rid of me, you can. Only you'll be put to 't wi' t' printing.'

The two young fellows surveyed each other. Then suddenly David said, pushing him to the door:

'You're a great ass, John—get out, and good night to you.'

But next day the atmosphere was cleared, and, with inexpressible relief on both sides, the two fell back into the old brotherly relation. Poor John! He kept an old photograph of Louie in a drawer at his lodging, and, when he came home to bed, would alternately weep over and denounce it. But, all the same, his interest in David's printing ventures was growing keener and keener, and whenever business had been particularly exciting during the day, the performance with the photograph was curtailed or omitted at night. Let no scorn, however, be thought, on that account, of the true passion!—which had thriven on unkindness, and did but yield to the slow mastery of time.

The war thundered on. To Manchester, and to the cotton and silk industries of Lancashire generally, the tragedy of France meant on the whole a vast boom in trade. So many French rivals crippled—so much ground set free for English enterprise to capture—and, meanwhile, high profits for a certain number at least of Manchester and Macclesfield merchants, and brisk wages for the Lancashire operatives, especially for the silk-weavers. This, with of course certain drawbacks and exceptions, was the aspect under which the war mainly presented itself to Lancashire. Meanwhile, amid these teeming Manchester streets with their clattering lurries and overflowing warehouses, there was at least one Englishman who took the war hardly, in whom the spectacle of its wreck and struggle roused a feeling which was all moral, human, disinterested.

What was Regnault doing? David kept a watch on the newspapers, of which the Free Library offered him an ample store; but there was no mention of him in the English press that he could discover, and Barbier, of course, got nothing now from Paris.

Christmas was over. The last month of the siege, that hideous January of frost and fire, rushed past, with its alternations of famine within and futile battle without—Europe looking on appalled at this starved and shivering Paris, into which the shells were raining. At last—the 27th!—the capitulation! All was over; the German was master in Europe, and France lay at the feet of her conqueror.

Out to all parts streamed the letters which had been so long delayed. Barbier and David, walking together one bitter evening towards Barbier's lodgings, silent, with hanging heads, met the postman on Barbier's steps, who held out a packet. The Frenchman took it with a cry; the two rushed upstairs and fell upon the letters and papers it contained.

There—while Barbier sat beside him, groaning over the conditions of peace, over the enthronement of the Emperor-King at Versailles, within sight of the statue of Louis Quatorze, now cursing '*ces imbéciles du gouvernement!*' and now wiping the tears from his old cheeks with a trembling hand—David read the news of the fight of Buzenval, and the death of Regnault.

It seemed to him that he had always foreseen it—that from the very beginning Regnault's image in his thought had been haloed with a light of tragedy and storm—a light of death. His eyes devoured the long memorial article in which a friend of Regnault's had given the details of his last months of life. Barbier, absorbed in his own grief, heard not a sound from the corner where his companion sat crouched beneath the gas.

Everything—the death and the manner of it—was to him, as it were, in the natural order—fitting, right, such as might have been expected. His heart swelled to bursting as he read, but his eyes were dry.

This, briefly, was the story which he read.

Henri Regnault re-entered Paris at the beginning of September. By the beginning of October he was on active service, stationed now at Asnieres, now at Colombes. In October or November he became engaged to a young girl, with whom he had been for long devotedly in love—ah! David thought of that sudden smile—the 'open door'! Their passion, cherished under the wings of war, did but give courage and heroism to both. Yet he loved most humanly! One night, in an interval of duty, on leaving the house where his *fiancee* lived, he found the shells of the bombardment falling fast in the street outside. He could not make up his mind to go—might not ruin befall the dear house with its inmates at any moment? So he wandered up and down outside for hours in the bitter night, watching, amid the rattle of the shells and the terrified cries of women and children from the houses on either side. At last, worn out and frozen with cold, but still unable to leave the spot, he knocked softly at the door he had left. The *concierge* came. 'Let me lie down awhile on your floor. Tell no one.' Then, appeased by this regained nearness to her, and by the sense that no danger could strike the one without warning the other, he wrapped himself in his soldier's cloak and fell asleep.

In November he painted his last three water-colours—visions of the East, painted for her, and as flower-bright as possible, 'because flowers were scarce' in the doomed city.

December came. Regnault spent Christmas night at the advanced post of Colombes. His captain wished to make him an officer. 'Thanks, my captain,' said the young fellow of twenty-three; 'but if you have a good soldier in me, why exchange him for an indifferent officer? My example will be of more use to you than my commission.' Meanwhile the days and nights were passed in Arctic cold. Men were frozen to death round about him; his painter's hand was frostbitten. 'Oh! I can speak with authority on cold!' he wrote to his *fiancee*; 'this morning at least I know what it is to spend the night on the hard earth exposed to a glacial wind. Enough! *Je me rechaufferai a votre foyer.* I love you—I love my country—that sustains. Adieu!'

On the 17th, after a few days in Paris spent with her and some old friends, he was again ordered to the front. On Thursday the fight at Buzenval began with a brilliant success; in the middle of the day his *fiancee* still had news of him, brought by a servant. Night fell. The battle was hottest in a wood adjoining the park of Buzenval. Regnault and his painter-comrade Clairin were side by side. Suddenly the retreat was sounded, and the same instant Clairin missed his friend. He sought him with frenzy amid the trees in the darkening wood, called to him, peered into the faces of the dying— no answer! Ah! he must have been swept backwards by the rush of the retreat—Clairin will find him again.

Three days later the lost was found—one among two hundred corpses of National Guards carted into Pere Lachaise. Clairin, mad with grief, held his friend in his arms—held, kissed the beautiful head, now bruised and stained past even *her* knowing, with its bullet-wound in the temple.

On his breast was found a medal with a silver tear hanging from it. She who had long worn it as a symbol of bereavement, in memory of dear ones lost to her, had given it to him in her first joy. 'I will reclaim it,' she had said, smiling, 'the first time you make me weep!' It was all that was brought back to her—all except a scrawled paper found in his pocket, containing some hurried and almost illegible words, written perhaps beside his outpost fire.

'We have lost many men—we must remake them—*better*—*stronger*. The lesson should profit us. No more lingering amid facile pleasures! Who dare now live for himself alone? It has been for too long the custom with us to believe in nothing but enjoyment and all bad passions. We have prided ourselves on despising everything good and worthy. No more of such contempt!'

Then—so the story ended—four days later, on the very day of the capitulation of Paris, Regnault was carried to his last rest. A figure in widow's dress walked behind. And to many standing by, amid the muffled roll of the drums and the wailing of the music, it was as though France herself went down to burial with her son.

David got up gently and went across to Barbier, who was sitting with his letters and papers before him, staring and stupefied, the lower jaw falling, in a trance of grief.

The young man put down the newspaper he had been reading in front of the old man.

'Read that some time; it will give you something to be proud of. I told you I knew him—he was kind to me.'

Barbier nodded, not understanding, and sought for his spectacles with shaking fingers. David quietly went out.

He walked home in a state of exaltation like a man still environed with the emotion of great poetry or great music. He said very little about Regnault in the days that followed to Ancrum or Barbier, even to Dora, with whom every week his friendship was deepening. But the memory of the dead man, as it slowly shaped itself in his brooding mind, became with him a permanent and fruitful element of thought. Very likely the Regnault whom he revered, whose name was henceforth a sacred thing to him, was only part as it were of the real Regnault. He saw the French artist with an Englishman's eyes—interpreted him in English ways—the ways, moreover, of a consciousness self-taught and provincial, however gifted and flexible. Only one or two aspects, no doubt, of that rich, self-tormented nature, reared amid the most complex movements of European intelligence, were really plain to him. And those aspects were specially brought home to him by his own mental condition. No matter. Broadly, essentially, he understood.

But thenceforward, just as Elise Delaunay had stood to him in the beginning for French art and life, and that ferment in himself which answered to them, so now in her place stood Regnault with those stern words upon his young and dying lips—'We have lost many men—we must remake them—better! Henceforward let no one dare live unto himself.' The Englishman took them into his heart, that ethical fibre in him, which was at last roused and dominant, vibrating, responding. And as the poignant images of death and battle faded he saw his hero always as he had seen him last—young, radiant, vigorous, pointing to the dawn behind Notre-Dame.

All life looked differently to David this winter. He saw the Manchester streets and those who lived in them with other perceptions. His old political debating interests, indeed, were comparatively slack; but persons—men and women, and their stories—for these he was instinctively on the watch. His eye noticed the faces he passed as it had never yet done—divined in them suffering, or vice, or sickness. All that he saw at this moment he saw tragically. The doors set open about him were still, as Keats, himself hurried to his end by an experience of passion, once expressed it, 'all dark,' and leading to darkness. There were times when Dora's faith and Ancrum's mysticism drew him irresistibly; other times when they were almost as repulsive to him as they had ever been, because they sounded to him like the formula of people setting out to explain the world 'with a light heart,' as Ollivier had gone to war.

But whether or no it could be explained, this world, he could not now help putting out his hand to meddle with and mend it; his mind fed on its incidents and conditions. The mill-girls standing on the Ancoats pavements; the drunken lurryman tottering out from the public-house to his lurry under the biting sleet of February; the ragged barefoot boys and girls swarming and festering in the slums; the young men struggling all about him for subsistence and success—these for the first time became realities to him, entered into that pondering of 'whence and whither' to which he had been always destined, and whereon he was now consciously started.

And as the months went on, his attention was once more painfully caught and held by Dora's troubles and Daddy's infirmities. For Daddy's improvement was short-lived. A bad relapse came in November; things again went downhill fast; the loan contracted in the summer had to be met, and under the pressure of it Daddy only became more helpless and disreputable week by week. And now, when Doctor Mildmay went to see him, Daddy, crouching over the fire, pretended to be deaf, and 'soft' besides. Nothing could be got out of him except certain grim hints that his house was his own till he was turned out of it. 'Looks pretty bad this time,' said the doctor to David once as he came out discomfited. 'After all, there's not much hope when the craving returns on a man of his age, especially after some years' interval.'

Daddy would sometimes talk frankly enough to David. At such times his language took an exasperating Shakespearean turn. He was abominably fond of posing as Lear or Jaques—as a man much buffeted, and acquainted with all the ugly secrets of life. Purcell stood generally for 'the enemy;' and to Purcell his half-mad fancy attributed most of his misfortunes. It was Purcell who had undermined his business, taken away his character, and driven him back to drink. David did not believe much of it, and told him so. Then, roused to wrath, the young man would speak his mind plainly as to Dora's sufferings and Dora's future. But to very little purpose.

'Aye, you're right—you're right enough,' said the old man to him on one of these occasions, with a wild, sinister look. 'Cordelia'll hang for 't. If you want to do her any good, you must turn old Lear out—send him packing, back to the desert where he was before. There's elbow-room there!'

David looked up startled. The thin bronzed face had a restless flutter in it. Before he could reply Daddy had laid a hand on his shoulder.

'Davy, why don't you drink?'

'What do you mean?' said the young man, flushing.

'Davy, you've been as close as wax; but Daddy can see a thing or two when he chooses. Ah, you should drink, my lad. Let people prate—why shouldn't a man please himself? It's not the beastly liquor—that's the worst part of it—it's the *dreams,* my lad, "the dreams that come." They say ether does the business cheapest. A teaspoonful—and you can be alternately in Paradise and the gutter four times a day. But the fools here don't know how to mix it.'

As he spoke the door opened, and there stood Dora on the threshold. She had just come back from a Lenten service; her little worn prayer-book was in her hand. She stood trembling, looking at them both—at David's tight, indignant lips—at her father's excitement.

Daddy's eye fell on her prayer-book, and David, looking up, saw a quick cloud of distaste, aversion, pass over his weird face.

She put out some supper, and pressed David to stay. He did so in the vain hope of keeping Daddy at home. But the old vagrant was too clever for both of them. When David at last got up to go, Daddy accompanied him downstairs, and stood in the doorway looking up Market Place till David had disappeared in the darkness. Then with a soft and cunning hand he drew the door to behind him, and stood a moment lifting his face to the rack of moonlit cloud scudding across the top of the houses opposite. As he did so, he drew a long breath, with the gesture of one to whom the wild airs of that upper sky, the rush of its driving wind, were stimulus and delight. Then he put down his head and stole off to the right, towards the old White Inn in Hanging Ditch, while Dora was still listening in misery for his return step upon the stairs.

A week later Dora, not knowing how the restaurant could be kept going any longer, and foreseeing utter bankruptcy and ruin as soon as the shutters should be up, took her courage in both hands, swallowed all pride, and walked up to Half Street to beg help of Purcell. After all he was her mother's brother. In spite of that long feud between him and Daddy, he would surely, for his own credit's sake, help them to escape a public scandal. For all his rodomontade, Daddy had never done him any real harm that she could remember.

So she opened the shop door in Half Street, quaking at the sound of the bell she set in motion, and went in.

Twenty minutes afterwards she came out again, looking from side to side like a hunted creature, her veil drawn close over her face. She fled on through Market Place, across Market Street and St. Ann's Square, and through the tall dark warehouse streets beyond—drawn blindly towards Potter Street and her only friend.

David was putting out some books on the stall when he looked up and saw her. Perceiving that she was weeping and breathless, he asked her into the back room, while John kept guard in the shop.

There she leant against the mantelpiece, shaking from head to foot, and wiping away her tears. He soon gathered that she had been to Purcell, and that Purcell had dismissed her appeal with every circumstance of cold and brutal insult. The sooner her father was in the workhouse or the lunatic asylum, and she in some nunnery or other, the sooner each would be in their right place. He was a vagabond, and she a Papist—let them go where they belonged. He was not going to spend a farthing of his hard-earned money to help either of them to impose any further on the world. And then he let fall a word or two which showed her that he had probably been at the bottom of some merciless pressure lately applied to them by one or two of their chief creditors. The bookseller's hour was come, and he was looking on at the hewing of his Agag with the joy of the righteous. So might the Lord avenge him of all his enemies.

Dora could hardly give an account of it. The naked revelation of Purcell's hate, of so hard and vindictive a soul, had worked upon her like some physical horror. She had often suspected the truth, but now that it was past doubting, the moral shock was terrible to this tender mystical creature, whose heart by day and night lived a hidden life with the Crucified and with His saints. Oh, how could he, how could anyone, be so cruel? her father getting an old man! and she, who had never quarrelled with him—who had nursed Lucy! So she wailed, gradually recovering her poor shaken soul—calming it, indeed, all the while out of sight, with quick piteous words of prayer and submission.

David stood by, pale with rage and sympathy. But what could he do? He was himself in the midst of a hard struggle, and had neither money nor credit available. They parted at last, with the understanding that he was to go and consult Ancrum, and that she was to go to her friends at St. Damian's.

Till now poor Dora had carefully refrained from bringing her private woes into relation with her life in and through St. Damian's. Within that enchanted circle, she was another being with another existence. There she had never asked anything for herself, except the pardon and help of God, before His altar, and through His priests. Rather she had given—given all that she had—her time, such as she could spare from Daddy and her work, to the Sunday-school and the sick; her hard-won savings on her clothes, and on the extra work, for which she would often sit up night after night when Daddy believed her asleep, to the poor and to the services of the Church. There she had a position, almost an authority of her own—the authority which comes of self-spending. But now this innocent pride must be humbled. For the sake of her father, and of those to whom they owed money they could not pay, she must go and ask—beg instead of giving. All she wanted was time. Her embroidery work was now better paid than ever. If the restaurant were closed she could do more of it. In the end she believed she could pay everybody. But she must have time. Yes, she would go to Father Vernon that night! He would understand, even if he could not help her.

Alas! Next morning David was just going out to dinner, when a message was brought him from Market Place. He started off thither at a run, and found a white and gasping Dora wandering restlessly up and down the upper room; while Sarah, the old Lancashire cook, very red and very tearful, followed her about trying to administer consolation. Daddy had disappeared. After coming in about eleven the night before and going noisily to his room—no doubt for the purpose of deluding Dora—he must have stolen down again and made off without being either seen or heard by anybody. Even the policeman on duty in Market Place had noticed nothing. He had taken what was practically the only money left them in the world—about twenty pounds—from Dora's cashbox, and some clothes, packing these last in a knapsack which still remained to him from the foreign tramps of years before.

The efforts made by Dora, David, and Ancrum, whom David called in to help, to track the fugitive, were quite useless. Daddy had probably disguised himself, for he had all the tricks of the adventurer, and could 'make up' in former days so as to deceive even his own wife.

Strange outbreak of a secret ineradicable instinct! He had been Dora's for twenty years. But life with her at Leicester, and during their first years at Manchester, had thriven too evenly, and in the end the old wanderer had felt his blood prick within him, and the mania of his youth revive. His business had grown hateful to him; it was probably the comparative monotony of success which had first reawakened the travel-hunger—then restlessness, conflict, leading to drink, and, finally, escape.

'He will come back, you know,' said Dora one night, sharply, to David. 'He served my mother so many times. But he always came back.'

They were sitting together in the shuttered and dismantled restaurant. There was to be a sale on the premises on the morrow, and the lower room had that day been filled with all the 'plant' of the restaurant, and all or almost all the poor household stuff from upstairs. It was an odd, ramshackle collection; and poor Dora, who had been walking round looking at the auction tickets, was realising with a sinking heart how much debt the sale would still leave unprovided for. But she had found friends. Father Vernon had met the creditors for her. There had been a composition, and she had insisted upon working off to the best of her power whatever sum might remain after the possession and goodwill had been sold. She could live on a crust, and she was sure of continuous work both for the great church-furniture shop in Manchester which had hitherto employed her and also for the newly established School of Art Needlework at Kensington. As an embroideress there were few more delicately trained eyes and defter hands than hers in England.

When she spoke of her father's coming back, David was seized with pity. She could not sit down in these days when her work was out of her hands. Perpetual movement seemed her only relief. The face, that seemed so featureless but was so expressive, had lost its sweet, shining look; the mouth had the pucker of pain; and she had piteous startled ways quite unlike her usual soft serenity.

'Oh, yes, he will come back—some time,' he said, to comfort her.

'I don't doubt that—never. But I wonder how he could go like that—how he had the heart! I did think he cared for me. I wasn't ever nasty to him—at least, I don't remember. Perhaps he thought I was. But only we two—and always together—since mother died!'

She began to tidy some of the lots, to tie some of the bundles of odds and ends together more securely—talking all the while in a broken way. She was evidently bewildered and at sea. If she could have remembered any misconduct of her own, it seemed to David, it would have been a relief to her. Her faith taught her that love was all-powerful—but it had availed her nothing!

The sale came; and the goodwill of the Parlour was sold to a man who was to make a solid success of what with Daddy had been a half-crazy experiment.

Dora went to live in Ancoats, that teeming, squalid quarter which lies but a stone's-throw from the principal thoroughfares and buildings of Manchester, and in its varieties of manufacturing life and population presents types which are all its own. Here are the cotton operatives who work the small proportion of mills still remaining within the bounds of Manchester—the spinners, minders, reelers, reed-makers, and the rest; here are the calico-printers and dyers, the warehousemen and lurrymen; and here too are the sellers of 'fents,' and all the other thousand and one small trades and occupations which live on and by the poor. The quarter has one broad thoroughfare or lung, which on a sunny day is gay, sightly, and alive; then to north and south diverge the innumerable low red-brick streets where the poor live and work; which have none, however, of the trim uniformity which belongs to the workers' quarters of the factory towns pure and simple. Manchester in its worst streets is more squalid, more haphazard, more nakedly poor even than London. Yet, for all that, Manchester is a city with a common life, which London is not. The native Lancashire element, lost as it is beneath many supervening strata, is still there and powerful; and there are strong well-defined characteristic interests and occupations which bind the whole together.

Here Dora settled with a St. Damian's girl friend, a shirt-maker. They lived over a sweetshop, in two tiny rooms, in a street even more miscellaneous and half-baked than its neighbours. Outside was ugliness; inside, unremitting labour. But Dora soon made herself almost happy. By various tender shifts she had saved out of the wreck in Market Place Daddy's bits of engravings and foreign curiosities, his Swiss carvings and shells, his skins and stuffed birds; very moth-eaten and melancholy these last, but still safe. There, too, was his chair; it stood beside the fire; he had but to come back to it. Many a time in the week did she suddenly rise that she might go to the door and listen; or crane her head out of window, agitated by a figure, a sound, as her mother had done before her.

Then her religious life was free to expand as it had never been yet. Very soon, in Passion Week, she and her friend had gathered a prayer-meeting of girls, hands from the mill at the end of the street. They came for twenty minutes in the dinner-hour, delicate-faced comely creatures many of them, with their shawls over their heads: Dora prayed and sang with them, a soft tremulous passion in every word and gesture. They thought her a saint—began to tell her their woes and their sins. In the evenings and on Sunday she lived in the coloured and scented church, with its plaintive music, its luminous altar, its suggestions both of a great encompassing church order of undefined antiquity and infinite future, and of a practical system full of support for individual weakness and guidance for the individual will. The beauty of the ceremonial appealed to those instincts in her which found other expression in her glowing embroideries; and towards the church order, with its symbols, observances, mysteries, the now solitary girl felt a more passionate adoration, a more profound humility, than ever before. Nothing too much could be asked of her. During Lent, but for the counsels of Father Russell himself, a shrewd man, well aware that St. Damian's represented the one Anglican oasis in an incorrigibly moderate Manchester, even her serviceable and elastic strength would have given way, so hard she was to that poor 'sister the body,' which so many patient ages have gone to perfect and adjust.

Half of the romance, the poetry of her life, lay here; the other half in her constant expectation of her father, and in the visits of David Grieve. Once a week at least David mounted to the little room where the two girls sat working; sometimes now, oh joy! he went to church with her; sometimes he made her come out to Eccles, or Cheadle, or the Irwell valley for a walk. She used various maidenly arts and self-restraints to prevent scandal. At home she never saw him alone, and she now never went to Potter Street. Still, out of doors they were often alone. There was no concealment, and the persons who took notice assumed that they were keeping company and going to be married. When such things were said to Dora she met them with a sweet and quiet denial, at first blushing, then with no change at all of look or manner.

Yet the girl who lived with her knew that the first sound of David's rap on the door below sent a tremor through the figure beside her, that the slight hand would go up instinctively to the coiled hair, straightening and pinning, and that the smiling, listening, sometimes disputing Dora who talked with David Grieve was quite different from the dreamy and ascetic Dora who sat beside her all day.

Why did David go? As a matter of fact, with every month of this winter and spring, Dora's friendship became more necessary to him. All the brotherly feeling he would once so willingly have spent on Louie, he now spent on Dora. She became in truth a sister to him. He talked to her as he would have done to Louie had she been like Dora. No other relationship ever entered his mind; and he believed that he was perfectly understood and met in the same way.

Both often spoke of Lucy, towards whom David in this new and graver temper felt both kindly and gratefully. She, poor child, wrote to Dora from time to time letters full of complaints of her father and of his tyranny in keeping her away from Manchester. He indeed seemed to have taken a morbid dislike to his daughter, and what company he wanted he got from the widow, whom yet he had never made up his mind to marry. Lucy chafed and rebelled against the perpetual obstacles he placed in the way of her returning home, but he threatened to make her earn her own living if she disobeyed him, and in the end she always submitted. She poured herself out bitterly, however, to Dora, and Dora was helplessly sorry for her, feeling that her idle wandering life with the various aunts and cousins she boarded with was excessively bad for her—seeing that Lucy was not of the stuff to fashion new duties or charities for herself out of new relations—and that the small, vain, and yet affectionate nature ran an evil chance of ultimate barrenness and sourness.

But what could she do? In every letter there was some mention of David Grieve or request for news about him. About the visit to Paris Dora had written discreetly, telling only what she knew, and nothing of what she guessed. In reality, as the winter passed on, Dora watched him more and more closely, waiting for the time when that French mystery, whatever it was, should have ceased to overshadow him, and she might once more scheme for Lucy. He must marry—that she knew!—whatever he might think. Anyone could see that, with the returning spring, in spite of her friendship and Ancrum's, he felt his loneliness almost intolerable. It was clear, too, as his manhood advanced, that he was naturally drawn to women, naturally dependent on them. In spite of his great intelligence, to her so formidable and mysterious, Dora had soon recognised, as Elise had done, the eager, clinging, confiding temper of his youth. And beneath the transformation of passion and grief it was still there—to be felt moving often like a wounded thing.

CHAPTER XV

It was a showery April evening. But as it was also a Saturday, Manchester took no heed at all of the weather. The streets were thronged. All the markets were ablaze with light, and full of buyers. In Market Place, Dora's old home, the covered glass booths beside the pavement brought the magic of the spring into the very heart of the black and swarming town, for they were a fragrant show of daffodils, hyacinths, primroses, and palms. Their lights shone out into the rainy mist of the air, on the glistening pavements, and on the faces of the cheerful chattering crowd, to which the shawled heads so common among the women gave the characteristic Lancashire touch. Above rose the dark tower of the Exchange; on one side was the Parlour, still dedicated to the kindly diet of corn—and fruit-eating men, but repainted, and launched on a fresh career of success by Daddy's successor; on the other, the gabled and bulging mass of the old Fishing-tackle House, with a lively fish and oyster traffic surging in the little alleys on either side of it.

Market Street, too, was thronged. In the great cheap shop at the head of it, aflame with lights from top to base, you could see the buyers story after story, swarming like bees in a glass hive. Farther on in the wide space of the Infirmary square, the omnibuses gathered, and a detachment of redcoats just returned from rifle-practice on the moors crowded the pavement outside the hospital, amid an admiring escort of the youth of Manchester, while their band played lustily.

But especially in Peter Street, the street of the great public halls and principal theatres, was Manchester alive and busy. Nilsson was singing at the 'Royal,' and the rich folk were setting down there in their broughams and landaus. But in the great Free Trade Hall there was a performance of 'Judas Maccabeus' given by the Manchester Philharmonic Society, and the vast place, filled from end to end with shilling and two-shilling seats, was crowded with the 'people.' It was a purely local scene, unlike anything of the same kind in London, or any other capital. The performers on the platform were well known to Manchester, unknown elsewhere; Manchester took them at once critically and affectionately, remembering their past, looking forward to their future; the Society was one of which the town was proud;

the conductor was a character, and popular; and half the audience at least was composed of the relations and friends of the chorus. Most people had a 'Susan,' an 'Alice,' or a 'William' making signs to them at intervals from the orchestra; and when anything went particularly well, and the applause was loud, the friends of Susan or Alice beamed with a proprietary pride.

Looking down upon this friendly cheerful throng sat David Grieve, high up in the balcony. It had been his wont of late to frequent these cheap concerts, where as a rule, owing to the greater musical sensitiveness of the English North as compared with the South, the music is singularly good. During the past winter, indeed, music might almost be said to have become part of his life. He had no true musical gift, but in the paralysis of many of his natural modes of expression which had overtaken him music supplied a need. In it he at least, and at this moment, found a voice and an emotion not too personal or poignant. He lost himself in it, and was soothed.

Towards the beginning of the last part he suddenly with a start recognised Lucy Purcell in the body of the hall. She was sitting with friends whom he did not know, staring straight before her. He bent forward and looked at her carefully. In a minute or two he decided that she was looking tired, cross, and unhappy, and that she was not attending to the music at all.

So at last her father had let her come home. As to her looks, to be daughter to Purcell was to be sure of disagreeable living; and perhaps her future stepmother had been helping Purcell to annoy her.

Poor little thing! David felt a strong wish to speak to her after the performance. Meanwhile he tried to attract her attention, but in vain. It seemed to him that she looked right along the bench on which he sat; but there was no flash in her face; it remained as tired and frowning as before.

He ran downstairs before the end of the last chorus, and placed himself near the door by which he felt sure she would come out. He was just in time. She and her party also came out early before the rush. There was a sudden crowd of people in the doorway, and then he heard a little cry. Lucy stood before him, flushed, pulling at her glove, and saying something incoherent. But before he could understand she had turned back to the two women who accompanied her and spoken to them quickly; the elder replied, with a sour look at David; the younger laughed behind her muff. Lucy turned away wilfully, and at that instant the crowd from within, surging outwards, swept them away from her, and she and David found themselves together.

'Come down those steps there to the right,' she said peremptorily. 'They are going the other way.'

By this time David himself was red. She hurried him into the street, however, and then he saw that she was breathing hard, and that her hands were clasped together as though she were trying to restrain herself.

'Oh, I am so unhappy!' she burst out, 'so unhappy! And it was all, you know, to begin with, because of you, Mr. Grieve! But oh! I forgot you'd been ill—you look so different!'

She paused suddenly, while over her face there passed an expression half startled, half shrinking, as of one who speaks familiarly, as he supposes, to an old friend and finds a stranger. She could not take her eyes off him. What was this new dignity, this indefinable change of manner?

'I am not different,' he said hastily, 'not in the least. So your father has never forgiven you the kindness you did me? I don't know what to say, Miss Lucy. I'm both sorry and ashamed.'

'Forgiven it!—no, nor ever will,' she said shortly, walking on, and forgetting everything but her woes. 'Oh, do listen! Come up Oxford Street. I must tell some one, or I shall die! I must see Dora. Father's forbidden me to go, and I haven't had a moment to myself yet. She hasn't written to me since she left the Parlour, and no one'll tell me where she is. And that *odious* woman! Oh, she is an abominable wretch! She wants to claim all my things—all the bits of things that were mother's, and I have always counted mine. She won't let me take any of them away. And she's stolen a necklace of mine—yes, Mr. Grieve, *stolen* it. I don't care *that* about it—not in itself; but to have your things taken out of your drawers without "*With* your leave" or "*By* your leave"!—She's made father worse than ever. I thought he had found her out, but he is actually going to marry her in July, and they won't let me live at home unless I make a solemn promise to "perform my religious duties" and behave properly to the chapel people. And I never will, not if I starve for it—nasty, canting, crawling, backbiting things! Then father says I can live away, and he'll make me an allowance. And what do you think he'll allow me?'

She faced round upon him with curving lip and eyes aflame. David averred truly that he could not guess.

'Thirty—pounds—a—year!' she said with vicious emphasis. 'There—would you believe it? If you put a dirty little chit of a nurse-girl on board wages, it would come to more than that. And he just bought three houses in Millgate, and as rich as anything! Oh, it's shameful, I call it, *shameful!*'

She put her handkerchief to her eyes. Then she quickly withdrew it again and turned to him, remembering how his first aspect had surprised her. In the glare of some shops they were passing David could see her perfectly, and she him. Certainly, in the year which had elapsed since they had met she had ripened, or rather softened, into a prettier girl. Whether it was the milder Southern climate in which she had been living, or the result of physical weakness left by her attack of illness in the preceding spring, at any rate her bloom was more delicate, the lines of her small, pronounced face more finished and melting. As for her, now that she had paused a moment in her flow of complaint, she was busy puzzling out the change in him. David became vaguely conscious of it, and tried to set her off again.

'But you'd rather live away,' he said, 'when they treat you like that? You'd rather be independent, I should think? I would!'

'Oh, catch me living with that woman!' she cried passionately.' She's no better than a thief, a common thief. I don't care who hears me. And *made up!* Oh, its shocking! It seems to me there's nothing I can talk about at home now—whether it's getting old—or teeth—or hair—I'm always supposed to be "passing remarks." And I wouldn't mind if it was my Hastings cousins I had to live with. But they can't have me any more, and now I'm at Wakely with the Astons.'

'The Aston's?' David echoed. Like most people of small training and intelligence, Lucy instinctively supposed that whatever was familiar to her was familiar to other people.

'Oh, don't you know? It's father's sister who married a mill-overseer at Wakely. And they're very kind to me. Only they're *dreadfully* pious too—not like father—I don't mean that. And, you see—it's Robert!'

'Who's Robert?' asked David amused by her blush, and admiring the trim lightness of her figure and walk.

'Robert's the eldest son. He's a reedmaker. He's got enough to marry on—at least he thinks so.'

'And he wants to marry you?'

She nodded. Then she looked at him, laughing, her naturally bright eyes sparkling through the tears still wet in them.

'Father's a Baptist, you know—that's bad enough—but Robert's a *Particular* Baptist. I asked him what it meant once when he was pestering me to marry him. "Well, you see," he said, "a man must *show* that his heart's changed—we don't take in everybody like—we want to be *sure* they're real *converted*." I don't believe it does mean that—father says it doesn't. Anyway I asked him whether if I married him he'd want me to be a Particular Baptist too. And he said, very slow and solemn, that of course he should look for religious fellowship in his wife, but that he didn't want to hurry me. I laughed till I cried at the thought of *me* going to that hideous chapel of his, dressed like his married sister. But sometimes, I declare, I think he'll make me do what he wants—he's got a way with him. He sticks to a thing as tight as wax, and I don't care what becomes of me sometimes.'

She pouted despondently, but her quick eye stole to her companion's face.

'Oh, no, you won't marry Robert, Miss Lucy,' said David cheerfully. 'You've had a will of your own ever since I've known you. But what are you at home for now?'

'Why, I told you—to pack up my things. But I can't find half of them; she—she's walked off with them. Oh, I'm going off again as soon as possible—I can't stand it. But I must see Dora. Father says I shan't visit Papists. But I'll watch my chance. I'll get there to-morrow—see if I don't! Tell me what she's doing, Mr. Grieve.'

David told her all he knew. Lucy's comments were very characteristic. She was equally hard on Daddy's ill-behaviour and Dora's religion, with a little self-satisfied hardness that would have provoked David but for its childish *naivete*. Many of the things that she said of Dora, however, showed real feeling, real affection.

'She *is* good,' she wound up at last with a long sigh.

'Yes, she's the best woman I ever saw,' said David slowly; 'she's beautiful, she's a saint.'

Lucy looked up quickly—her dismayed eyes fastened on him—then they fell again, and her expression became suddenly piteous and humble.

'You're still getting on well, aren't you?' she said timidly. 'You were glad not to be turned out, weren't you?'

Somehow, for the life of her, she could not at that moment help reminding him of her claim upon him. He admitted it very readily, told her broadly how he was doing and what new connections he was making. It was pleasant to tell her, pleasant to speak to this changing rose-leaf face with its eager curiosity and attention.

'And you were ill when you were abroad?—so Dora said. Father, of course, made unkind remarks—you may be sure of that!—He'll set stories about when he doesn't like anybody. I didn't believe a word.'

'It don't matter,' said David hotly, but he flushed. His desire to wring Purcell's neck was getting inconveniently strong.

'No, not a bit,' she declared. Then she suddenly broke into laughter. 'Oh, Mr. Grieve, how many assistants do you think father's had since you left?'

And she chatted on about these individuals, describing a series of dolts, their achievements and personalities, with a great deal of girlish fun. Her companion enjoyed her little humours and egotisms, enjoyed the walk and her companionship. After the strain of the day, a day spent either in the toil of a developing business or under a difficult pressure of thought, this light girl's voice brought a gay, relaxed note into life. The spring was in the air, and his youth stirred again in that cavern where grief had buried it.

'Oh, *dear*, I must go home,' she said at last regretfully, startled by a striking clock. 'Father'll be just mad. Of course, he'll hear all about my meeting you—I don't care. I'm not going to be parted from all my friends to please him, particularly now he's turned me out for good—from Dora and—'

'From you,' she would have said, but she became suddenly conscious and her voice failed.

'No, indeed! And your friends won't forget you, Miss Lucy. You'll go and see Dora to-morrow?'

'Yes, if I can give them the slip at home.'

There was a pause, and then he said—

'And will you allow me to visit you at Wakely some Sunday? I know those moors well.'

She reddened all over with delight. There was something in the little stiffness of the request which gave it importance.

'I wish you would; it's not far,' she stammered. 'Aunt Miriam would be glad to see you.'

They walked back rapidly along Mosley Street and into Market Place. There she stopped and shyly asked him to leave her. Almost all the Saturday-night crowd had disappeared from the streets. It was really late, and she became suddenly conscious that this walk of hers might reasonably be regarded at home as a somewhat bold proceeding.

'I wish you'd let me see you right home,' he said, detaining her hand in his.

'Oh, no, no—I shall catch it enough as it is. Oh, they'll let me in! Will it be next Sunday, Mr. Grieve?'

'No, the Sunday after. Can I do anything for you?'

He came closer to her, seeming to envelope her in his tall, protecting presence. It was impossible for him to ignore her girlish flutter, her evident joy in having seen and talked to him again, in spite of her dread of her father. Nor did he wish to ignore them. They were unexpectedly sweet to him, and he surprised himself.

'Oh no, nothing,—but it's very good of you to say so,' she said impulsively; '*very*. Good night again.'

And instinctively she put out another small hand, which also he took, so holding her prisoner a moment.

'Look here,' he said, 'I'll just slip down that side of the Close and wait till I see you get safe in. Good night; I *am* glad I saw you!'

She ran away in a blind whirl of happiness up the steps into the passage of Half Street. He slipped down to the left and waited, looking through the railings across the corner of the Close, his eyes fixed on that upper window, where he had so often sat, parleying alternately with the cathedral and Voltaire.

Lucy rang, the door opened, there were loud sounds within, but she was admitted; it closed behind her.

David was soon in his back room, kindling a lamp and a bit of fire to read by. But when it was done he sat bent forward over the blaze, till the cathedral clock chimed the small hours, thinking.

She was so unformed and childish, that poor little thing!—surely a man could make what he would of her. She would give him affection and duty; the core of the nature was sound, and her little humours would bring life into a house.

He had but to put out his hand—that was plain enough. And why not? Was any humbler draught to be for ever put aside, because the best wine had been poured to waste?

Then the rebellions of an unquenched romance, an untamed heart, beset him. Surging waves of bitterness and pain, the after-swell of that tempest in which his youth had so nearly foundered, seemed to bear him away to seas of desolation.

After all that had happened, the greed for personal joy he every now and then detected in himself surprised and angered him by its strength. The truth was that in whole tracts of his nature he was still a boy, still young beyond his years, and it was the conflict in him between youth's hot immaturity and a man's baffling experience which made the pain of his life.

He meant to go to Wakely on the next Sunday but one—that he was certain of—but as to what he was to do and say when he got there he was perhaps culpably uncertain. But in his weakness and *sehnsucht* he dwelt upon the thought of Lucy more and more.

Then Dora—foolish saint!—came upon the scene.

Lucy found her way to the street in Ancoats where Dora lived, the morning after her talk with David, and the two cousins spent an agitated hour together. Lucy could hardly find time to ask Dora about her sorrows, so occupied was she in recounting all her own adventures. She was to go back to Wakely that very afternoon. Purcell had been absolutely unapproachable since the cousin who had escorted Lucy to the Free Trade Hall the night before had in her own defence revealed the secret of that young lady's behaviour. Pack and go she should! He wouldn't have such a hussy another night under his roof. Let them do with her as could.

'I thought he would have beaten me this morning,' Lucy candidly confessed. There was a red spot on each cheek, and she was evidently glorying in martyrdom. 'He looked like a devil—a real devil. Why can't he be fond of me, and let me alone, like other girls' fathers? I believe he *is* fond of me somehow, but he wants to break my spirit—'

She tossed her head significantly.

'Lucy, you know you ought to give in when you can,' said the perplexed Dora, with rebuke in her voice.

'Oh, nonsense!' said Lucy. 'You can't—it's ridiculous. Well, he'll quarrel with that woman some day—I'm sure *she's* his match—and then maybe he'll want me back. But perhaps he won't get me.'

Dora looked up with a curious expression, half smiling, half wistful. She had already heard all the story of the walk.

'O Dora!' cried the child, laying down her head on the table beneath her cousin's eyes, 'Dora, I do believe he's beginning to care. You see he *asked* to come to Wakely. I didn't ask him. Oh, if it all comes to nothing again, I shall break my heart!'

Dora smoothed the fine brown hair, and said affectionate things, but vaguely, as if she was not quite certain what to say.

'He does look quite different, somehow,' continued Lucy. 'Why do you think he was so long away over there, Dora? Father says nasty things about it—says he fell into bad company and lost his money.'

'I don't know how uncle Purcell can know,' said Dora indignantly. 'He's always thinking the worst of people. He was ill, for Mr. Ancrum told me, and he's the only person that *does* know. And anyone can see he isn't strong yet.'

'Oh, and he is so handsome!' sighed Lucy, 'handsomer than ever. There isn't a man in Manchester to touch him.'

Dora laughed out and called her a 'little silly.' But, as privately in her heart of hearts she was of the same opinion, her reproof had not much force.

When Lucy left, Dora put away her work, and, lifting a flushed face, walked to the window and stood there looking out. A pale April sun was shining on the brewery opposite, and touched the dark waters of the canal under the bridge to the left. The roofs of the squalid houses abutting on the brewery were wet with rain. Through a gap she could see a laundress's back-yard mainly filled with drying clothes, but boasting besides a couple of pink flowering currants just out, and holding their own for a few brief days against the smuts of Manchester. Here and there a man out of work lounged, pipe in mouth, at his open door, silently absorbing the sunshine and the cheerfulness of the moist blue over the house-tops. There was a new sweetness and tenderness in the spring air—or were they in Dora's soul?

She leant her head against the window, and remained there with her hands clasped before her for some little time—for her, a most unusual idleness.

Yes, Lucy was very obstinate. Dora had never thought she would have the courage to fight her father in this way. And selfish, too. She had spoken only once of Daddy, and that in a way to make the daughter wince. But she was so young—such a child!—and would be ruined if she were left to this casual life, and people who didn't understand her. A husband to take care of her, and children—they would be the making of her.

And he! Dora's eyes filled with tears. All this winter the change in him, the silent evidences of a shock all the more tragic to her because of its mystery, had given him a kind of sacredness in her eyes. She fell thinking, besides, of the times lately he had been to church with her. Ah, she was glad he had heard that sermon, that beautiful sermon of Canon Welby's in Passion Week! He had said nothing about it, but she knew it had been meant for clever, educated men—men like him. The church, indeed, had been full of men—her neighbours had told her that several of the gentlemen from Owens College had been there.

That evening David knocked at the door below about half-past eight. Dora got up quickly and went across to her room-fellow, a dark-faced stooping girl, who took her shirt-maker's slavery without a murmur, and loved Dora.

'Would you mind, Mary?' she said timidly. 'I want to speak to Mr. Grieve.'

The girl looked up, understood, stopped her machine, and, hastily gathering some pieces together that wanted buttonholes, went off into the little inner room and shut the door.

Dora knelt and with restless hands put the bit of fire together. She had just thrown a handkerchief over her canaries. On the frame a piece of her work, a fine altar-cloth gleaming with golds, purples, and pale pinks, stood uncovered. The deal table, the white walls on which hung Daddy's old prints, the bare floor with its strip of carpet, were all spotlessly clean. The tea had been put away. Daddy's vacant chair stood in its place.

When David came in he found her sitting pensively on a little wooden stool by the fire. Generally he gossipped while the two girls worked busily away—sometimes he read to them. To-night as he sat down he felt something impending.

Dora talked of Lucy's visit. They agreed as to the folly and brutality of Purcell's treatment of her, and laughed together over the marauding stepmother.

Then there was a pause. Dora broke it. She was sitting upright on the stool, looking straight into his face.

'Will you not be cross if I say something?' she asked, catching her breath. 'It's not my business.'

'Say it, please.' But he reddened instantly.

'Lucy's—Lucy's—got a fancy for you,' she said tremulously, shrinking from her own words. 'Perhaps it's a shame to say it—oh, it may be! You haven't told me anything, and she's given me no leave. But she's had it a long time.'

'I don't know why you say so,' he replied half sombrely.

His flush had died away, but his hand shook on his knee.

'Oh, yes, you do,' she cried; 'you must know. Lucy can't keep even her own secrets. But she's got such a warm heart! I'm sure she has. If a man would take her and be kind to her, she'd make him happy.'

She stopped, looking at him intently.

Then suddenly she burst out, laying her hand on the arm of his chair—Daddy's chair:

'Don't be angry; you've been like a brother to me.'

He took her hand and pressed it, reassuring her.

'But how can I make her happy?' he said, with his head on his hand. 'I don't want to be a fool and deny what you say, for the sake of denying it. But—'

His voice sank into silence. Then, as she did not speak, he looked up at her. She was sitting, since he had released her, with her arms locked behind her, frowning in her intensity of thought, her last energy of sacrifice.

'You would make her happy,' she said slowly, 'and she'd be a loving wife. She's flighty is Lucy, but there's nothing bad in her.'

Both were silent for another minute, then, by a natural reaction, both looked at each other and laughed.

'I'm making rather free with you, I'm bound to admit that,' she said, with a merry shamefaced expression, which brought out the youth in her face.

'Well, give me time, Miss Dora. If—if anything did come of it, I should have to let Purcell know, and there'd be flat war. You've thought of that?'

Certainly, Dora had thought of it. They might have to wait, and Purcell would probably refuse to give or leave Lucy any money. All the better, according to David. Nothing would ever induce him to take a farthing of his ex-master's hoards.

But here, by a common instinct, they stopped planning, and David resolutely turned the conversation. When they parted, however, Dora was secretly eager and hopeful. It was curious how little the father's rights weighed with so scrupulous a soul. Whether it was his behaviour to her father which had roused an unconscious hardness even in her gentle nature, or whether it was the subtle influence of his Dissent, as compared with the nascent dispositions she seemed to see in David—anyway, Dora's conscience was silent; she was entirely absorbed in her own act, and in the prospects of the other two.

CHAPTER XVI

When David reached home that night he found a French letter awaiting him. It was from Louie, still dated from the country town near Toulouse, and announced the birth of her child—a daughter. The letter was scrawled apparently from her bed, and contained some passionate, abusive remarks about her husband, half finished, and hardly intelligible. She peremptorily called on David to send her some money at once. Her husband was a sot, and unfaithful to her. Even now with his first child, he had taken advantage of her being laid up to make love to other women. All the town cried shame on him. The priest visited her frequently, and was all on her side.

Then at the end she wrote a hasty description of the child. Its eyes were like his, David's, but it would have much handsomer eyelashes. It was by far the best-looking child in the place, and because everybody remarked on its likeness to her, she believed Montjoie had taken a dislike to it. She didn't care, but it made him look ridiculous. Why didn't he do some work, instead of letting her and her child live like pigs? He could get some, if his dirty pride would let him. It wasn't to be supposed, with this disgusting Commune going on in Paris, and everybody nearly ruined, that anyone would want statues—they had never even sold the Maenad—but somebody had wanted him to do a monument, cheap, the other day for a brother who had been killed in the war; and he wouldn't. He was too fine. That was like him all over.

It was as though he could hear her flinging out the reckless sentences. But he thought there were signs that she was pleased with the baby—and he suddenly remembered her tyrannous passion for the Mason child.

As to the money, he looked carefully into his accounts. For the last six months he had been gathering every possible saving together with a view to the History of Manchester, which he and John had planned to begin printing in the coming autumn. It went against him sorely to take from such a hoard for the purpose of helping Jules Montjoie to an idler and easier existence. The fate of his six hundred pounds burnt deep into a mind which at bottom was well furnished with all the old Yorkshire and Scotch frugality.

However, he sent his sister money, and he gave up in thought that fortnight's walking tour in the Lakes he had planned for his holiday. He must just stay at home and see to business.

Then next morning, as it happened, he woke up with a sudden hunger for the country—a vision before his eyes of the wide bosom of the Scout, of fresh airs and hurrying waters, of the sheep among the heather. His night had been restless; the whole of life seemed to be again in debate— Lucy's figure, Dora's talk, chased and tormented him. Away to the April moorland! He sprang out of bed determined to take the first train to Clough End. He had not been out of Manchester for months, and it was luckily a Saturday. Here was this letter of Louie's too—he owed the news to Uncle Reuben. Since Reuben's visit to Manchester, a year before, there had been no communication between him and them. Six years! How would the farm— how would Aunt Hannah look? There was a drawing in him this morning towards the past, towards even the harsh forms and memories of it, such as often marks a time of emotion and crisis, the moment before a man takes a half-reluctant step towards a doubtful future.

But as he journeyed towards the Derbyshire border, he was not in truth thinking of Dora's counsels or of Lucy Purcell at all. Every now and then he lost himself in the mere intoxication of the spring, in the charm of the factory valleys, just flushing into green, through which the train was speeding. But in general his attention was held by the book in his hand. His time for reading had been much curtailed of late by the toils of his business. He caught covetously at every spare hour.

The book was Bishop Berkeley's 'Dialogues.'

With what a medley of thoughts and interests had he been concerned during the last four or five months! His old tastes and passions had revived as we have seen, but unequally, with morbid gaps and exceptions. In these days he had hardly opened a poet or a novelist. His whole being shrank from them, as though it had been one wound, and the books which had been to him the passionate friends of his most golden hours, which had moulded in him, as it were, the soul wherewith he had loved Elise, looked to him now like enemies as he passed them quickly by upon the shelves.

But some of his old studies—German, Greek, science especially—were the saving of him. Among some foreign books, for instance, which he had ordered for a customer he came upon a copy of some scientific essays by Littre. Among them was a survey of the state of astronomical knowledge written somewhere about 1835, with all the luminous charm which the great Positivist had at command. David was captured by it, by the flight of the scientific imagination through time and space, amid suns, planets and nebulae, the beginnings and the wrecks of worlds. When he laid it down with a sigh of pleasure, Ancrum, who was sitting opposite, looked up.

'You like your book, Davy?'

'Yes,' said the other slowly, staring out of the twilight window at the gloom which passes for sky in Manchester. Then with another long breath,—'It makes you a new heaven and a new earth!'

A similar impression, only even richer and more detailed, had been left upon him by a volume of Huxley's 'Lay Sermons.' The world of natural fact in its overpowering wealth and mystery was thus given back to him, as it were, under another aspect than that torturing intoxicating aspect of art— one that fortified and calmed. All his scientific curiosities which had been so long laid to sleep revived. His first returning joy came from a sense of the inexhaustibleness and infinity of nature.

But very soon this renewed interest in science began to have the bearing and to issue in the mental activities which, all unknown to himself, had been from the beginning in his destiny. He could not now read it for itself alone. That new ethical and spiritual susceptibility, into which agony and loss had become slowly transformed, dominated and absorbed all else. For some time, beside his scientific books, there lay others from a class not hitherto very congenial to him, that which contains the great examples in our day, outside the poets, of the poetical or imaginative treatment of ethics—Emerson, Carlyle, Ruskin. At an age when most young minds of intelligence amongst us are first seized by these English masters, he had been wandering in French paths. 'Sartor Resartus,' Emerson's 'Essays,' 'The Seven Lamps,' came to him now with an indescribable freshness and force. Nay, a too great force! We enjoy the great prophets of literature most when we have not yet lived enough to realise all they tell us. When David, wandering at night with Teufels-drockh through heaven and hell, felt at last the hard sobs rising in his throat, he suddenly put the book and others akin to it away from him. As with the poets so here. He must turn to something less eloquent—to paths of thought where truth shone with a drier and a calmer light.

But still the same problems! Since his Eden gates had closed upon him, he had been in the outer desert where man has wandered from the beginning, threatened with all the familiar phantoms, illusions, mist-voices of human thought. What was consciousness—knowledge—law? Was there any law—any knowledge—any *I?*

Naturally he had long ceased to find any final sustenance or pleasure in the Secularist literature, which had once convinced him so easily. Secularism up to a certain point, it began to seem to him, was a commonplace; beyond that point, a contradiction. If the race should ever take the counsel of the Secularists, or of that larger Positivist thought, of which English secularism is the popular reflection, the human intellect would be a poorer instrument with a narrower swing. So much was plain to him. For nothing can be more certain than that some of the finest powers and noblest work of the human mind have been developed by the struggle to know what the Secularist declares is neither knowable nor worth knowing.

Yet the histories of philosophy which he began to turn over were in truth no more fruitful to him than the talk of the *Reasoner*. They stimulated his powers of apprehension and analysis; and the great march of human debate from century to century touched his imagination. But in these summaries of the philosophical field his inmost life appropriated nothing. Once by a sort of reaction he fell upon Hume again, pining for the old intellectual clearness of impression, though it were a clearness of limit and negation. But he had hardly begun the 'Treatise' or the 'Essays' before his soul rose against them, crying for he knew not what, only that it was for nothing they could give.

Then by chance a little Life of Berkeley, and upon it an old edition of the works, fell into his hands. As he was turning over the leaves, the 'Alciphron' so struck him that he turned to the first page of the first volume, and evening after evening read the whole through with a devouring energy that never flagged. When it was over he was a different being. The mind had crystallised afresh.

It was his first serious grapple with the fundamental problems of knowledge. And, to a nature which had been so tossed and bruised in the great unregarding tide of things, which had felt itself the mere chattel of a callous universe, of no account or dignity either to gods or men, what strange exaltation there was in the general *suggestion* of Berkeley's thought! The mind, the source of all that is; the impressions on the senses, merely the speech of the Eternal Mind to ours, a Visual Language, whereof man's understanding is perpetually advancing, which has been indeed contrived for his education; man, naturally immortal, king of himself and of the senses, inalienably one—if he would but open his eyes and see—with all that is Divine, true, eternal: the soul that had been crushed by grief and self-contempt revived at the mere touch of these vast possibilities like a trampled plant. Not that it absorbed them yet, made them its own; but they made a healing stimulating atmosphere in which it seemed once more possible for it to grow into a true manhood. The spiritual hypothesis of things was for the first time presented in such a way as to take imaginative hold without exciting or harrowing the feelings; he saw the world reversed, in a pure light of thought, as Berkeley saw it, and all the horizon of things fell back.

Now—on this April afternoon—as the neighbourhood of Manchester was left behind, as the long woodclad valleys and unpolluted streams began to prophesy of Derbyshire and the Peak, David, his face pressed against the window, fell into a dream with Berkeley and with nature. Oh for knowledge! for verification! He began dimly and passionately to see before him a life devoted to thought—a life in which science after science should become the docile instrument of a mind still pressing on and on into the shadowy realm, till, in Berkeley's language, the darkness part, and it 'recover the lost region of light'!

But in the very midst of this overwhelming vision he said suddenly to himself:

'There is another way—another answer—Dora's way and Ancrum's.'

Aye, the way of faith, which asks for no length of years in which to win the goal, which is there at once—in the beat of a wing—safe on the breast of God! He thought of it as he had seen it illustrated in his friend and in Dora, with the mixture of attraction and repulsion which, in this connection, was now more or less habitual to him. The more he saw of Dora, the more he wondered—at her goodness and her ignorance. Her positive dislike to, and alienation from knowledge was amazing. At the first indication of certain currents of thought he could see her soul shrivelling and shrinking like a green leaf near flame. As he had gradually realised, she had with some difficulty forgiven him the attempt to cure Daddy's drinking through a doctor; that anyone should think sin could be reached by medicine—it was in effect to throw doubt on the necessity of God's grace! And she could not bear that he should give her information from the books he read about the Bible or early Christianity. His detached, though never hostile, tone was clearly intolerable to her. She could not and would not suffer it, would take any means of escaping it.

Then that Passion-week sermon she had taken him to hear; which had so moved her, with which she had so sweetly and persistently assumed his sympathy! The preacher had been a High Church Canon with a considerable reputation for eloquence. The one o'clock service had been crowded with business and professional men. David had never witnessed a more tempting opportunity. But how hollow and empty the whole result! What foolish sentimental emphasis, what unreality, what contempt for knowledge, yet what a show of it!—an elegant worthless jumble of Gibbon, Horace, St. Augustine, Wesley, Newman and Mill, mixed with the cheap picturesque—with moonlight on the Campagna, and sunset on Niagara— and leading, by the loosest rhetoric, to the most confident conclusions. He had the taste of it in his mouth still. Fresh from the wrestle of mind into which Berkeley had led him, he fell into a new and young indignation with sermon and preacher.

Yet, all the same, if you asked how man could best *live*, apart from thinking, how the soul could put its foot on the brute—where would Dora stand then? What if the true key to life lay not in knowledge, but in *will*? What if knowledge in the true sense was ultimately impossible to man, and if Christianity not only offered, but could give him the one thing truly needful—his own will, regenerate?

But with the first sight of the Clough End streets these high debates were shaken from the mind.

He ran up the Kinder road, with its villanous paving of cobbles and coal dust, its mills to the right, down below in the hollow, skirting the course of the river, and its rows of workmen's homes to the left, climbing the hill—in a tremor of excitement. Six years! Would anyone recognize him? Ah! there was Jerry's 'public,' an evil-looking weather-stained hole; but another name swung on the sign; poor Jerry!—was he, too, gone the way of orthodox and sceptic alike? And here was the Foundry—David could hardly prevent himself from marching into the yard littered with mysterious odds and ends of old iron which had been the treasure house of his childhood. But no Tom—and no familiar face anywhere.

Yes!—there was the shoemaker's cottage, where the prayer-meeting had been, and there, on the threshold, looking at the approaching figure, stood the shoemaker's wife, the strange woman with the mystical eyes. David greeted her as he came near. She stared at him from under a bony hand put up against the sun, but did not apparently recognise him; he, seized with sudden shyness, quickened his pace, and was soon out of her sight.

In a minute or two he was at the Dye-works, which mark the limit of the town, and the opening of the valley road. Every breath now was delight. The steep wooded hills to the left, the red-brown shoulder of the Scout in front, were still wrapt in torn and floating shreds of mist. But the sun was everywhere—above in the slowly triumphing blue, in the mist itself, and below, on the river and the fields. The great wood climbing to his left was all embroidered on the brown with palms and catkins, or broken with patches of greening larch, which had a faintly luminous relief amid the rest. And the dash of the river—and the scents of the fields! He leapt the wall of the lane, and ran down to the water's edge, watching a dipper among the stones in a passion of pleasure which had no words.

Then up and on again, through the rough uneven lane, higher and higher into the breast of the Scout. What if he met Jim Wigson on the way? What if Aunt Hannah, still unreconciled, turned him from the door? No matter! Rancour and grief have no hold on mortals walking in such an April world—in such an exquisite and sunlit beauty. On! let thought and nature be enough! Why complicate and cumber life with relations that do but give a foothold to pain, and offer less than they threaten?

There is smoke rising from Wigson's, and figures moving in the yard. Caution!—keep close under the wall. And here at last is Needham farm, at the top of its own steep pitch, with the sycamore trees in the lane beside it, the Red Brook sweeping round it to the right, the rough gate below, the purple Scout mist-wreathed behind. There are cows lowing in the yard, a horse grazes in the front field; through the little garden gate a gleam of sun strikes on the struggling crocuses and daffodils which come up year after year, no man heeding them; there is a clucking of hens, a hurry of water, a flood of song from a lark poised above the field. The blue smoke rises into the misty air; the sun and the spring caress the rugged lonely place.

With a beating heart David opened the gate into the field, walked round the little garden, let himself into the yard, and with a hasty glance at the windows mounted the steps and knocked.

No answer. He knocked again. Surely Aunt Hannah must be about somewhere. Eleven o'clock; how quiet the house was!

This time there was a clatter of a chair on a flagged floor inside, and a person with a slow laboured step came and opened.

It was Reuben. He adjusted his spectacles with difficulty, and stared at the intruder.

'Uncle Reuben!—I thought it was such a fine day, I'd just run over and see the old place, and bring you some news,' said David, smiling and holding out his hand.

Reuben took it, stupefied. 'Davy,' he said, trembling. Then with a sudden movement he whipped the door to behind him, and shut it close.

'Whist!' he said, putting his old finger to his lip. 'T' servant's just settlin her i' t' kitchen. She's noa ready yet—she's been terr'ble bad th' neet. Coom yo here.' And he descended the steps with infinite care, and led David to the wood-shed.

'Is Aunt Hannah ill?' asked David, astonished.

Reuben leant against the wall of the shed, and took off his spectacles, as though to wipe them with his old and shaking hands. Then David saw a sort of convulsion pass across his ungainly face.

'Aye,' he said, looking down, 'aye, she's broken is Hannah. Yo didna knaw?'

'I've heard nothing.'

Reuben recounted the facts. Since her stroke of last spring, and the partial recovery which had followed upon it, there had been little apparent change, except perhaps in the direction of slowly increasing weakness. She was a wreck, and likely to remain so. Hardly anybody but Reuben could understand her now, and she rarely let him out of her sight. He could not get time to attend to the farm, was obliged to leave things to the hired man, and was in trouble often about his affairs.

'Bit yo see, she hasna t' reet use of her speach,' he said, excusing himself humbly to this handsome city nephew. 'An' she conno gie ower snipin aw at onst. 'Twudna be human natur'. An't' gell's worritin' an' I mun tell her what t' missis says.'

David asked if he might see her, or should he just turn back to the town? Reuben protested, his hospitality and family feeling aroused, his poor mind torn with conflicting motives.

'I believe she'd fratch if she didna see tha,' he said at last. 'A'll just goo ben, and ask.'

He went in, and David remained in the wood-shed, staring out at the familiar scene, at Louie's window, at the steps where he and she had fed the fowls together.

The door opened again, and Reuben reappeared on the steps, agitated and beckoning.

David went in, stepping softly, holding his blue cloth cap in his hand. In another instant he stood beside the old cushioned seat in the kitchen, looking down at Hannah.

This Hannah! this his childhood's enemy! this shawled and shrunken figure with the white parchment face and lantern cheeks!

He stooped to her and said something about why he had come. Reuben listened wondering.

'Louie's married and got a babby—dosto hear, Hannah? And he—t' lad—did yo iver see sich a yan for growin?'

He wished to be mildly jocular. Hannah's face did not move. She had just touched her nephew with her cold wasted hand. Now she beckoned to him to sit down at her right. He did so, and then for the first time he could believe that Hannah, the old Hannah, was there beside them. For as she slowly studied his dress, the Inverness cape then as now a favourite garb in Manchester, the hand holding the cap, refined since she saw it last by commerce with books and pens rather than hurdles and sheep, the broad shoulders, the dark head, her eye for the first time met his, full, and a weird thrill went through him. For that eye—dulled, and wavering—was still Hannah. The old hate was in it, the old grudge, all that had been at least for him and Louie the inmost and characteristic soul of their tyrant. He knew in an instant that she had in her mind the money of which he and his sister had robbed her, and beyond that the offences of their childhood, the infamy of their mother. If she could, she would have hurled them all upon him. As it was, she was silent, but that brooding eye, like a smouldering spark in her blanched face, spoke for her.

Reuben tried to talk. But a weight lay on him and David. The gaunt head in the coarse white nightcap turned now to one, now to the other, pursued them phantom-like. Presently he insisted that his nephew must dine, avoiding Hannah's look. David would much rather have gone without; but Reuben, affecting joviality, called the servant, and some food was brought. No attempt was made to include Hannah in the meal. David supposed that it was now necessary to feed her.

Reuben talked disjointedly of the neighbours and his stock, and asked a few questions, without listening to the answers, about David's affairs, and Louie's marriage. In Hannah's presence his poor dull wits were not his own; he could in truth think of nothing but her.

After the meal, however, when a draught of ale had put some heart in him, he got up with an air of resolution.

'I mun goo and see what that felly's been doin' wi' th' Huddersfield beeasts,' he said; 'wilta coom wi' me, Davy? Mary!'

He called the little maid. Hannah suddenly said something incoherent which David could not understand. Reuben affected not to hear.

'Mary, gie your mistress her dinner, like a good gell. An' keep t' house-door open, soa 'at she can knock wi' t' stick if she wants owt.'

He stood before her restless and ashamed, afraid to look at her. Then he suddenly stooped and kissed her on the forehead. David felt a lump in his throat. As he took leave of her the spell, as it were, of Reuben's piteous affection came upon him. He saw nothing but a dying and emaciated woman, and taking her hand in his, he said some kind natural words.

The hand dropped from his like a stone. As he stood at the door behind Reuben, the servant came forward with a plate of something which she put down inside the fender. As she did so, she awkwardly upset the fire-irons, which fell with a crash. Hannah started upright in her chair, with a rush of half-articulate words, grasping fiercely for her stick with glaring eyes. The servant, a wild moorland lass, fled terrified, and at the 'house' door turned and made a face at David.

Outside Reuben slowly mastered himself, and woke up to some real interest in Louie's doings. David told him her story frankly, so far as it could be separated from his own, and, pressed by Reuben's questions, even revealed at last the matter of the six hundred pounds. Reuben could not get over it. Sandy's "six hunderd pund" which he had earned with the sweat of his brow, all handed over to that minx Louie, and wasted by her and a rascally French husband in a few months—it was more than he could bear.

'Aye, aye, marryin's varra weel,' he said impatiently. 'A grant tha it's a great sin coomin thegither without marryin. But Sandy's six hunderd pund! Noa, I conno abide sich wark.'

And he fell into sombre silence, out of which David could hardly rouse him. Except that he said once, 'And we that had kep' it so long. I'd better never ha gien it tha.' And clearly that was the bitter thought in his mind. The sacrifice that had taxed all his moral power, and, as he believed, brought physical ruin on Hannah, had been for nothing, or worse than nothing. Neither he nor David nor anyone was the better for it.

'I must go over the shoulder to Frimley,' said David at last. They had made a half-hearted inspection of the stock in the home fields, and were now passing through the gate on to the moor. 'I must see Margaret Dawson again before I take the train back.'

Reuben looked astonished and shook his head as though he did not remember anything about Margaret Dawson. He walked on beside his nephew for a while in silence. The Red Brook was leaping and dancing beside them, the mountain ashes were just bursting into leaf, the old smithy was ahead of them on the heathery slope, and to their left the Downfall, full and white, thundered over its yellow rocks.

But they had hardly crossed the Red Brook to mount the peak beyond when Reuben drew up.

'Noa'—he said restlessly—'noa. I mun goo back. T' gell's flighty and theer's aw maks o' mischief i' yoong things.' He stood and held his nephew by the hand, looking at him long and wistfully. As he did so a calmer expression stole for an instant into the poor troubled eyes.

'Very like a'st not see tha again, Davie. We niver know, Livin's hard soomtimes—soa's deein, folks say. I'm often freet'nt of deein'—but I should na be. Theer's noan so mich peace here, and we *knaw* that wi' the Lord theer's peace.'

He gave a long sigh—all his character was in it—so tortured was it and hesitating.

They parted, and the young man climbed the hill, looking back often to watch the bent figure on the lower path. The spell had somehow vanished from the sunshine, the thrill from the moorland air. Life was once more cruel, implacable.

He walked fast to Frimley, and made for the cottage of Margaret's brother. He remembered its position of old.

A woman was washing in the 'house' or outer kitchen. She received him graciously. The weekly money which in one way or another he had never failed to pay since he first undertook it, had made him well known to her and her husband. With a temper quite unlike that of the characteristic northerner, she showed no squeamishness at all about the matter. If it hadn't been for his help, they would just have sent Margaret to the workhouse, she said bluntly; for they had many mouths to feed, and couldn't have burdened themselves with an extra one. She was quite 'silly' and often troublesome.

'Is she here?' David asked.

'Aye, if yo goo ben, yo'll find her,' said the woman, carelessly pointing to an inner door. 'I conno ha her in here washin days, nor the children noather.'

David opened the door pointed out to him. He found himself in a rough weaving shed almost filled by a large hand-loom, with its forest of woodwork rising to the ceiling, its rolls of perforated pattern-paper, its great cylinders below, and many-coloured shuttles to either hand. But to-day it stood idle, the weaver was not at work. The room was stuffy but cold, and inexpressibly gloomy in this silence of the loom.

Where was Margaret? After a minute's search, there, beyond the loom, sitting by a fireless grate, was a little figure in a bedgown and nightcap, poking with a stick amid the embers, and as it seemed crooning to itself.

David made his way up to her, inexpressibly moved.

'Margaret!'

She did not know him in the least. She had a starved-looking cat on her lap, which she was huddling against her breast. The face had fallen away almost to nothing, so small and thin it was. She was dirty and unkempt. Her still brown hair, once so daintily neat, straggled out beneath her torn cap; her print bed-gown was pinned across her, her linsey skirt was in holes; everywhere the same tale of age neglected and unloved.

When David first stood before her she drew back with a terrified look, still clutching the cat tightly. But, as he smiled at her, with the tears in his eyes, speaking her name tenderly, her frightened look relaxed, and she remained staring at him with the shrinking furtive expression of a quite young child.

He knelt down beside her.

'Margaret, dear Margaret—don't you know me?'

She did not answer, but her wrinkled eyes, still blue and vaguely sweet, wavered under his, and it seemed to him that every now and then a shiver of cold ran through her old and frail body. He went on gently, trying to recall her wandering senses. In vain. In the middle she interrupted him with a piteous lip.

'They promised me a ribbon for't,' she said, complainingly, in a hoarse, bronchitic voice, pointing to the animal she held, and to its lean neck adorned with a collar of plaited string, on which apparently she had just been busy, to judge from the odds and ends of string lying about.

At the same moment David became aware of a couple of children craning their heads round the corner of the loom to look, a loutish boy about eleven, and a girl rather younger. At sight of them, Margaret raised a cry of distress and alarm, with that helpless indefinable note in the voice which shows that personality, in the true sense, is no longer there.

'Go away!' David commanded.

The children did not stir, but grinned. He made a threatening movement. Then the boy, as quick as lightning, put his tongue out at Margaret, and caught hold of his sister, and they clattered off, their mother in the next room scolding them out into the street again.

And this the end of a creature all sacrifice, a life all affection!

He took her shivering hand in his.

'Margaret, listen to me. You shall be better looked after. I will see to that. No one shall be unkind to you any more. If they won't do it here, my — my — wife shall take care of you!'

He lifted her hand and kissed it, putting all the pity and bitter indignation of his heart into the action. Margaret, seeing his emotion, whimpered too; otherwise she was impassive.

He left her, went into the next room, and had a long energetic talk with Margaret's sister-in-law. The woman, half ashamed, half recalcitrant, in the end promised amendment. What business it was of his she could not imagine; but the small weekly addition which he offered to make to Margaret's payments, while it showed him a greater fool than before, made it impossible to put his meddling aside. She promised that Margaret should be brought into the warm, that she should have better clothes, and that the children should be kept from plaguing her.

Then he departed, and mounting the moor again, spent an hour or two wandering among the boggy fissures of the top, or sitting on the high edges of the heather, looking down over the dark and craggy splendour of the hill immediately around and beneath him, on and away through innumerable paling shades of distance to the blue Welsh border. His speculative fervour was all gone. Reuben, Hannah, Margaret, these figures of suffering and pain had brought him close to earth again. The longing for a human hand in his, for a home, wife, children to spend himself upon, to put at least for a while between him and this unconquerable 'something which infects the world,' became in this long afternoon a physical pain not to be resisted. He thought more and more steadily of Lucy, schooling himself, idealising her.

It was the Sunday before Whitsunday. David was standing outside a trim six-roomed house in the upper part of the little Lancashire town of Wakely, waiting for Lucy Purcell.

She came at last, flushed and discomposed, pulling the door hastily to behind her.

They walked on a short distance, talking disconnectedly of the weather, the mud, and the way on to the moor, till she said suddenly:

'I wish people wouldn't be so good and so troublesome!'

'Did Robert wish to keep you at home?' inquired David, laughing.

'Well, he didn't want me to come out with—anybody but him,' she said, flushing. 'And it's so bad, because one can't be cross. I don't know how it is, but they're just the best people here that ever walked!'

She looked up at him seriously, an unusual energy in her slight face.

'What!—a town of saints?' asked David, mocking. It was so difficult to take Lucy seriously.

She tossed her head and insisted.

Talking very fast, and not very consecutively, she gave him an account, so far as she was able, of the life lived in this little town, a typical Lancashire town of the smaller and more homogeneous kind. All the people worked in two large spinning mills, or in a few smaller factories representing dependent industries, such as reed-making. Their work was pleasant to them. Lucy complained, with the natural resentment of the idle who see their place in the world jeopardised by the superfluous energy of the workers, that she could never get the mill girls to say that the mill hours were too long. The heat tried them, made appetites delicate, and lung mischief common. But the only thing which really troubled them was 'half-time.' Socially everybody knew everybody. They were passionately interested in each other's lives and in the town's affairs. And their religion, of a strong Protestant type expressed in various forms of Dissent, formed an ideal bond which kept the little society together, and made an authority which all acknowledged, an atmosphere in which all moved.

The picture she drew was, in truth, the picture of one of those social facts on which perhaps the future of England depends. She drew it girlishly, quite unconscious of its large bearings, gossiping about this person and that, with a free expenditure of very dogmatic opinion on the habits and ways which were not hers. But, on the whole, the picture emerged, and David had never liked her talk so well. The little self-centred thing had somehow been made to wonder and admire; which is much for all of us.

And she, meanwhile, was instantly sensible that she was in a happy vein, that she pleased. Her eyes danced under her pretty spring hat. How proud she was to walk with him—that he had come all this way to see her! As she shyly glanced him up and down, she would have liked the village street to be full of gazers, and was almost loth to leave the public way for the loneliness of the moor. What other girl in Wakely had the prospect of such a young man to take her out? Oh! would he ever, ever 'ask her'—would he even come again?

At last, after a steep and muddy climb, through uninviting back ways, they were out upon the moor. An apology for a moor in David's eyes! For the hills which surround the valley of the Irwell, in which Wakely lies, are, for the most part, green and rolling ground, heatherless and cragless. Still, from the top they looked over a wide and wind-blown scene, the bolder moors of Rochdale behind them, and in front the long green basin in which the Irwell rises. Along the valley bottoms lay the mills, with their surrounding rows of small stone houses. Up on the backs of the moors crouched the old farms, which have watched the mills come, and will perhaps see them go; and here and there a grim-looking colliery marked a fold of the hill. The landscape on a spring day has a bracing bareness, which is not without exhilaration. The wind blows freshly, the sun lies broadly on the hills. England, on the whole at her busiest and best, spreads before you.

They were still on the top when it occurred to them that they had a long walk in prospect—for they talked of getting to the source of the Irwell—and that it was dinner-time. So they sat down under one of the mortarless stone walls which streak the moors, and David brought out the meal that was in his pockets. They ate with laughter and chat. Pigeons passed overhead, going and coming from an old farm about a hundred yards away; the sky above them had a lark for voice singing his loudest; and in the next field a peewit was wheeling and crying. The few trees in sight were struggling fast into leaf. Nature even in this cold north was gay to-day and young.

Suddenly, in the midst of their meal, by a natural caprice and reaction of the mind, as David sat looking down on slate roofs and bare winding valley, across the pale, rain-beaten grass of the moor, all the northern English detail vanished from his eyes. For one suffocating instant he saw nothing but a great picture gallery, its dimly storied walls and polished floor receding into the distance. In front Velazquez' 'Infanta,' and before it a figure bent over a canvas. Every line and tint stood out. He heard the light varying voice, caught the complex grace of the woman, the strenuous effort of the artist.

Enough! He closed his eyes for one bitter instant; then raised them again to England and to Lucy.

There under the wall, while they were still lingering in the sun, he asked Lucy Purcell to be his wife. And Lucy, hardly believing her own foolish ears, and in a whirl of bliss and exultation past expression, nevertheless put on a few maidenly airs and graces, coquetted a little, would not be kissed all at once, talked of her father and the war that must be faced, and finally surrendered, held up her scarlet cheek for her lord's caress, and then sat speechless, hand in hand with him.

But Nature had its way. They rambled on, crossing the stone stiles which link the bare green fields on the side of the moor. When a stile appeared, Lucy would send him on in front, so that she might mount decorously, and then descend trembling upon his hand.

Presently they came to a spot where the path crossed a little streamlet, and then climbed a few rough steps in a steep bank, and so across a stile at the top.

David ran up, leapt the stile, and waited. But he had time to study the distant course of their walk, as well as the burnt and lime-strewn grass about him, for no Lucy appeared. He leant over the wall, and to his amazement saw her sitting on one of the stone steps below, crying.

He was beside her in an instant. But he could not loosen the hands clasped over her eyes.

'Oh, why did you do it?—why did you do it? I'm not good enough—I never shall be good enough!'

For the first time since their formal kiss he put his arms round her. And as she, at last forced to look up, found herself close to the face which, in its dark refinement and power, seemed to her to-day so far, so wildly above her deserts, she saw it all quivering and changed. Never had little Lucy risen to such a moment; never again, perhaps, could she so rise. But in that instant of passionate humility she had dropped healing and life into a human heart.

Yet, was it Lucy he kissed?—Lucy he gathered in his arms? Or was it not rather Love itself?—the love he had sought, had missed, but must still seek—and seek?